Inside the shrine room ⌂▪▪▪▪▪▪▪▪▪ *im to,* *Gabriel gazed with breathless disbelief.*

Suffocated by vines and tree roots at the far end of the chamber, clotted with decades of dried mud and impacted dust, was a giant bronze statue of a grotesque figure, pointing one bony sculpted finger toward the center of the room. Underlit by torchlight it was positively ghoulish, a nightmare vision, an evil god. The scaling and tarnish on the bronze made the looming statue appear to be leprous.

It took the better part of two hours for Gabriel to clean, hack, and chip away the main debris around the base of the statue, uncovering an iron panel. The panel, nearly a foot thick, gradually inched backward until there was a gap into which Gabriel could shove a lantern. He popped a flare and dropped it through. That was when he first saw that the metal floor below was writhing with worms and salamanders, some as much as a foot long . . .

Enjoy these other Gabriel Hunt adventures:

**HUNT AT THE WELL OF ETERNITY
HUNT THROUGH THE CRADLE OF FEAR
HUNT AT WORLD'S END
HUNT BEYOND THE FROZEN FIRE
HUNT THROUGH NAPOLEON'S WEB** *

* coming soon

GABRIEL HUNT

HUNT

Among the Killers of Men

AS TOLD TO DAVID J. SCHOW

LEISURE BOOKS NEW YORK CITY

A LEISURE BOOK®

July 2010

Published by

Dorchester Publishing Co., Inc.
200 Madison Avenue
New York, NY 10016

in collaboration with Winterfall LLC

ISBN 10: 0-8439-6256-9
ISBN 13: 978-0-8439-6256-7
E-ISBN: 978-1-4285-0895-8

Printed in the United States of America.

10 9 8 7 6 5 4 3 2 1

Visit us online at www.dorchesterpub.com or
www.HuntForAdventure.com

HUNT

Among the Killers of Men

Prologue

The sign was in eleven languages including Arabic, German, Dutch, English, Russian, and both Mandarin and Cantonese variants for the locals. The English interpretation read:

The Chinese Cooperative Confederation
Welcomes Its Honored Guests
(private reception)

In any language the message was clear: *Keep Out.*

If this polite suggestion was vague, the men keeping watch over all ingress and egress were heavy with implied threat. They were all uniformed members of the People's Armed Police Force, carrying the authority of the Central Military Committee. Dressed in tightly belted army greens, they bore both sidearms and automatic weapons; in comportment they looked the same as the officer directing the hectic traffic mere blocks away, not far from the world-famous bronze statue of Mao Tse-Tung pointing boldly toward the future. The statue still stood outside the Peace Hotel on the Bund, though Mao's historical significance had lately been overshadowed by the political and economic reforms of his successors.

At night the Bund is brilliant with golden light, presently competing with an ever-increasing array of garish neon advertisements in all languages. The most unusual building found on the Bund sits in Pudong Park in Lujiazui. It is called "the Pearl"—short for the Oriental Pearl TV Tower. It looks like a recently landed spaceship from another planet. A massive tripod base supports three nine-meter-wide columns of stainless steel that encase a variety of metallic spheres and globes. The topmost globe, at an elevation of nearly 1,500 feet, is called the "space module." From the large lower sphere, one can see all the way to the Yangtze River. The design aesthetic was to create "twin dragons playing with pearls," derived from the presence of the Yangpu Bridge to the northeast and the Nanpu Bridge to the southwest.

The Pearl is home to commerce, recreation, and history. The Shanghai Municipal History Museum is housed in its pedestal. The topmost sphere features a revolving restaurant. In between are shops, more restaurants, hotel facilities and the transmission headquarters for nearly two dozen television channels and FM radio stations. The Pearl is so dominant on the Bund that it can be seen from twenty miles inland; lit up at nighttime, it is a truly eerie, otherworldly sight.

Zhongshan Road was seething with traffic—everything from skate-sized diesel automobiles to pedicabs and bicycles (thousands of bicycles)—binding and blending with pedestrians (thousands more). Every twenty minutes the Sin Shan Ferry brought more people, more vehicles. A roiling, complex sea of humanity.

At night the abundance of artificial light from the Bund, and from the Pearl, makes the Huangpu River appear almost black.

Qingzhao Wai Chiu, whose given name meant "clear illumination and understanding," understood appearances and how to manipulate them. Klaxons sounded for the docking ferry, and she debarked, pulling her little wheeled suitcase behind her.

There was a beggar trying to negotiate the upward slope of the ferry ramp. It was a legless old woman, hauling herself along on a wheeled platform by means of wooden blocks, totally alone on the concrete ramp until the steel mesh gates withdrew and the complement of ferry passengers surged toward her in an unbroken wave. She kept her eyes down, as is common for beggars. Inevitably her cup was jostled and a few meager coins pinwheeled down the ramp or disappeared beneath the shoes of the incoming.

The disparity between the old wretch and Qingzhao could not have been more striking. Qingzhao was tall for a Chinese woman—five foot nine, rendered even taller by expensive spike heels so new the soles were barely scuffed. Unlike many women, she knew how to walk in those heels. Her stride itself could be a weapon, a statement. Her full, lush fall of ebony black hair concealed many scars. Her gaze could be as steely dark as espresso but it was shielded now behind tinted glasses. She walked with a purpose.

She tucked a one hundred-yuan note into the beggar's cup, noticing the depth of the ragged woman's platform. It was designed to conceal her lower legs. She was a fake. She looked skyward and off-center at the sound of paper rustling in the cup and Qingzhao saw her milky, cataracted eyes. She probably was not really blind, either. No matter. Qingzhao was faking, too.

The beggar was swallowed by the crowd as Qingzhao made her way toward the rocketship, the TV tower—the Pearl.

The policemen flanking the sign ate her up head-to-toe with expressions just shy of leering. She knew what they were thinking: *An entertainer, probably a prostitute.* That was what she needed them to think.

First hurdle cleared.

In the Tower lobby there was more security on behalf of the reception for the CCC—double guards and a walk-through booth twice the size of an airport scanner. Qingzhao knew this was a recently emplaced piece of Japanese technology that could present a body scan in X-ray schematic.

The scan of her trolley case revealed that it contained, among other things, a flamboyant, metallic wig—the sort of thing a dancer might wear. Or a stripper.

The guards made her open the case anyway, mostly so they could sneak peeks down her cleavage. Her silk blouse and leather jacket had been strategically chosen and just as strategically deployed. These baboons would never see the big X of scar tissue beneath her left breast, or care.

Qingzhao was waved toward a lift with brushed aluminum doors. The car shot up nearly a thousand feet in fifteen seconds; she felt her ears pop.

Second hurdle cleared.

The Chinese Cooperative Confederation was the brainchild of a financier who had changed his name to Kuan-Ku Tak Cheung, although Qingzhao knew the man was Russian by birth. It represented a new sociopolitical horizon for 21st Century China, which irritated all the traditionalists and old Party members but represented an enticing commercial future for China's so-called "new generation." As far as the old school was concerned, giving Cheung a political foothold would be akin to the Mafia fielding a presidential candidate in the United States. But it did not really matter as long as the correct palms were silvered. And Cheung, ever the tactician, was perpetually developing inroads to curry the favor of his harshest opponents.

Of course, politics had nothing to do with the reasons Qingzhao had come to kill Cheung, whose real name was Anatoly Dragunov.

The noise level was painfully high in the middle of the Moire Club, overlooking the Huangpu from the midsection of the Pearl.

On a revolving chromium stage, expressionless dancers in white body stockings and face paint moved like robots, tracking the gyrations of naked men and women being projected onto them from hidden lenses.

At least five hundred guests and noteworthies were portioned into pie-wedge areas sectioned by hanging panes of soundproof karaoke glass. In the midst of chaos, silence could be had. The glass was also bulletproof, grade six, arranged to accommodate any sized group and isolate them in plain sight. Each alcove of glass was a different projected color. The support wires could also transmit billing information from any of the glass-topped scanner tables.

The servers were all *Takarazuka*—female Japanese exotics dressed as tuxedoed men, supervised by a matron dolled up in an elaborate fringed gown and a mile-high pile of spangled hair, himself a transplant from a Dallas, Texas, drag show where he had specialized in Liza Minnelli.

At the mâitre d' station there was another body scanner. Even an amateur could have picked out guest from bodyguard. The watchdogs were too confident, too arrogant, too chest-puffy. They had seen too much Western television and been inspired by too many Western films.

Ivory was disappointed by this crew, but it was not his place to say so. His job was not only to watch the crowd, but to watch the watchers. He was a dark-haired, sharp-eyed son of Heilongjiang Province—although those records had been erased long ago. His current name was Longwei Sze Xie—nickname, "Ivory," source unknown—and he looked like he was in charge of everything.

An immaculate, six-foot blonde Caucasian woman had just raised the hackles of the mâitre d' at the scanner. She was packing a sleek .380 in a spine retention holster just below the elaborate calligraphy of the tattoo on the small of her back. Vistas of exposed flesh, yards of leg, a good weight of ample bosom, and yet she could still artfully hide a firearm inside the slippery, veiled thing she was almost wearing.

Ivory quickly interceded: "She's one of Cheung's." Meaning: *Her gun is permitted.* Just like the similar gun concealed amidst the charms of her opposite number, an equally statuesque African goddess named Shukuma—Cheung's other arm doily for the evening.

Kuan-Ku Tak Cheung, a.k.a. Anatoly Dragunov, was holding forth from a VIP area near the center of the swirling carnival. Ivory put the man to be in his midfifties; barrel chest, huge hands, a face like unfinished sculpture. From his vantage Ivory could see that

Shukuma had Cheung's back at all times. Good. Either she or the blonde, Vulcheva, would signal if Ivory needed to be called into play.

Down in the VIP pit, Cheung placed a denominational bill on the glass table before each of his honored guests, four in focus: Japanese yen for Mr. Igarishi, a new Euro for Mr. Beschorner, modern rubles for Mr. Oktyabrina and good old U.S. of A. dollars for Mr. Reynaldo.

Mr. Igarishi said, "We are equally honored." He spoke with a Kyoto inflection.

Cheung said, "I respect the charm of a gesture." Turning to Beschorner, he added, "True wealth is invisible, ja?" in Frankfurt German. To Mr. Oktyabrina he added, "Ones and zeros are what we are really after," and completed the sentence in English for the benefit of Mr. Reynaldo: ". . . so we cannot deny the purity." He had just delivered an unbroken speech in four languages. He was showing off. They were all multilingual. But it helped to choose a negotiative tongue that could not be readily comprehended by, say, the average waiter.

"Paper currency is almost extinct," he told his familiars. "What you see is the last gasp of that outmoded idiom, and I guarantee it will pass muster anywhere in the world. Paper currency will erect our economical siege machine. In the aftermath of what we do, digital currency will make us all wealthy beyond the belief of ordinary human beings."

"*If* you can deliver China as promised," said Beschorner.

"I anticipate all phases complete within the next two years," said Cheung.

Ivory monitored all this via earbud. New dancers,

tricked out in painfully complex PVC fetishwear, had taken the circular chrome stage.

Then somebody opened fire on Cheung, Ivory's boss, and people started diving for cover. Except for Ivory, still standing, eyes unfazed, gun already drawn.

Qingzhao quickly approached the backstage corral as the white–body-stockinged dancers hustled off. She smiled as her "fellow performers" passed. Half of them returned her expression, no doubt thinking: *What was her name again? I'm sure I've met her.* The men got deferential avoidance of eye contact, otherwise they might spend too much time later trying to place her face.

The hosed and goggled PVC outfits had been wheeled to the prep floor on a giant mobile rack whose casters creaked with the weight of the gear. All the evening's entertainments had been either calculatedly androgynous or garishly sexual, and Qingzhao could advantage either opportunity as it arose. The next troupe went on in another ten minutes.

The only privacy backstage was found in the staff toilets. Performers had a splendid nonchalance about nudity, which meant that Qingzhao could use her breasts, ass and million-watt smile as further distractions from the fact that she was not supposed to be there at all. She stripped off her wrap skirt, her jacket, her blouse, while striding purposefully toward her destination. On the way, she lifted one of the PVC costumes from the rack.

In the loo she cracked open her little wheeled suitcase. The wig inside matched the gear for the PVC dancers.

After opening the case handle, popping the hidden

seam on the heavy-duty hinges, and unclicking a concealed hatch on the wig mount, Qingzhao assembled the components for her pistol—a big AutoMag IV frame jazzed up to resemble the prop space guns that were also part of the forthcoming presentation. A steel tube disgorged a full magazine's worth of specialty ammunition. They were heavy-caliber loads with black and yellow hazard striping on the cartridge casings.

Miraculously, the assembled gun actually fit the holster that was part of the stage costume—an unanticipated plus, there.

The white facial pancake and black lipstick and liner she rapidly applied made her indistinguishable from the others, male or female. This, she had counted on.

Feeling like an ingénue in a chorus line, she filed onstage with the rest, having no idea whatsoever about marks, timing, position, or the number to which they were supposedly herky-jerking around. It did not matter. She needed five seconds, tops, before she was blown.

Outside the Pearl, a dirigible bloated with neon circled the convex windows.

In a single liquid move, Qingzhao pivoted, crouched, sighted and fired.

The bullet rocketed across the room and hit the Plexi about a foot away from Kuan-Ku Tak Cheung's head. The tempered material spiderwebbed but did not shatter. The round left a broad, opaque splatter like a paintball round.

Which began to effervesce. Acid.

Immediately, Ivory and the two female bodyguards Shukuma and Vulcheva triangulated to shield Cheung, guns out.

The highly paid bodyguards of Cheung's international guests lacked such reaction time. They were still unholstering their weaponry and trying to acquire a target. By the time they found their senses, Qingzhao had fired twice more.

The compromised Plexi disintegrated and the unfortunate Mr. Igarishi took a round in the head that nearly vaporized his skull.

Ivory brought up his pistol in a leading arc and returned auto-rapidfire through the breached glass single-handedly—something not many men could do with a sense of control. The OTs-33 "Pernach" in his grasp stuttered, instantly reducing its double-stack 27-round mag by half in the first burst. "Pernach" meant "multivaned mace" in Russian, and a jagged line of Parabellum rounds chased Qingzhao's wake as she dived off the stage.

Ivory did not pause in astonishment as Qingzhao hit the circular lip of the stage, shooting back while in midfall. He already knew how capable she was.

Vulcheva's shooting arm violently parted company with her body, the spray causing everyone to duck. The hanging Plexi all around the club was jigging now with bullet hits as other enforcers tried to determine what threat, from where, and filled the night with panic fire.

Ivory broadsided Cheung and caught two hits in the chest. He did not go down. It took him less than a tenth of a second to register the acid and he quickly stripped his jacket, which was lined with whisper-thin body armor of Japanese manufacture. Spotlights exploded above him.

Ivory and Shukuma bulldogged Cheung into the body scanner at the mâitre d' station. Ivory hit the device's panic button, which dropped chainmail-style rollups to enclose his boss. Cheung's skeleton showed on the screen in blue, but no bullet could harm him there. The less-lucky mâitre d' was slumped across the dais, having interrupted the travel of several conventional rounds fired by other bodyguards.

Ivory only had eyes for Qingzhao, who was now boxed in near the panoramic windows with no place to run. The blimp cruised past behind her, flashing advertising in polyglot: *CortCom. Vivitrac. Eat Nirasawa-Mega-Output Beverage!*

Qingzhao brought an entire framework of glass panels down on Ivory's head. Then she put the rest of her clip into the big curved window, which disassembled itself and succumbed to gravity.

Ivory had her dead in his sights as she jumped. He spent the rest of his clip trying to wing her on the way out.

He ran to the window, icy night air scything inward. From this high up, the light of the Bund made it impossible to see the river. No parachute, no falling body, just blackness.

Qingzhao, Ivory knew, would have counted on that.

Chapter 1

"I give up."

Gabriel Hunt was widely known for solving mysteries and rising to challenges. This time, however, frustration had bested him.

"I give up. You do it."

He relinquished the Rubik's Cube, placing it onto the table (itself a Chinese antique gifted by a beneficiary of a Hunt Foundation grant) next to a more obscure and even more difficult puzzle called the Alexander Star.

"It's a toy, Gabriel. Children do it."

"So give it to a child then," Gabriel said.

Michael picked the cube up, began idly turning its sides. Instead of colors, each square was labeled with a piece of the Hunt Foundation logo against a different metallic background—silver, copper, bronze, gold—and the toy itself was made of stainless steel rather than plastic. "You give up on things too quickly," he said. In his hands, the facets slowly reorganized themselves.

"Name one thing I've given up on," Gabriel said. "Just one. Other than this toy."

"The Dufresne report."

"I brought back the mask. Dufresne should be happy."

"He wants a report."

"Here's your report: I brought back the mask, close quotes, signed, Gabriel Hunt. What else does he want to know?"

Michael shook his head. "He has a board of trustees he has to answer to. It's not enough to hand him a carton and say, *here, here's your mask*. That's not the way things are done in the foundation world. You should know that."

Why was it that every time Michael opened his mouth, he sounded like he was the older brother rather than the younger? Gabriel was his senior by six years and change.

Michael set down the Rubik's Cube, its sides neatly arranged, entropy defeated once again.

"Never mind," he said, heaving a familiar sigh. "I'll write it."

"Make it good," Gabriel said. "Tell them I had to sneak past a tribe of cannibals to get it."

"In the south of France?"

"Gourmet cannibals."

"I'd appreciate it, Gabriel, if you could show a modicum of seriousness about these things."

"I know you would, Michael. It's what I love about you. You use words like 'modicum' with a straight face."

They were a study in contrast, Gabriel and his brother.

Both were still in tuxedos—how often had *that* fate befallen them?—the evening's entertainment having consisted of the Hunt Foundation's annual Martin J. Beresford Memorial Awards dinner two floors below.

But where Michael wore his bespoke tailored suit with quiet dignity, Gabriel had untied the bowtie and cummerbund of his rented number and undone the shirt studs halfway down his chest. Michael was scholarly, almost tweedy, bespectacled; the pallor of his skin reflected a life spent largely indoors, these days behind a computer screen much of the time, or else talking on the telephone to similarly pale men halfway around the globe. Gabriel was darker—hair as black as shoe crème, skin browned by the sun of many lands. He was chiseled, the muscles of his long arms ropy. The last time he'd found himself behind a computer he'd been using the thing as a shield. You can't beat a nice solid IBM laptop for stopping a bullet.

The aegis of the Hunt Foundation had made both brothers moderately famous in their respective ways, and to an extent they depended on one another for their success. Gabriel's discoveries in the field and unearthments of historical significance would not have been possible without the Foundation's financial support. Michael, in turn, acknowledged grudgingly that much of the Foundation's prestige derived from the attention Gabriel's higher-profile successes had brought in—the kind of risk-taking that is indefensibly reckless until it yields something suitable for publication.

"Your presentation went over well," Michael said in a conciliatory tone.

"It had pictures. Everyone likes pictures."

"Oh, you're in one of your *moods*," Michael said.

"Four hours of speeches from guys in penguin suits will put anyone in a mood. Anyone but you."

"Maybe so." Michael sorted through some of the neatly arranged papers on the table, pulled a sheet and

turned it to face Gabriel. "Before you go." He uncapped a fountain pen and held it out. "You still have
to cosign the endowment for the Indonesian group."
All significant expenditures of the Hunt Foundation
needed to bear the signatures of both brothers, though
Michael handled all other aspects of the organization's
administration on his own.

"The Molucca figures," said Gabriel. "Right." He
reached out for the pen, and at that moment both
brothers heard the sound of footsteps outside the office door. The knob turned, the door swung toward
them, and a member of the Foundation staff stuck his
head inside. "Mr. Hunt?"

"Yes?" Michael said. "What is it, Roger?"

But Roger said, "Not you, sir," and turned to Gabriel.

"Me?"

"There's a woman, sir, asking for you. Quite . . .
informally dressed. She insists on speaking with you. I
let her know you were occupied with Foundation business, but she insisted she has something of utmost
importance to discuss with you . . . in private, sir."

"Do you know who this is, Gabriel?" Michael
asked. "Some old paramour of yours?"

"Probably," Gabriel said. "Though how any of them
would know to look for me here I don't know."

"Possibly your last name on the plaque by the door,"
Michael said, "next to the word 'Foundation,' had
something to do with it."

"Where is she?" Gabriel asked Roger.

"In the club room, sir." Roger's expression was un-
readably neutral. He was very good at his job.

Gabriel bent over the Indonesian papers, signed

them swiftly in triplicate, re-capped the pen and followed Roger to the door. "Don't wait up for me," he told Michael.

"Oh, I know better than that," Michael said.

As Roger led him down a gently curving and lushly carpeted flight of stairs, Gabriel ran through in his head the women who could possibly have tracked him down here. Annabelle? Rebecca? No; they were both still in Europe and lacked visas to travel to the U.S. Joyce Wingard? Fiona Rush? Unlikely in the former case, strictly impossible in the latter. Then who? He could have continued guessing indefinitely without ever thinking of the woman who turned from the window at the far end of the room to face him after he entered the club room and shut the door behind him.

"Hello, Gabriel."

"Lucy?"

He saw her bristle at the name.

Lucy Hunt had been born Lucifer Artemis Hunt, thanks to parents whose knowledge of classical antiquity and Biblical scholarship exceeded their ability to anticipate the taunting a girl might be forced to endure from her peers if they named her Lucifer. They'd meant well, naming all three of their children after archangels from the Bible, but Gabriel and Michael had gotten the long end of that particular stick and Lucy the short. When she'd run away from home at age seventeen, her name hadn't been the cause, or at least not the sole cause—but all the same, she'd taken to calling herself Cifer. She'd also severed all ties to the family, the Foundation and her prior life. Gabriel had seen her a grand total of two times in the past nine years, neither of them here in the building where they'd grown up; and he knew Michael hadn't seen her even once. He'd exchanged e-mail with the mysterious "Cifer" from time to time, but had no idea who it really was, because at Lucy's request Gabriel had never told him.

"What are you doing here?" Gabriel asked.

She came forward. She was wearing scuffed, mud-spattered sneakers and well-worn leather pants; a battered denim jacket with a black T-shirt underneath; and a canvas rucksack over one shoulder. She had obviously just thundered in out of the rain. Her wet hair was dyed brick red and chopped short and she had a large Celtic tattoo Gabriel didn't remember decorating one side of her neck. She'd filled out a bit since Gabriel had seen her last, put on some weight that she'd badly needed; she was in her midtwenties now and quite pretty, and cleaned up she'd be a killer. But that was about as likely to happen, Gabriel knew, as a televangelist refusing a tithe.

She stopped beside him. "I can only stay a short time, Gabriel. I'm not even supposed to be in the country. I'm supposed to be under house arrest in Arezzo." She lifted one leg of her pants to reveal a bit of high-tech apparatus clamped around her ankle; a red LED on it flashed silently every few seconds. "I hacked it so it says I'm still there. But they do visual sweeps every three days, which only gives me till tomorrow night to get back."

"Jewelry-wise, you might want to go with something a bit more spidery," Gabriel said. "So I repeat, what are you doing here?"

"When I heard about Mitch, I had to come. She

needs help. Which means I need *your* help." She took note of Gabriel's monkey suit, nodded toward it. "Hey. Wedding or funeral?"

"Funeral would have been more fun," said Gabriel.

"Why I got the hell out," she muttered. "So, what about it? Talk?"

"Sure, what the heck? We can get Michael down here, make it a real family reunion. There's got to be some ice cream in a freezer around here someplace. Marshmallows. We can put on our pj's and talk all night."

"Serious," she said, shucking water like a cat. She took him by the wrist, tugged him toward the door.

"What's wrong with talking here? It's wet out there." But she kept tugging. "Fine." Gabriel grabbed an umbrella from an elephant-foot stand, buttoned up his shirt with his other hand. "After you," he said.

"I've got this friend, Mitch," Lucy began. "Short for Michelle."

She had steered Gabriel to a caffeine dive in the Village where the espresso ran extra-strong and the lights were kept mercifully low. On the way out of the townhouse, Gabriel had abandoned his suit jacket for a nicely broken-in A2, US Army Air Corps vintage circa 1942, with the emblem of the Eighth Air Force and the Flying Eight-Balls on one shoulder. He was still wearing the white piquet tuxedo shirt under it, though.

"Mitch is air force—or she was, before they threw her to the wolves for a helicopter crash, a training flight accident. They needed a scapegoat and wouldn't nail the pilot because of rank. Plus they hate the idea of a woman in the program, needless to say."

"Is this going to be another feminist soapbox thing?" said Gabriel. "Or does it get interesting?"

"Just shut up and listen and I'll get to it."

"Okay." Gabriel took another sip. The coffee here really was very good; the kind of drink that made you want to sit and contemplate deeper mysteries.

"So: Mitch gets defrocked. She comes back to New York to stay with her sister, Valerie, who works in the records department of a company called Zongchang Limited. But the day Mitch arrives, Valerie goes to a meeting with Zongchang's foreign corporate heads at a hotel. The police find her heels-up in a Dumpster at 1 A.M. the next day with the stale Caesar salad. Her throat's been cut, and she's been shot through the heart."

"Both?"

"Yeah—and that's not even the interesting part. Do the cops go hunting for someone who might have done it? No—they nail Mitch for it. For the murder of her own sister. No way in hell, but that's what they've decided. She Twittered it on the way to jail. I snuck myself onto the next flight over."

"Twittered?"

"Think of it as a way you can update a blog from your cell phone—" She saw Gabriel's blank stare. "Never mind. Point is, she told me what was happening. They're only calling her a 'material witness' for now, but it's obvious they think she did it. The only good part of the whole thing is that, over the prosecutor's objections, the judge has set bail. Which by the way means I need some bail money."

"If what you want's money," Gabriel said, "Michael's got the checkbook."

"I can't ask him. Can you picture that, first time I

see him in a decade, it's *Hey, Michael, can you get my friend out of jail? And by the by, I'm sort of under arrest myself . . .*" Lucy shook her head. "Anyway the money's not all I want. Listen. The high muckety-mucks in this company have something to do with 'ethnographic Chinese antiquities.' "

"I think I remember reading something about that," Gabriel said, "the head of Zongchang being a collector. Ching, or Chung, something like that."

"Yeah, well, Mitch is pretty sure Ching-or-Chung whacked her sister because she found out something she wasn't supposed to. But now the men who did it have high-tailed it back to China—to the CCC. You know what that is?"

Gabriel pinched the bridge of his nose. The CCC. He knew this political movement-cum-Mafia only by ruthless reputation, since he had somehow managed to avoid a hands-on run-in with them. "The Chinese Cooperative Confederation. It's a lot like Russia after the Soviet Union fell apart. Like Morocco during World War Two."

"Bastards who play for keeps, was how Mitch put it," said Lucy. "They're outside international law. No extradition—"

"No diplomatic inquiry," said Gabriel, nodding.

"Once someone's tucked away in there, there's no getting them out."

"And you want to get someone out?"

"Mitch does. And unless they keep her locked up for the rest of her life, she's going to go after him herself. Neither of which is a great alternative. I mean, Mitch can take care of herself, but I wouldn't want to see her go up against an organization like this."

"Unlike me, for instance," Gabriel said.

Lucy nodded, and the look of utter confidence in her eyes shot right through Gabriel's defenses. It was like when she was eight years old and he was twenty, freshly back from a year in North Africa, and she'd listened to his exaggerated tales of his exploits with rapt attention each night after Michael had headed off to bed. She'd believed he could do anything. He'd believed it for a while himself.

"And who is this woman?" asked Gabriel. "Why is it so important to you to help her?"

Lucy paused before answering. "She's a friend," Lucy said. "I've known her a long time. She got me through some very bad stuff. I owe her a lot."

"All right," Gabriel said. He mulled over the possibilities. "The CCC," he said. "Well, moving around inside China's easier than it used to be, though you'd still want cover for something like this. One possibility, Michael was telling me about a lecture series he's setting up at a bunch of Chinese universities. He's supposed to give the lectures himself—but who'd really complain if I showed up with him?"

Lucy allowed herself the ghost of a smile. "Or instead of him. You'd really wake up some of those rooms."

"No doubt," Gabriel said. "So, tell me straight: what exactly is it you want me to do?"

"First thing is help me get Mitch out of jail," said Lucy. "And then convince her that she doesn't need to fly to China to kill this guy."

"Because I'll do it for her? I'm not some sort of assassin, Lucy."

"You'll think of something," Lucy said. "You always do."

Chapter 2

Michelle "Mitch" Quantrill was a piece of work indeed. Twenty-nine years old, tall and square-cut, sturdy and practical, strong, attractive but not glamorous, zero makeup. Blonde hair, cut indifferently. Eyes of milky green.

For Gabriel, it was worth the bail money just to meet her. And to see her and Lucy together provided some interstitial links.

"*Not* what you think," chided Lucy, but Gabriel had a feeling it was exactly what he thought.

"You're Lucy's brother?" said Mitch. Her handshake grip was strong and to the point.

"One of them," Gabriel said.

"Well, I appreciate your getting me out of there. I was beginning to lose my mind."

They caught a cab outside the precinct house and told the cabbie to take them to Valerie's apartment, a building near 45th and Eighth.

"Have you ever heard of Kangxi Shih-k'ai?" said Mitch, who was in the backseat with Gabriel. Lucy was turned around in the passenger seat up front, watching them through the Plexiglas divider.

"Sure. The warlord of warlords," Gabriel said.

"Around the turn of the century—the last century—he mantled himself the Favorite Son of China. He's said to have personally killed twenty thousand enemies. He died in, what, 1901 or 1902, something like that? Assassinated by his own bodyguards, as I recall."

"Right. Well, Valerie told me that working at Zong-chang she'd uncovered some kind of dirt on a guy named Cheung—the guy in charge of the CCC, the one they're saying will be the new Mao? She said she'd found proof he wasn't Chinese at all—he's really a Russian trying to pose himself as a Chinese. Specifically, as a blood descendant of Kangxi Shih-k'ai, who was known to have over two hundred children."

"Cheung is the guy who collects the statues," said Lucy.

"What statues?" said Gabriel.

"The terra-cotta warriors. Life size."

"You mean the famous ones?" said Gabriel. "Those are all in government hands. They have been since they first started digging them up in the 1970s."

Gabriel dredged up what he knew about China's First Emperor and his statue-making predilection.

In 246 B.C., the then 13-year-old Emperor Qin had tasked over 700,000 workers with building his mausoleum. The project, including the terra-cotta army of over 8,000 figures, took nearly forty years to complete. When a group of farmers digging for a well in Shaanxi Province uncovered the first terra-cotta head in 1974, they had no idea they had uncovered the archeological find of the 20th Century. It dwarfed even Howard Carter's 1922 uncovering of Tutankhamen's tomb—yes, Qin's tomb was larger, the size of two entire cities, complete with a pearl-inlaid ceiling to simulate nighttime stars. Besides the figures of soldiers, generals (the tallest figures, averaging six feet in height), acrobats, strongmen and musicians, there were 130 chariots drawn by 520 terra-cotta horses, not to mention another 150 additional horses for the cavalry. The "four divine animals"—dragon, phoenix, tortoise and a sort of giraffe-like chimera called a *qilin*—were represented, as well as the unicorn, or *xiezhi*. Diggers found the remains of artisans and craftsmen (in addition to all of Qin's barren concubines), suggesting that they were sealed inside the complex to prevent them from divulging their knowledge of the tombs . . . or of the 30-meter-high adjacent building discovered nearby in 2007 by Chinese archeologists. The side building remained unexplored to this day.

"Cheung has offered a flat ten million dollars to anybody who can find the terra-cotta warrior of Kangxi Shih-k'ai," said Mitch.

"But that makes no sense," said Gabriel. "Kangxi Shih-k'ai lived at the end of the 19th Century—the terra-cotta warriors are two thousand years older."

"Kangxi Shih-k'ai apparently had his *own* terra-cotta army made," Mitch said. "That's what Valerie told me. And it has never been found."

"Hold on," Gabriel said. "You're saying he built an entire second terra-cotta army and buried it somewhere in modern China and nobody has ever heard about it except your sister?"

"No, Mr. Hunt," Mitch said. "Except my sister and this guy Cheung. And he's looking for it."

"Did she say what he wants with it?"

"The main resistance Cheung is getting to the rise of the CCC is from old-school Chinese traditionalists. If he can prove he's somehow related to Kangxi Shih-k'ai, that resistance evaporates."

"And how would the statue prove anything?"

"Because it contains Kangxi Shih-k'ai's skeleton," she said. "Sheathed in lead and gold. Or at least his skull—Valerie wasn't clear which. But *something*. Something Cheung could use to perpetrate a bit of DNA flummery, I guess, or maybe that wouldn't even be necessary. It's such a powerful cultural icon, just possessing it would give him enormous credibility."

"Your sister told you this?"

"Yeah," said Mitch. "Right before she went to a meeting with Cheung and wound up dead."

The cab drew up to the curb beside Valerie's building. Gabriel gave the driver a twenty and followed Mitch out the door.

They plodded through the typically New York experience of the walk-up: twelve steps, turn; twelve steps more. Mitch had a fistful of keys out, but it was Lucy who reached the apartment door first. She paused, then raised one hand in a silencing gesture.

"Hang on," she whispered. "It's already open."

Upon sighting the forced door and the visual evidence of damage to the jamb and molding from a professional jimmy—someone had come prepared enough to outfox the overkill of multiple locks in Manhattan—each of the three people in the stairwell reacted differently.

Lucy, experienced in urban rat-traps, flattened against the wall so as to provide herself with maximum cover should an assault issue from the doorway.

Mitch's hand automatically flew down to draw a gun she did not possess. It was a flicker, a notion instantly replaced by the reset of her body into a defensive combat stance, one forearm up to shield, the other to strike, sharp key-points extending between her knuckles.

Gabriel had already moved past both of them to be first through into possible hazard. "Hold it," he whispered. "I don't hear anything inside."

They were at his back (in a classic triangle defense pattern, he noticed; good for them) as he toed the door open. His perimeter senses were keyed up full. His shoulders relaxed.

"Whatever happened here, I think they've already come and gone."

Mitch sagged as though she knew what they would find. The one-bedroom was in a state of disarray that suggested a thorough yet not particularly malicious burglary—drawers dumped, knickknacks scattered. Mitch's eyes went straight to the desk where it looked Valerie had had her computer setup.

"They took her hard drives," Mitch said numbly. She dropped the keys in the newly empty space on her sister's desk.

Gabriel scanned the room. "Two men, I'll bet. One for lookout, one for the turnover." He ran a finger over the surface of the computer table. "Powder," he noted. "They came in wearing latex gloves." He turned to Mitch. "I don't suppose she told you what kind of evidence she had?"

"There wasn't any time," said Mitch. "She picked me up at Newark when I came in. We had lunch at some fancy joint, one of those places where they have a whole separate menu for water. We couldn't talk too openly there, with all the waiters listening. She was going to tell me later—but first she had this meeting. I thought it was weird that it was so late at night, but she said these guys had come in internationally, were still on Shanghai time. It was a 'face' thing. And the meeting was important to her—she was going to confront them with what she'd found, tell them she couldn't be involved in any sort of cover-up; she wasn't telling them what to do, just backing out gracefully herself. You see how well that worked. I was sitting around here like a patsy when the cops showed up, and meanwhile the Zongchang boys were private-jetting it back to the CCC."

"So," Gabriel said, "the first, best hope for the new, modern China, the dedicated wannabe chief big grand kahuna of the CCC, this guy who is Russian pretending to be Chinese, the guy hunting for a one-of-a-kind statue of a dead Chinese warlord, comes to New York and, confronted with evidence that he's not what he says he is, kills the woman who found it and ransacks her apartment?" Gabriel was looking around the apartment—the leftovers of Valerie's life—with a renewed intensity in his gaze.

"Yeah," said Mitch. "Or it was done on his orders."

Gabriel turned to Lucy. "Okay, *now* I'm interested." He picked up the ring of keys. "Your sister gave you these?"

Mitch nodded. "In case I needed to go out before she got back."

The bundle contained four door keys, a main entry key, a foyer key, a mailbox key, a trash-door key and a riot of dead weight in the form of a pewter Empire State Building, a rabbit's foot (dyed pink), a big rubber sandal with the name VAL embossed on it . . . and something else.

"What's this?" said Gabriel, peering closer.

It was a silver charm in the form of a little hardcover

book about a half-inch tall. The cover was engraved with the legend DRINK ME.

Gabriel pried the seam with a thumbnail and the tiny book popped open like a locket to reveal its cargo.

"Aha," he said, looking at the narrow black sliver inside. It was plastic and had tiny metal contacts at one end. "It's a . . . thing."

"Give me that," Lucy said. Gabriel plucked it out of the book and handed it over. He could navigate the tunnels of the Paris sewer system in the dark and tell you where an obsidian blade was made by the strike pattern on the stone edge; modern technology, though, was not his bailiwick.

Fortunately, it was his sister's. "Memory stick," she said, turning the sliver over. "Four gigs. The kind you plug into a cell phone."

"Like this one?" Mitch held up a unit she'd unplugged from a charger dock that lay overturned on the floor. It looked like the kind of biz-crazy portable device that did everything except unzip your duds and make you see the face of God.

"We have a winner," Lucy said, popping a hatch on the back of the thing and sliding the stick inside.

Mitch, meanwhile, was staring into one of the desk drawers, riffling its contents. "Her passport's still here. Some credit cards. ID." A tear leaked from one eye, dropped and spattered across the back of her hand.

"Let me see that," said Gabriel while Lucy worked on the phone. "I'd like to see her face."

The family resemblance was undeniable.

"This is some bizarre stuff," said Lucy, scrolling through data on the phone's tiny screen. "Mostly spreadsheets, it looks like. Amounts of money, invoices, bills of lading."

"She must have known something was going to happen to her," said Mitch, straining to keep the tremor in her voice from showing. Gabriel could tell she was the sort who wanted to be in control, in charge of her messier emotions, and who would beat herself up for any public display she thought looked weak. "To leave all this stuff behind."

"We need to print this out," Lucy said. "You can't read it properly on a screen this size."

"I'm sure Michael's got a setup we can use, back at the town house," Gabriel said. And to Mitch he said, "You want to come with us? I'm not sure it's good for you to stay here alone." He put a hand on Mitch's shoulder, but she shook it off.

"I'm fine," she said roughly, sounding anything but.

"I'll stay," Lucy said. "I don't have to be on a plane till tomorrow morning—"

"I'm *okay*," Mitch said. "You don't have to get yourself in trouble on my account." She turned to Gabriel. "And you don't have to take care of me, either. I'm not a fragile flower. I'm a soldier, goddamn it. Or I used to be. I'm not going to sit around moaning or feeling frightened—I'm going to find the men who did this and make them sorry they did."

"Maybe," Gabriel said. "Or maybe they'll make you sorry you did. I don't think you know the kind of power you're talking about taking on."

"Listen, stud, if you're scared and want to drop out, that's fine," Mitch said. "You posted bail. That's plenty."

"If you want to go up against the CCC and you want to live to tell about it," Gabriel said patiently, "you'll listen to me and you'll do it very, *very* carefully."

"He can be a pain," Lucy said, "but he does know what he's talking about, Mitch."

Mitch threw up her hands. "All right. You've got something to say, I'll listen. But I'm not waiting long."

"Fair enough," Gabriel said. And to Lucy: "I'll be back as quick as I can. Couple hours at most. You guys can stick around here that long, right?" Lucy looked anxiously over at Mitch, who was pacing impatiently. She nodded.

"All right. Call me if anything happens."

Gabriel left them to pick up the pieces at the apartment while he headed back to Sutton Place with the cell phone and the memory stick.

Michael would be able to print the document, and from there, well . . . they'd see what they would see. He shared Mitch's preference for action and distaste for waiting around, but jumping into a conflict with the CCC wasn't something you did lightly.

Or at least it wasn't something *he* would do lightly.

It wasn't two hours later that Valerie's cell phone, now sitting in a docking station attached to one of Michael's computers, started vibrating, and when Gabriel opened it and brought it to his ear, he heard Lucy's voice shouting at him. "Gabriel? That you?"

"Yes."

"She's gone," Lucy said. "I went to take a shower, and when I got out . . ."

"No Mitch," Gabriel said.

"She left a note," Lucy said. "Just one line."

"And what's that?"

" 'Enough's enough,' " Lucy read. " 'I'm going to get those bastards.' "

Chapter 3

"For god's sake, Gabriel, you don't know anything about the Han Dynasty," Michael grumbled. "The *Later* Han Dynasty? The Three Kingdoms and the Period of Disunion? You'll never get away with it."

"For one or two lectures? I think I can. And then you can take over from me after that, finish the tour yourself."

"What, are you going to speak to Mandarin students in Cantonese?"

"I'll speak English. They'll chalk it up to American arrogance and move on. They're used to it."

"You . . . you don't even have a *degree*!" Michael protested, flustered. If you started counting up Michael's assorted doctorates on your fingers, you'd be compelled before long to remove your shoes.

"We're not talking about a debate, Michael. I don't need to hold my own. You'll give me your slides and I'll work off them. Not like I can't regurgitate names and dates with the best of them."

Michael switched gears: "You don't even know if this Cheung had anything to do with that woman's death."

"Well, according to *you*, these documents show

he's guilty of plenty else." He waved the sheaf of print-outs in Michael's face. "Arms trafficking, drug smuggling, racketeering, not to mention a murder or five."

Michael flushed crimson. "Gabriel . . . it's a different country. Different laws. We'd be intruding where we're not invited."

"My specialty," said Gabriel, with slightly more pride than he needed to drive his point home. "One day of travel in, one day out. In between, a couple of days of poking around the edges of things. See what spills forth. Michael—it's what the Foundation does *best*, don't kid yourself. You clear the paperwork and I kick down the doors."

"You really think," Michael said, "there's a second terra-cotta army out there no one's ever seen, waiting to be discovered."

"I do," Gabriel said. "And even if there isn't, there's a young woman out there who's going to get herself arrested and executed for trying to kill somebody who, as you point out, we don't even know has done anything—not to her, at least."

"This is the girlfriend of your . . . what was she again, one of your nurses in the hospital in Khartoum?"

Gabriel had made up a story, at Lucy's request; she didn't want Michael to know she was in New York. So Gabriel had, but he unfortunately no longer remembered what it was he'd said. "Something like that. Look, Michael, it won't cost much—"

"It's not about the money, Gabriel. It's the principle of the thing."

"I agree. And as a matter of principle, I don't like to let innocent people get themselves killed when I can prevent it."

"I suppose," Michael said in a resigned tone, "you'll be taking the jet."

"Yes," said Gabriel. "For two reasons. One: I can't go as you on a commercial flight—they'll check my passport."

"What's the other reason?"

"Because I don't want to run *this* through baggage check."

Gabriel hoisted up his work-belt, worn around the world in one situation or another. It was tooled steer-hide with faded intaglio, furry at some of the rivets, an old friend and constant companion that had seen him through more than one tough scrape. Lashed to the belt was a big holster. Sheathed inside was an even bigger sidearm, itself a pricey antique, Gabriel's own restored single-action Colt Peacemaker—a first-generation Cavalry model circa 1880 with the 7 1/2-inch barrel, chambered for the .45 "Long Colt" cartridge. The original heavily distressed ivory grips had been replaced, by Gabriel himself, with burnished mahogany.

Nearly two centuries ago, Samuel Colt had been the man who did not understand the meaning of the word "impossible" when naysayers told him the idea of a repeating handgun could never be realized. While he did not actually invent the revolver, he won his first patent in the early 1800s and was instrumental in introducing the use of interchangeable, mass-produced parts.

Whenever people said "impossible," or that a thing *should not* be done or *could not* be done, Gabriel always thought of old Sam Colt.

Michael was staring at his older brother with an odd tilt of his head, like an explorer mantis or a curious puppy. "Okay," he began carefully. "What part *aren't* you telling me? What are you leaving out?"

"There is one thing," Gabriel said.

"I knew it."

"The name of the man behind the second terra-cotta army," said Gabriel, not without a dramatic flourish. "It's Kangxi Shih-k'ai, Michael. The Favored Son of China. The last real-man warlord before the modern world stomped them down. The Vlad the Impaler of Chinese history—the history that the Cultural Committee never talks about during stuff like the Olympics. We're not talking about an ordinary monarch, Michael. We're talking about one of the most frightening figures of his time, or any time. You remember what he called his champions while he was alive?"

"The Killers of Men," Michael murmured.

"The Killers of Men, that's right. And this is the man who constructed a second terra-cotta army as a monument to his ego, and nobody has ever *seen* it. Can you imagine what those figures must be like? Wouldn't you want us to be the first in the world to see them, to bring them to light?"

Gabriel hefted an original hardcover first edition of *Space, Time & Earthly Gods* by Ambrose and Cordelia Hunt, first published in 1982, the year their daughter Lucy had been born. "Take a closer look at Appendix III—the one where they listed what they thought were the greatest undiscovered treasures of the modern world."

The Hunt Foundation's foundation (as it were) was the success enjoyed by Gabriel and Michael's parents through a series of improbably popular books that conjoined history, religion, linguistics and anthropol-

ogy for the modern reader. Ambrose and Cordelia
Hunt were hailed as the new Will and Ariel Durant,
and at the time of their mysterious disappearance (to
this day, even Michael was hesitant to say "death"),
their fame had spread worldwide.

Gabriel gestured with the book; did not open it. "It's
right there at big number four, before the Bermuda
Triangle pirate shipwrecks and after the 'lost pyra-
mid' scroll that supposedly explains the destiny of the
world. It doesn't say what it is, exactly, but it talks
about 'the legacy of Kangxi Shih-k'ai.' Check Dad's
journal library and you'll find a lead he recorded, right
outside Shanghai. It's one of the last entries before they
vanished."

During the Mediterranean leg of a Millennium-
themed speaking tour at the end of 1999, Ambrose
and Cordelia Hunt were among the passenger contingent of the *Polar Monarch*, a luxuriously appointed
cruise ship of Norwegian registry. The ship disappeared from sea radar for three days, then reappeared
near Gibraltar without a living soul on board. Three
crew members were found in the wheelhouse with
their throats slit. Subsequently, bodies and stores began to wash ashore, but a dozen or so passengers were
never recovered in any form—including Ambrose and
Cordelia Hunt.

"You're not making this up, are you?" said Michael.

"Kangxi Shih-k'ai was on Mom and Dad's Most
Wanted list. They were on the verge of something and
they knew it; they just never had the time to pursue it. Now, I'm not saying there's a connection to
Michelle Quantrill and this Russian who wants to run
China . . . but it's enough to make me think there really is something there in China for us to find. It's

time, Michael. We should have gone after this years ago."

"Time for you to ruin my reputation on the lecture circuit, you mean," Michael said sourly.

"Come on, no one will pay attention to the lectures themselves," said Gabriel. "You know how it goes in China—they'll want to wine and dine us and tour us around to demonstrate their cultural diversity and goodwill. And I'll be perfectly charming, I promise."

Michael put a hand to his forehead and massaged the deep furrows that had appeared there. "This is sounding worse and worse," he said. Then, as he usually did, he diplomatically tabled the topic. "Let me think about it."

Which was all the approval Gabriel needed.

It was still startling for Mitch to see uniformed police and soldiers carrying automatic weapons in an airport, even in a foreign country.

The Customs official was unreadable: Round head, military crop, unblinking eyes, a knife scar on one side of his mouth. "Remove glasses," he said to Mitch, speaking in fractured English.

They examined each other. The official spot-checked the entry form boxes on *Criminal convictions* and *Contagious diseases*. Mitch had the feeling she had been processed and found lacking, no doubt an impression the uniforms cultivated deliberately.

He did not stamp Mitch's passport. "Stand in blue area, please."

Mitch was directed to a gauntlet of interview cubicles, where a burly Chinese soldier eviscerated her carry-on bag. She was directed to strip down to her underwear and was scanned with a multiband detector. Then into a scanning booth, to insure no contraband was up her ass or down her throat. Only then did a uniformed female supervisor show up, a black Eurasian who gave Mitch the once-over with disdain. It was designed to be as humiliating and intimidating as possible.

The soldier handed a business card to the supervisor. She squinted first at it, then at Mitch. "Your work is in computers," she said in flawlessly mellow Oxford English.

"Yes," said Mitch, trying to find her shirt in the tangle of clothing on the table.

"You are a consultant for Zongchang, Ltd." Nothing the humorless supervisor said was a question. It was rhetorical prodding, bald statements of facts intended to provoke a confirmation or denial.

"Yes."

"That is a good job for a foreigner to have."

"Yes it is."

About an hour later, Mitch finally made it to the overburdened taxicab queue. If one arrived at the city's more modern Pudong Airport, one had the option of taking the MagLev train the thirty kilometers or so into downtown. Mitch had flown into Hongqiao International, and as an outsider unfamiliar with the grid, was stuck with cabbing it. She knew that if the meter crested more than 200 *renminbi* she would have to have words with the "*helpfull, clean, professional, English-spakeing Driver*"—as a sign on the inside of the door informed her.

Most commercial cabs in China are compact cars with a Plexi-shield folded around the driver's seat only, giving the pilots an odd, bottled aspect and muffling nearly everything they say.

"Is biggest of all large bridges," the driver told her as they chugged across the modernist swath of Nanpu Bridge. "Most excellent photo opportunity!"

"We *are* going to downtown Shanghai, right?" said Mitch.

The driver nodded enthusiastically. "Three times! In 1997!"

It was all right. She could already see the spire of the Oriental Pearl TV Tower on the Bund.

Outside the Dongfeng Hotel, the scene was a casserole of Grand Central Station rush hour mixed with Casablanca; a huge and bustling open-air marketplace full of hucksters, eccentrics, exotics and bums. Even the poorest citizen was proud of his suit jacket; in fact, there was a thriving subindustry whereby designer labels could be sewn onto the sleeve of virtually any garment. The visible labels (usually on the left cuff) were a weird sort of status symbol, whether you were riding a bike or stepping out of a limousine. The sheer crush of human bodies was fantastic: thousands of people, hundreds of bicycles (ten abreast and moving fast on each side of Zhongshan Road), citizens hustling about in a floral rainbow of ponchos, pushcart cages of live food. Mitch saw one intrepid cyclist precariously transporting enough strapped-on TV sets to fill a 4x4.

A liveried doorman took her shoulder bag at the entrance to the Dongfeng.

The rooms at the Dongfeng featured card-access slots on the doors but still used old-fashioned keys. Mitch slumped on a double bed, trying not to let all her energy leak out, wondering where the surveillance camera might be hidden. They certainly were omnipresent in every other part of the hotel, particularly the elevators, which seemed to have two per car. She thought about this as she undressed, thought about the bored government functionary charged with watching this particular room's feed. Probably just made his day, she thought as she pulled a black dress out of her bag and slipped it on over her head.

Downstairs, a very polite but very confused concierge tried to help her get where she needed to go.

Mitch tapped Valerie's business card. "This? Here? Zongchang? Yes?"

The concierge seemed conflicted; apparently there was more than one destination called Zongchang. "A taxi can take you from hotel if you really wish to go," he said, implying that perhaps she did *not* want to go.

"I have an appointment with Mr. Kuan-Ku Tak Cheung," she said.

"Oh. I see." He scribbled a square note to be handed off to the next cabbie. "This is the Zongchang you seek."

"She's lost her mind," Lucy said.

Gabriel and Lucy sat in the war zone that had once been Valerie Quantrill's apartment.

"Near as I can figure, she took all the cards," said Lucy. "The business stuff, the photo ID, the credit cards. She left the keys so I'm guessing she wasn't planning to come back."

Gabriel still had a clear mental image of Valerie Quantrill's photo ID. The sisters had looked close enough to one another for Mitch to pass the quick scrutiny she'd get at an airport counter, especially if she'd done something to make her hair match. "A last-minute ticket to Shanghai's not cheap . . . but if Mitch maxed out the credit cards she could've swung it. And if she got a style cut or a wig . . ."

"She could pass for Valerie," Lucy said. "Fly on her passport. It's soon enough, maybe nobody knows Valerie is dead yet."

"The people who killed Valerie know."

"Goddamn it," Lucy said. "Why'd she pull something like this?"

"She's your friend. Don't ask me."

"Gabriel, if I'm not on a plane in four hours, I'll have the police forces of two countries after me!"

"So get on a plane," Gabriel said.

"*Someone's* got to help Mitch," Lucy said.

Gabriel Hunt picked up a little snow globe from the floor. Something belonging to Valerie. Little Statue of Liberty, swirling fake snow. Big heart, for NYC.

Lucy cleared her throat. "Will you do it?" she asked.

"Like I've ever been able to say no to you," Gabriel said.

Chapter 4

It was the first time Mitch had worn a dress in over six years, and the last time had been at a funeral. She felt askew in her rakish feminine attire, but it was necessary if she wanted to blend.

Zongchang Ltd. had tentacles all over urban Shanghai, and the destination to which her cabbie took her turned out to be a casino.

A floating casino.

A floating casino housed inside a converted aircraft carrier anchored in the harbor. The word "Zongchang" was painted on its side in four-foot-high red characters, English and Chinese both.

Inside a buoy-marked perimeter, scuba-capable security staff patrolled from one-man speed skiffs featuring gun mounts.

Loudspeakers advised potential trespassers to stay clear of the boat zone.

At the dock, more security men assisted patrons onto custom mini-ferries that ran to and from the ship's ornate gangplank. The security men were dressed in no-nonsense, upscale eveningwear, rather like Mitch was.

Except Mitch was not toting a visible MAC-10 with

a huge, priapic SIONICS suppressor stretching the barrel.

The carrier shell had been hollowed out and structurally reinforced to provide for broad, windowed views of the shimmering Bund, with outdoor restaurants on the flight deck. Inside, French staircases curved from level to level. Some bled off toward premium members-only gambling areas.

The main casino floor was anything but Vegas, favoring baccarat and *chemin de fer*, though tables for blackjack, roulette and Texas Hold 'Em were also in view.

At the armored cash windows, the currency of many different countries was being exchanged for the casino's special chips.

Mitch passed through another body scanner at the entry. There was no way she could have come in armed. She thought: *Play it as cool as dry ice. You're not Michelle Quantrill. You're Valerie. You're not dead. You're seeking your employer. You're a guest. Simple. Just ask. Don't panic.*

A tray of drinks was being offered to her before she'd even found her focus on the gambling floor. Mitch hesitated. Chose a martini.

"I'm looking for Mr. Cheung," she said, but the server had already departed.

She tried again with a passing security man who apparently "did not have the English." He arched an eyebrow at her and strode away.

Insane bass-heavy house/trance music thundered at her as she crossed an opaque dance floor of solid glass.

Mitch didn't know it yet, but she had already been made.

* * *

Qingzhao Wai Chiu took note of the blonde woman crossing the dance floor. Another lost, clueless American. Another despised tourist.

Qingzhao looked quite different from her previous public appearance, when an aerodynamic suit with a concealed mini-chute had permitted her to disappear into the blackness of the Huangpu River . . . instead of hitting flat water from a 300-meter drop, which would have been like landing on stone.

Tonight she was dressed to kill, literally and figuratively. New wig of cascading black curls. Tinted designer glasses. She had applied makeup so as to cause light to change the planes of her face. Enough exposure of thigh and décolletage to ensure she could steer men. The prostitutes in the casino were tawdry and obvious. Qingzhao prided herself as a chameleon.

She, too, had entered unarmed.

She, too, sought the man known as Kuan-Ku Tak Cheung.

Qingzhao found herself a likely security man. A bald East Indian, supersized, muscle packed atop more muscle.

"Ladies' toilet?" she said in a high, squeaky voice.

The idol-huge man rolled his eyes, then jerked a thumb. "That way, gorgeous."

Qingzhao giggled, as though from too much champagne. In her real life, she almost never laughed anymore.

The East Indian would not do. She needed somebody more reckless, younger, a hotshot on staff here.

"Don't mind Dinanath," said a voice behind her. "He's never polite."

She turned. Bingo. This guy was like a horny raptor with the eyes of a pit viper. He could be steered.

"You're *funny*," she said vacantly. "Listen . . . I need to find the toilet. I might need a little help getting there without becoming embarrassed."

He offered his arm. "Certainly. My name is Romero."

Qingzhao and Romero navigated across the dance floor, Qingzhao keeping her pace just halting enough to be convincing. By the time they reached the nearest restroom, Romero had already brushed her breasts twice and her ass once, strictly to guide her.

"Wait here, okay?" She gave him a little wave and tottered inside.

What she had been doing while in transit was noting the locations of the security cameras in the non-gambling zones. While there was a spy-eye (much more discreet) in the powder room, there were none in the individual toilets, which were set up in Western-style stalls.

Once inside a stall, she levered loose the stainless steel clip-lid of the toilet tank. The plunger works came loose easily enough. She bent the flimsy metal to form a spiked punch she could wrap around one fist.

Then she ventured a shy around-the-corner peek at Romero through the bathroom door. "Hey," she said. "This thing doesn't work." He stepped toward her. She smiled, grabbed his belt buckle, and pulled him along.

The cameras would only see two hard partiers headed for a stall and perhaps a taste of inebriated hanky-panky.

Qingzhao made sure Romero kept his eyes on her smile and other assets as she boxed him into the stall and quickly punched a gushing hole into his neck. One more strategic punch and the man was soundlessly down. She quickly stripped him of an automatic pistol and spare magazine, concealing the gun in the only place her show-offy dress would allow.

Done, armed, and not a drop of blood on her. So far so good.

Longwei Sze Xie had few peers or intimates, but nearly everybody called him "Ivory." Even his employer, Kuan-Ku Tak Cheung, used this familiar form. Other times, when matters were more grave, Cheung called him "Long." It had happened once or twice in nearly twenty years.

He was taking a break in the Zongchang's security nest—surrounded by monitors and exchanging monotonous chitchat with a console monkey named Zero—when he saw the blonde American stride across the dance floor. The whites of his eyes went stark with surprise at such naked boldness. He snapped his fingers and Zero backed up the feed in order to print out a photo of the woman, after choosing the best vantage.

Ivory's initial shock had come from seeing what he thought was a woman he knew to be dead, right there, seemingly alive, her body language practically broadcasting the rough retribution she sought for her own demise. Then his rational mind processed the image. *No, it's not her. Close, but no.* He was already on the move.

Ivory had feared something like this. Had prepared for its eventuality.

Cheung was holding forth with some financiers in the craps alcove. This woman would spot him eventually, or locate him indirectly. Then nine kinds of hell would break out—if he didn't get to her first.

He glided up behind her. Took a breath. Spoke calmly.

"Do you wish to enjoy Shanghai, Miss Quantrill?"

Mitch spun, slopping her untouched drink. Sandbagged. "Who the hell are you?"

"My name is Longwei Sze Xie," said the handsome Asian. "Please call me Ivory."

"Do you know Kuan-Ku Tak Cheung?"

Ivory was astonished at her directness. She was processing minor shock, he could tell, yet remained bullishly American.

"Yes," he said.

"I don't suppose you could point him out to me?"

Ivory dipped into his vest pocket, his free hand cautioning her against rash action. He withdrew a packet of airline tickets. "First class back to New York City, with my compliments."

Mitch eyed him suspiciously. "What're *you* supposed to be?"

"I am the greatest friend you have in the world right now, Miss Quantrill."

Past the woman's shoulder, Ivory saw Dinanath, the big bald operative, signaling to him from across the gambling floor. Summoning him.

Ivory clenched his teeth as though mildly pained. "Come with me."

Kuan-Ku Tak Cheung made a habit of keeping tabs on his Number One, Ivory, and when he spotted his head of security chatting up a strangely familiar blonde, he snapped his fingers and Dinanath jumped to.

It wasn't quite an arrest, but had more insistence than a mere escort.

Cheung excused himself from the company of his

supporters after making sure they had drinks all around. Extra security, all first string except for Romero (who was MIA somewhere), formed an outer ring for privacy as Dinanath, Ivory and their visitor came over. She was not a beautiful woman, noted Cheung. More . . . handsome. But there was something compelling about her, something about the hardness in her eyes.

Mitch stared. It was not polite, but she couldn't help herself. Cheung was burly, bristly. Nothing about him seemed Chinese except for the epicanthic folds of his eyelids, and she realized, with a jolt, that the man had probably had surgery to acquire the look. In any event, his eyes were bright blue.

"And, this is . . . ?" said Cheung, not speaking to Mitch, but to Ivory.

"I've come about Valerie Quantrill," said Mitch.

Dinanath was upending her small clutch purse on a vacant table, rummaging.

"Who is Valerie Quantrill?" said Cheung, again to Ivory.

"A woman you left dead in a Dumpster in New York," said Mitch, reddening.

Upon hearing this, Dinanath turned to Cheung and shrugged. *It was all we could find. A garbage bin.* As if to say, *so what?*

Cheung looked around to his fellows as though he had missed something, like a punch line. *"And . . . ?"*

"And I want to know what you had to do with it," said Mitch.

Cheung splayed his fingers across his mouth, pondering. "Hmm. All the way from the United States? Seems like a lot of trouble just to hurl an accusation. Why bother?"

"She was my sister."

Cheung seemed truly at sea. Mitch wondered if he was going to toy with her, string her out, maximize the pain. But what he said was infinitely colder. He again turned to Ivory and said, "What does she want? Money? Then pay her some money."

"I don't want your money," Mitch said through clenched teeth.

He looked at Mitch as though truly seeing her for the first time. "You want an apology?" He shrugged. "Very well—you have my apologies for your loss."

Mitch said, "That's not all. You *know* that's not all."

Cheung had already turned to resume other business, but allowed himself a parting shot: "That's all *you* get, my dear."

Mitch's thumb snapped the martini glass she was holding at its stem. With the base held against her palm, she shucked Dinanath's light grasp and lunged at Cheung's face, putting her shoulder into the thrust.

Ivory was there instantly, his hand arresting her wrist in a vise-grip, as though he had snatched a fly in midair. The jagged stem of the glass hovered inches from his own eyes. He had stepped in to shield Cheung with unnatural speed. Stoically, he nerve-pinched the glass from Mitch's hand.

Cheung was grinning—not smiling. The expression was vulpine. "See if you can find another Dumpster," he said to Dinanath. "And don't alarm the *dakuan*." Cheung needed the high-rollers to remain unagitated.

The backwash of adrenaline in Qingzhao's system was nauseating.

In a vital confluence of dozens of moving people and wavering vantage points, she'd briefly had the perfect shot at Cheung's head—maybe time to get two or three rounds in before general panic ruined the target. And that American bitch had spoiled everything!

Now this . . . this *amateur* was being escorted to the security nest.

But wait: after a beat, she saw Cheung and his head of security (that son of a bitch, Ivory) headed the same way.

She still might have a chance.

Qingzhao moved across the grand hall as quickly as she could, blending.

"This is really good for headaches," said the Chinese security man, who wore Buddy Holly glasses and a goatee, and was apparently named Chino. He was referring to a leather glove on his right hand. The glove had rivets across the knuckles. He punched Mitch a second time in the side of the head. "Got one, yet?"

His first punishing blow had been dealt to the left side of her head, so it was only fair that he rock her back the way she came. For balance.

Mitch lolled in the chair, half-conscious.

Chino automatically became less cocky when Cheung and Ivory entered the security room. Zero kept to his monitors.

"Oh, don't do it *here*," Cheung said, piqued.

Before further debate could ensue there came a businesslike rap on the door. Chino yanked it open, prepared to repel all invaders. "*What*!" he said, full up with brine.

Qingzhao shot him in the head.

Mitch tried to scoot her chair out of the way of Chino's falling corpse and wound up dumping herself backward on the floor. One chair arm cracked violently loose and the bindings securing her fell slack. She freed herself as quickly as she could.

More gunfire. She saw Ivory tackle Cheung and both men disappeared through the slanted observation window in a hailstorm of glass.

Zero huddled in a quivering ball beneath the console where his monitors were disintegrating from bullet hits as Qingzhao tried to track Cheung.

No go.

Qingzhao was holding her hand out to Mitch.

"Come on. We've got to go now."

The moment Chino answered the door was the same moment that Gabriel Hunt, freshly arrived from America, entered the Zongchang casino ship for the first and only time in his life.

Chapter 5

Gabriel Hunt's first view of the Zongchang was impressive—the ship was one of the four Kiev class warships built for the Soviet Navy in the mid-1970s and decommissioned in 1995. One was sold to the Indian Navy for modernization; one was scrapped and the other two were sold to China as "recreational pieces." The nonmilitary paint job incorporated a lot of dead black and silver, in sweeping lines that reminded Gabriel of formula race cars back in the hero days, before all the advertising sponsorships.

He wondered if any of the ship's firepower was still functional.

Gabriel had just gotten his first taste of the vast main gambling floor when two men came exploding through a slanted, one-way observation window at the far end.

Flashes of gunfire, from within the chamber.

And a split-second glimpse of the only person in this place that Gabriel might recognize—Mitch Quantrill, dolled up as her own sister. Blood on her face.

Gabriel moved as the main floor erupted into chaos.

A Frenchman in the poker pit stood up and stopped a stray round, his busted flush flying into the air like cast-off flower petals. Half the clientele hit the deck while the other half was galvanized into directionless flight. Gabriel shoved one runner aside in time to save his life. The man cursed him in Arabic. The casino's black-suited security men had unlimbered a frightening variety of snubbed full-autos and were handing their disorganization back to the crowd in the form of scattered bullet-sprays at anything and everything that might be an antagonist. Gabriel knew that, in a firefight, those little earphone-buds only worked in the movies, so if the shooters were trying to communicate or coordinate, right now they couldn't hear a damned thing.

The racket was incredible inside what was still essentially a huge metal room. Flat-nosed slugs chuddered up a balustrade and destroyed a fake Grecian urn next to Gabriel's head.

The two acrobats who had made their grand entrance by defenestrating from the security portal were still trying to find their wits and their feet. One man was yelling and pointing. The other was trying to shield his boss.

Forgoing the increasing availability of weapons as a good contingent of assorted bodyguards and security men inadvertently shot each other, Gabriel bypassed his instinctual craving for a firearm (if anything, he would have wanted his Colt, but he'd left that stashed back on the Foundation jet) and made for the vacant security window. Mitch was up there. Alive, dead or compromised—he had no way of knowing except through immediate action.

Slugs tore across the baize at his heels as he hit a *chemin de fer* table at full tilt and vaulted toward the gaping eye of the blown observation port. Its rubberized mount was fanged with shards of glass but Gabriel managed to pull himself up and over.

He found himself in the security nest with a couple of dead guys and one gibbering employee still stashed beneath the console. Equipment was sparking and blowing out all around him as incoming fire destroyed costly electronics the way rock breaks scissors.

Outside the nest door was a secondary corridor more in keeping with the ship's utilitarian naval origins—a lot of cast iron and shatterproof lights.

Thirty yards ahead, Qingzhao and Mitch encountered two security men rushing toward the danger zone. Qingzhao flat-handed one in the face, pile-driving his palate back toward his spine. He collided with his buddy, whose legs Mitch took away in a fast and clumsy sweep-kick. It was enough. The man bonked rivets and decking with his head all the way down. Qingzhao quickly disarmed them and handed off the extra firearm to Mitch.

They had no time for a huddle. No time to exchange numbers. No time to recognize each other as anything but an ally.

"Where to?" said Mitch.

"Out," said Qingzhao.

They untethered a blistering spray of bullets back the way they had come, just as Gabriel Hunt ran into their field of fire.

Gabriel flattened out in a home-run slide. An inch higher, a split second sooner, and he would have caught a bullet in his left nostril.

The women were firing at the gunmen who had crowded into the passage in Gabriel's wake. Men who were shooting back just as ferociously as the women tried to flee.

Hornet swarms of lead exchanged position above Gabriel as he pulled himself into an opening in the wall—steam piping, cold now, unused in the new incarnation of the aircraft carrier. There would come an eyeblink instant when all shooters had to reload, and that was what Gabriel was waiting for.

The volley ebbed and Gabriel mad-dashed for the next hatchway, knowing from seafaring experience how to grab the upper ledge and swing through without giving himself a skull fracture.

Mitch had spotted him during the exchange. She had even uttered his name—"*Gabriel?*"—but this had gone unheard in the cannonade. She hesitated. Qingzhao had to drag her along with a snort of frustration.

Her yanked arm erupted with sudden pain and Mitch looked down to see a bullet hole in her left shoulder. Dammit, she'd been hit! *Stupid!*

They were trying to figure out which way to abandon ship when Gabriel came soaring at them from the hatchway in a flying tackle. Expertly catching both women by the neck in the crooks of his arms, Gabriel used his momentum to take them over the observation deck edge and tumbling down into the drink.

The water was clammy and stale.

Gunners were already shooting at them from the upper deck—automatic swath-fire that sent bullets down into the dark water like deadly snail darters.

Qingzhao had kicked off her heels and was already stroking for the surface, swimming toward one of the patrol boats. Gabriel saw her since she was three feet away. But when they had splashed down, he'd lost his grip on Mitch and had no idea where she was. He tried to see her through the murky water, tried to reach for her, but it was hopeless.

Current was pulling them, still submerged.

"Help!" A voice that blurred as Gabriel surfaced and water decanted from his ears.

It was Qingzhao, ploshing about to attract the attention of one of the security men on a skiff. His face was split in a grin of rough good fortune; here was an enticing female delivered unto him by the sea!

When Qingzhao got a grip on his extended hand, she swung her gun out of the water and shot him.

Modern technology had some advantages, Gabriel conceded. Wet guns could still fire. Modern cartridges had to be submerged for some time to become useless. Otherwise, nobody could ever have a shootout in the rain.

Qingzhao used her leverage to tumble the perforated guard into the water. She quickly took control of the boat, as though this had been her exit strategy all along.

There was still no sign of Mitch, and other boat sentries were catching up in a big hurry.

Gabriel felt a sting at his temple as a bullet passed within millimeters. Enough.

He swung one arm over the side of the skiff and pulled himself in just as Qingzhao floored it. Gabriel was hurled indecorously back against a padded vinyl seat as Qingzhao throttled the boat up full.

"Sit down," she barked over the howl of the engine.

With at least three speed-skiffs behind them, they were ramrodding into a tighter section of the waterway, dodging sampans and houseboats. Qingzhao could not bank fast enough to avoid hitting a *hua-tzu*—one of the smaller, narrower, canoe-like boats used by fishermen. The steel-reinforced ramming prow of the skiff cut the *hua-tzu* in half as Gabriel saw the occupant jack-in-the-box himself skyward in panic.

Their pursuers chopped through in their wake, destroying what was left.

Gabriel felt the sea air cool the sweat on his forehead. The skiff was headed at high speed directly for an elaborate floating restaurant in the middle of the harbor. It was the size of a city block, lit up like a Christmas tree with strung lights, and completely encased in a service latticework of bamboo.

Diners inside enjoying the splendid view of the river were no doubt dismayed by the sudden sight of a speedboat rocketing toward them with no possibility of detour, followed by a contingent of similar boats firing lots and lots of bullets in the direction of the windows.

Qingzhao banked the craft hard, attempting a bootlegger's reverse, but the skiff crashed gratingly into the bamboo superstructure and got hung up with its prow sticking through a shattered window.

Gabriel had a flashpop-image of Qingzhao jamming an extra magazine from the skiff pilot's pistol into her décolletage. Then she was diving into the eatery, the patrons and staff of which had taken some small notice of their cacophonous arrival. Gabriel plunged in after her.

Cheung's men were already coming in the shoreline entrance.

As Gabriel pounded through the swinging double doors of the kitchen, he saw Qingzhao jam the extra magazine of bullets into a flaming brazier.

An instant later, the bullets began exploding. Cheung's men collided with each other in their haste to find sparse cover and evade what they thought was ambush fire.

Gabriel pushed his way through hanging skinned fowl and fish dangling from cleaning hooks. The cooks were all yelling and taking cover. Steps ahead of him, Qingzhao appropriated a gigantic silver meat cleaver from a bracket on the wall.

Cheung's men would be gathering outside the kitchen door about now, massing an assault.

Gabriel and Qingzhao went out the back, shot glances in every direction. At the southern end of the floating restaurant was a loading spur as crowded as a parking lot with assorted boats that arrived hourly to meet the needs of a business that advertised *fresh-fresh-fresh*. Gabriel took Qingzhao's arm, careful to avoid getting within striking distance of that cleaver, and aimed her in the direction of one particular vessel that had what seemed, from this distance, to be an empty hold. She searched his face for an instant, apparently didn't find whatever signs of incipient betrayal she was looking for, and followed his lead.

The gunners stood down when Ivory cut through the destruction in the restaurant. He stopped and stood staring out at the water for a moment.

"Did you know who that was?" said Dinanath breathlessly, trundling up behind Ivory.

"My responsibility," said Ivory, more to himself than to his coworker.

"Stop the traffic and search these boats."

The junk was captained by an old-school river rat named Lao, whose grin revealed he had had all his teeth replaced with steel substitutes decades ago. He was the first to be allowed to leave the supply berth at the Floating Feast Superior Restaurant, since all he carried was a hold full of tuna that could not be delayed, for spoilage.

When he put a little distance between himself and the Floating Feast, he saw the tuna piled in his hold begin to move.

Gradually, as though surfacing through a muck of cloudy fish jelly, Gabriel and Qingzhao materialized amidst the odiferous cargo. They had jumped into the belly of the empty hold and Qingzhao had used the cleaver to cut the net holding the fish overhead, burying them summarily.

The smell was . . . memorable.

Lao extended a courtly hand to help Qingzhao up to the deck first. He jabbered at her in reedy, mutated Mandarin.

"What did he say?" said Gabriel.

"He thanks us for the marvelous new knife," said Qingzhao, indicating the cleaver, which Lao was turning over in his hands like a rare jewel.

His smile matched the metal cutting edge.

Gabriel wanted to say something ironic, tough and competent. But he raised one hand to his temple instead, where the bullet had stung him earlier and where he now was suddenly conscious of wetness welling. Instead of fish oil or the dank, frigid bilge water of the hold, his fingertips were smeared, he saw, with blood. The last thing he thought before he lost consciousness was: *Well, I guess the whole lecture thing is pretty much blown.*

Chapter 6

When Gabriel opened his eyes, he was staring at a parked motorcycle.

Which was odd, because he seemed to be indoors.

A series of smells hit his nose—smoke, burning wood, incense, packed dirt, pine-scented air, charred paper, and beneath all that a subtle tang of gasoline, gun oil and engine lubricant.

Most enticing of all was the smell of coffee.

The bike appeared to be a vintage German BMW R-71 from 1938. Four-stroke, 750cc, with a sidecar, just like dozens seen in every World War II movie ever made. This one looked newer, and was more likely one of the painstaking Chinese rebuilds called Changjiangs, very popular with motorcycle clubs in this part of the world.

He heard light rain pattering down into what sounded like a Japanese water garden.

He tried to rise and found he was lying on a rawhewn wooden pallet and facing a huge rope candle on a rusted bronze stand. The candle was fashioned on the same principle as the gigantic coils of incense Gabriel had seen in assorted Eastern houses of worship.

It could burn for hundreds of hours if fed through the windproof receiver judiciously.

Wick-smoke twisted ceilingward and the sudden light of the flame made his head throb. The chamber was roughly circular, the walls formed of ancient cut stone blocks.

There was a dressing on his head. He touched it gingerly. He didn't seem to be bleeding anymore, which was nice. He figured the bullet must've come closer than he'd realized, must have hit him a glancing blow, perhaps scoring a neat groove in his thick skull. He'd made it a while on adrenaline alone, but when that had run out . . .

He tried to stand up and experienced whirling vertigo. At first he thought it was from his injury but a moment later he realized that the floor of the room actually was slanted, and a moment after that he realized it was necessary to compensate for the incline of the building itself. The effect was disorienting, though he suddenly knew where he was: in one of the leaning pagodas outside Shanghai.

Through a small alcove he caught sight of the temple ruins outside.

He was halfway up a mountainside, inside snaggle-toothed fortifications choked by wild foliage. The leaning pagoda jutted crookedly toward the stars, like Pisa.

Several centuries ago temples like this had served as waystations for travelers as well as locations for worship and ritual. They generally consisted of three sequential courtyards, each with its own shrine. He made his way through an overgrown courtyard to the nearest of the shrine rooms. It was so large Gabriel could see clusters of bird nests near the holes in the domed ceiling. It was mustier in here where the damp had gotten through to the limestone. Vines had claimed the walls.

Gabriel saw Qingzhao toss a packet of ceremonial money into the flames licking up from an iron urn. Greasy smoke corkscrewed into the air.

He cleared his throat and Qingzhao's free hand shot up holding a gun whose barrel looked a foot long. Gabriel tried not to react. Turning her head his way, Qingzhao recognized him and gestured idly toward a small cookstove—pointing with the gun, of course.

"Coffee. All Americans like coffee," she said, her voice having an almost African lilt concealed within it.

She saw him look at the money she was burning. "You wonder why I would burn—"

"For the dead to use in the next world," said Gabriel. "Don't burn enough, and you're considered cheap. That's the superstition, anyway. How much have you burned?"

"You can never burn enough."

She offered him a tin cup of strong coffee that smelled just the way Nirvana is supposed to.

Gabriel's eyes had adjusted to the sputtering light long enough for him to now make out a mural of a frothing demon on the far wall, obscured by wear and time and the overgrowth of underbrush. He touched the bandage on his head while Qingzhao, apparently, read his mind.

"You are embarrassed," she said. "You are a strong American man, it is your job to save the girl, and here I have saved you instead." She almost smiled. Almost. "I will not tell anyone and thus embarrass you further."

Gabriel was silent for a moment. Then he said, "Why did you bring me with you?"

"I think you and I wish to kill the same man."

"Sorry to say, lady, you've got that wrong. I'm not here to kill anybody."

She stopped what she was doing and regarded him.

"I came here to find someone in trouble who needed help," he said. "She jumped the gun and came here sloppy. Emotions on high-burn, full up with revenge. She didn't even have a plan worthy of the name."

"The blonde woman at the Zongchang."

Gabriel nodded. "Now *she* did want to kill the same man you do—she believed Cheung murdered her sister in New York City, or had her murdered."

"I sensed we had a connection," Qingzhao said quietly.

"Wanting to kill Cheung? I think you've probably got that in common with quite a few people."

"No. Something deeper. This woman wished to avenge her sister, who has been murdered." She tossed some more money into the fire. "Cheung murdered me, as well."

In a high-security chamber with walls of pumice situated atop the Peace Hotel, Cheung conducted his own rituals in the incense-choked, churchlike ambience.

Seated behind an artful, almost ephemeral desktop of hewn onyx, Cheung was working with a leather rollup of antique carving tools, delicately carving a detailed cherrywood casket about ten inches long.

Past the altarlike desk, past the bank of flat-screen monitors, several of his operatives worked damage control by phone, but none would proffer information or news, good or bad, until Cheung addressed them directly.

Finally, Cheung looked up and lit a long, poisonous-looking cigarette.

"Mr. Fleetwood," he said.

Fleetwood, a rangy Anglo wearing octagonal glasses wired around his completely shaved head, terminated the call on his headset.

"How much will last night cost us?" said Cheung, meaning the free-for-all at the Zongchang, including janitorial services.

"Ten days to reopen at a cost of $2.6 million New Pacific dollars. That's the repair versus the lost income."

"They're robbing us because they think we're desperate," Cheung said. He picked up a hardwood abacus and started clicking the beads on the device's lower deck, bottom-to-top, right-to-left, carrying totals to the upper deck, where each bead represented five times more value. It was the simplest base-ten counting system in the world.

"Get everything right. Tell them they have twenty days to reopen. Give them one point one. More time, but less loss."

"What about General Zhang's military loan?" said Fleetwood. "What about the interest the police owe us?"

Cheung waved this away because Longwei Sze Xie had entered.

"Ivory," Cheung said. "My Immortal. Tell me true things."

After a formal bow, Ivory exhibited several printouts salvaged from the surveillance cameras at the casino ship.

"The Nameless One," he said, unnecessarily. "Same as at the Oriental Pearl Tower. And here, again. And again."

"Is she a ghost?"

"No," said Ivory.

"Tell me," said Cheung, his voice succoring. "Is she a genuine threat, or is she just crazy and lucky?" The implication that Ivory's job hung in the balance was clear.

"She will be no threat. I will see to it."

Cheung rose and—very uncharacteristically—laid an avuncular hand on Ivory's shoulder. He rarely touched any of his employees.

"Longwei Sze Xie," he said, using respect language, "I shall need you close by at all times. You help enable my . . . mad little schemes, and I shall always be grateful. There is one small errand to which I would like you to attend."

"Name it and it is done," said Ivory.

He whispered into Ivory's ear.

"Sir, Nairobi's finally calling back on line two," Fleetwood announced.

"I'll take it," said Cheung, who picked up his phone and began speaking in perfect Kenyan dialect.

Ivory had already vanished from the room.

Qingzhao was punching holes in a sheet of tin with a mallet and chisel. Each time she smacked the metal the perforation made a *pank!* sound that echoed inside the shrine room.

"Was she a soldier, this woman?" she asked.

"Yes," said Gabriel. "A U.S. Air Force pilot."

"Then she knew about soldiers in battle. They die."

"Her sister was no soldier. She was a database

engineer at the American office of a Chinese corporation."

"Cheung's?"

Gabriel nodded.

"Cheung is a warrior. Anyone who works for him has to be prepared for the worst."

"Bet they don't tell employees that before they take the job."

Qingzhao shrugged this away.

"What's your connection to Cheung?" Gabriel asked. "Were you an employee, too? Before you were . . . what did you say, murdered?"

She flared with anger: "You have no right to show disdain. Have *you* fought and killed another man? Ever been wounded in battle?"

In his nearly twoscore years on the planet Gabriel had been shot six times and stabbed or cut with edged weapons over a hundred.

"Lady, trust me, I've been wounded plenty," he said.

"Lady," Qingzhao repeated as though testing a new word and finding it inadequate.

Qingzhao inverted the holed metal so the sharp-lipped edges of the punctures were facing her. Then she punched the metal with her bare fist.

Gabriel winced.

Qingzhao pounded the metal like a boxer, then turned to a basket of lemons at the base of the shrine. She squeezed one freehanded until it burst, and worked the juice into both bleeding hands. Gabriel knew the pain must be incredible, but Qingzhao's expression did not change.

"Toughens the skin," she said, as though that was answer enough. It ended their conversation.

Some lady, Gabriel thought.

* * *

At the archway to the pagoda, there had once been a gate guarded by immense stone lions of marble. Now there remained only weathered pedestals and severed stone paws, one holding a child, the other, a globe of the world.

Gabriel stood between them watching the setting sun, trying to frame an argument. Mitch Quantrill was lost; swallowed by the Huangpu with a bullet in her. The odds that she had survived were low. Lucy would be distraught when she found out. And furious with him. Still—was it his responsibility to pick up her doomed mission? Would that make things right?

No.

Then there was this woman, with the motorcycle and the tough skin and the story about having been murdered. All right, chalk some of it up to the language barrier, but still, she seemed mildly crazy. And whatever mission she was on seemed fraught with who knew what sort of damage in her past. If she wanted to go after Cheung, was that his problem?

No.

It would be the easiest thing in the world to make his way back to the city. By Gabriel's reckoning they were perhaps fifty miles into the mountains along the Yangtze River. He could jet back to the States. Michael could reschedule the lecture tour, make apologies for Gabriel's mysterious absence. And all this would become a bad bit of history. It made sense.

So why did he feel no desire to do it?

Gabriel tried to kid himself that he was still recovering from the bullet skid to the temple, but he knew better. Maybe he was attracted to Qingzhao; was that it?

He was still trying to work out the answer to that one when she appeared silently beside him.

"Don't let them see you."

Gabriel's senses instantly hit high alert. "Who?"

"The soldiers."

His body tensed, automatically crouching down and scanning the grounds for cover. "*What* soldiers?" he said.

"My army," said Qingzhao. "The Killers of Men."

The pair of Tosa dogs were schooled aggressors, each nearly 200 pounds. Also known as Japanese Fighting Mastiffs or "Sumo Dogs," their jaws could render nearly 600 pounds of crush pressure, and this brindle pair stood 25 inches at the shoulder. Highly prized as fighters, this type of dog had been banned in the UK, Ireland, New Zealand and Australia. As a breed they were alert, agile, and quick to respond with unbelievable reserves of stamina, which meant that gladiatorial training amplified all their most dangerous traits.

Dinanath had overseen the training of this pair. Neither dog had a name. Right now, Ivory was holding the remote fob keyed to their electronic discipline collars.

In his other hand he held the gleaming meat cleaver he had just confiscated from Lao, the fisherman.

Aboard his sampan, Lao was busy pleading for his life in Mandarin.

"It appears," Ivory said, "that Qingzhao Wai Chiu had not one ally, but two."

"This is getting out of hand," said Dinanath.

Ivory sighed and nodded. He was tired of trying to maintain a standard of honor that was increasingly irrelevant.

He keyed the fob and the Tosa dogs tore into the terrified Lao. His screams disappeared down chomping gullets, and Ivory rendered the man the small mercy of shooting him in the head before it was all over.

Gabriel gazed with breathless disbelief at one of the full-sized terra-cotta warriors inside the shrine room Qingzhao had led him to.

There were four in all, half-buried in deep dirt trenches, broken and weathered like long-vandalized tombstones. Two vacant slots suggested two figures had already been removed.

But that was not the most awe-inspiring thing in the shrine room.

Suffocated by vines and tree roots at the far end of the chamber, clotted with decades of dried mud and impacted dust, was a large bronze statue of a Chinese grotesque, pointing one bony sculpted finger toward the center of the room. Underlit by torchlight it was positively ghoulish, a nightmare vision, an evil god. The scaling and tarnish on the bronze made the looming grotesque appear to be leprous.

"Is this supposed to be Kangxi Shih-k'ai?" asked Gabriel. "The Favored Son of China? He looks like Nosferatu."

The reference was lost on Qingzhao. "I do not know. I only know of Kangxi Shih-k'ai's history because of Cheung's obsession with him. Whether this statue depicts him, I cannot say. But the phrase 'Killers of Men' struck me as appropriate for the others. My soldiers here help my cause." She pointed out one of the terra-cotta figures, missing an arm. "He was a bowman."

"Now he doesn't have a bow or an arm to draw it with," said Gabriel, marveling at the possibilities. "His face is almost gone."

"They all had weapons of bronze, a long time ago. They did not need shields, nor helmets. Cunning and ferocity were their protection."

Was she referring to the men who'd been the models for these figures or the figures themselves? Gabriel wasn't sure.

"You found them here? Out in the open? Or did you excavate them yourself?"

"They were buried," she said. "I dug them out."

"How did you find them?" She didn't answer. "How did you know they were here?"

"I knew." It was all she said.

"Does Cheung know they're here?"

She shook her head. "I found them; he does not know."

"And were there more? More figures?" She shook her head. "Not necessarily in this room," Gabriel said. "Maybe one of the other shrine rooms, or . . . is there a way *into* this mountain? A path to the inside?"

"You mean like a secret chamber?" She seemed amused. "No. I have seen all the caves and passageways this mountain has to offer. I was hoping to find more of the Killers of Men myself; I would certainly have use for them. These are all that there are."

Gabriel began scraping debris off the base of the huge bronze statue against the far wall. Maybe she was right that she'd found everything there was to find. But maybe she wasn't. A half-mad assassin using one of the leaning pagodas as a hideout would not search the way Gabriel Hunt could search.

"How do you use the warriors?" he asked as he

continued to work his way around the sculpture's base.

"Tonight I will take the bowman to a friend at the Night Market," said Qingzhao. "Perhaps if you come you will find out what you wish to know. I would welcome your help."

She very pointedly did not remind him that he was in her debt.

What the hell, thought Gabriel. He could give China one more day.

Chapter 7

Trash fires choked the street with milky smoke. The pedicab in which Gabriel and Qingzhao rode, with their inanimate charge wedged between them, threaded its way through the riot of human shapes that constituted the nightlife beyond the favored, protected realm of the Bund. Here were thousands of vendors, prostitutes, thieves, *huanquiande* bartering for money, DVD hucksters, homeopathic herbal medicine men, pirate electronics dealers, clothiers, all blurring past. Open petrol and propane tanks warned in English *NO NAKED LIGHT*, meaning fire.

They stopped at the Beggar's Arch, which was a long stone tunnel like a Roman aqueduct, its shadows lined on both sides by castoffs and derelicts. According to beggar etiquette, the seated and squatting men kept their eyes down and their cups (or cupped hands) up as Gabriel and Qingzhao passed, carrying the canvas-wrapped statue of the bowman carefully between them.

They emerged into one of Shanghai's many Night Markets, a tightly packed maze of tents reminiscent of an American swap meet or flea market, interspersed with solo hustlers and other racketeers working out of the shells of now-useless automobiles. Gabriel saw several more people burning ceremonial cash at drumfires, and a man putting trained birds through their paces inside an entire corridor of bird-sellers.

"It's like Mardi Gras," Gabriel said.

"More dangerous," said Qingzhao.

"You've never drunk a Hurricane, I bet."

Qingzhao ignored the remark. Wit, charm or humor were not her coinage.

Presently they emerged into a large open area completely engirded in stonemasonry, with drains in the floor. It could have been a covered outdoor patio or a deceptively big space between buildings with a canopy overhead. It reminded Gabriel a bit of an abandoned food court. There was a scatter of tables and chairs. At one, a wizened, skeletal man ceaselessly folded squares of paper into origami shapes and dropped them into an iron pot. Across from him, an equally ancient woman sat surrounded by disassembled cell phones, probing them with tiny jeweler's tools. They were both clad in simple Maoist tunics and the woman smiled at Gabriel as they passed. Every other tooth was missing.

Qingzhao spoke briefly to the old man in a dialect Gabriel could not place.

"Who are we talking to here?" Gabriel asked.

"Sentries."

"Sentries," said Gabriel.

Now the old man was grinning, too. Apparently he had scored all the woman's missing teeth.

Qingzhao whispered a monosyllable, and the next thing Gabriel knew, two guns were pointed right at his head.

* * *

The old folks were still smiling at him.

A big, booming, basso laugh rebounded from the rock walls.

The entryway to the next chamber in the maze filled up with a large black man, six-six easy in flat slippers, with a calm Buddha face and vaguely Asian eyes below a close-cropped crewcut.

"Your expression!" The big man thundered with mirth. "Priceless!" He took a moment to settle. "Forgive me."

The oldsters stowed their firepower and resumed their innocuous activities, the woman still smiling sweetly at Gabriel.

"I know what *you* want, I'm sure of it!" The big man embraced Qingzhao. Even more surprisingly, Qingzhao allowed this.

"And I know what *you* want," she said before the breath could be squeezed out of her.

The big man stuck out a hand the size of a catcher's mitt toward Gabriel. "*Ni chi le ma?*" It was a common greeting for a stranger—*have you eaten?*—testifying to the centrality of food in most Asian culture. Gabriel shook the proffered hand in the Western fashion. A more traditional Chinese handshake would have consisted of the men interlocking their fingers and waving them up and down a few times; but today this was done mostly by the very elderly or the very etiquette-conscious.

"Tuan, at your service," boomed the big man, "and the service of our little snapdragon, here."

Like some grandiose, benevolent street pasha, Tuan escorted Qingzhao and Gabriel through the heart of his domain, which rose in tiers from the cobblestoned street into a labyrinth of subdivisions and alcoves overpopulated with mercantile bustle. Over here, you could get your head massaged, cheap. Over there, your ears swabbed out. It was indoor-yet-outdoor; the grandest treehouse of all.

Besides Beggar's Arch, three other tunnels fed into the amphitheater. At one end was a traditional Chinese teahouse accessed by a zigzaggy footbridge over a turbid flow of water.

"Four people are in charge of the Bund, now," said Qingzhao as they trailed Tuan, their fragile burden held between them.

"Like gang turf?" said Gabriel.

"More akin to social castes."

"Classes."

"Tuan runs street level. All you can see."

"It is my privilege," chimed the big man leading them. "An entrepreneur named Hellweg has a lock on municipal services such as power, water. You may have noticed his petroleum tower—the Fire in the Sky. He's some sort of European; Danish, or Scandanavian at any rate.

"Our local army of mercenary police is owned by Lo Pei Zhang, who was once a military general. The soldiers are all ex–Red Army."

"And the fourth is Cheung?" said Gabriel.

"Yes. Qingzhao's former employer," said Tuan, and Gabriel realized it was the first time he'd heard the woman's name. "I believe he made his millions in currency speculation. His *first* millions."

Gabriel fired a glance back at Qingzhao. "So you *were* an employee of his."

"Mr. Cheung arrived in our fair land just as Communism was gasping its last," Tuan rattled on. "The CCC is the new land of opportunity, but it is all quite subsurface now. That's why Occidentals fear it so much, I think."

"And you," said Gabriel to Qingzhao, "used to work for this guy? The one you've been trying to—"

Her hand was on his forearm, extended across the body of the bowman between them. "Yes." Her eyes added: *Not now. Not in front of Tuan. Please.*

This was one raincheck Gabriel was going to follow up on.

Next to a booth whose sign proclaimed CHANGE YOUR I.D., Tuan pointed out an ammo hawker with half a face, masked as though by a giant eyepatch. Most of the man's fingers were missing or truncated.

"Do not purchase ammunition from that man," Tuan said. "Unreliable. Misfires."

"The man or the ammunition?" asked Gabriel.

"Both."

Tuan led them into another cubbyhole with signage halfway-hidden from the commonweal: SU-LIN GUN MERCHANT. It stank of gunpowder and gun oil, and was a cramped warren of firepower old and new. Su-Lin was a gnomish woman with a calm Easter Island gaze; she weighed maybe 75 pounds. Tuan bent from his enormous height to grace her cheek with a kiss.

"You must use the keyboard," said Qingzhao. Two laptops were set up collaborator-style on a small counter, with Su-Lin perched behind one as though ready to commence a game of *Battleship*. "This translates. First you type the proper greeting."

They set down the bowman and Qingzhao typed: YOUR PIG MOTHER EATS NIGHT SOIL, which transposed to Chinese characters on Su-Lin's screen.

Su-Lin typed back: I LOVE YOU, TOO.

Gabriel's attention meanwhile had been arrested

by a very special gun hanging from a clip on the back wall. His eye coded it as a close cousin to his faithful Colt Peacemaker, which he still wished he had strapped to his hip. That one was out of reach. This wasn't.

"You have seen something you like?" said Tuan.

It was a large Colt revolver—age-burnished, true, but Gabriel recognized it as the treasure it was. "If this is what I think it is . . ."

Tuan lifted it off the wall and handed it to him. The gun sprang open cleanly at his touch. There wasn't a spot of rust on it anywhere.

"This," Gabriel said, as if he were introducing an old friend to a new one, "looks like an old Navy Colt, .36 caliber—from when they first started converting cap-and-ball 'percussion pistols' to the more newfangled revolver. They called them 'wheelguns.' " He glanced back at Su-Lin. "How much do you think she might take for it?"

"That depends on whether you *like* it," Tuan goaded.

"I like it very much," said Gabriel. "Anyone who knows about guns would."

"Then it is yours," Tuan said. "For your trouble. With my compliments."

"Why?"

"You are a guest. Qingzhao said you helped to save her life. That is a favor bestowed upon me as well. Please allow me to repay this debt in a way that pleases you."

Gabriel nodded his thanks. He was always ill at ease accepting gifts, because you never knew what obligations might accompany them. But he wasn't about to turn down this one. He had a feeling he might need a good gun very soon.

* * *

The place Tuan called his Pleasure Garden featured a cabaret stage—empty just now—and about a million varieties of flowering plant life nourished by misting nozzles and artificial sunlight, here in the middle of a city of stone.

The newly unwrapped terra-cotta warrior—Qingzhao's bowman—watched silently as they ate from a table carved from a monkey-puzzle tree, laden with about forty dishes of food.

Tuan held up a goblet of absinthe for a toast.

"To my newest soldier," he said.

The licorice-flavored drink went down hard and sizzled with an afterbite of burned sugar.

Apparently, Qingzhao bartered the terra-cotta warriors with Tuan for supplies and intelligence. The figures she had discovered near the idol in the shrine room had great value, even as damaged as they were. The two empty slots Gabriel had noticed were remnants of earlier deals between Qingzhao and Tuan; their collaboration had been ongoing for the better part of a year.

"Barter being the best form of trade?" asked Gabriel.

Tuan nodded.

Gabriel surveyed the table. "My apologies, but this seems like an awful lot of food for three people."

"I am showing off," Tuan smiled. "Forgive me."

"It will feed others when we are done," said Qingzhao. "Tuan is responsible for filling many bellies."

"So," Gabriel said, returning to the subject of the clay warriors, "value for value. Like the black market in religious ikons in Russia."

"Not quite," said Tuan. "The Russian way provided

an interesting lesson on the subject of smuggled antiquities, because so many of their black- and gray-market religious ikons were forgeries. Of course, one of my business interests is a thriving popular outlet for *replica* warriors. We've copied most of the basic templates from the warriors found in the Xian pits and the army of Emperor Qin. We do custom paint jobs. We even have a service whereby your own features can be worked onto the terra-cotta warrior replica of your choice. My artisans use photographs of the subject. You'd be surprised at how many people want a recreation for their garden or foyer. How many people actually collect them."

"At a couple grand a pop, no doubt," said Gabriel. It was no different to him than some spinster collecting plates from the Franklin Mint. "But the replica market provides cover for moving the real warriors to private collectors who can't show them because it would be illegal to possess them."

"They pay for that privilege," said Tuan. "The funny thing is, the replica company actually started turning a profit last year. And most people cannot even discern authenticity, which has allowed the market in art forgeries to thrive the way it has."

It was true. Forgers had become so painstaking at their craft that the difference between a fake masterpiece (which hung in galleries and toured worldwide to the acclaim of millions) and the genuine article (which hung in someone's expensive, climate–controlled cellar and was available for viewing only by an elite few) had been reduced almost to nil. As far as the world was concerned, the fake was real. The real paintings only increased in value every time a subterranean auction was held, and sometimes the aficionados tried to screw each other. Michael had told him that half the Impressionists in the last Getty exhibition were bogus, but no one wanted to say so. What was the point in starting *that* blaze of controversy unless the whereabouts of the real ones were known?

The epidemic had gotten so dire that within the last five years, even the Mona Lisa had come under serious doubt. Which might explain her goofy, cryptic smile at last. *I'm a fake, boys.*

Tuan pushed back his seat. "My honored guest," he said. "Permit me the ill manner of a private conversation with Qi."

"Qi?" said Gabriel.

"My diminutive for our delectable little fighter. You have no doubt already felt the strange attraction she exerts."

She lowered her gaze.

"No doubt," Gabriel said.

He handed Gabriel a puzzle box of closely worked unlacquered cedar. "We have a few small affairs of business to transact that are not for all ears to hear."

Gabriel accepted the box with mild interest. It called to mind nothing so much as the Rubik's Cube he'd held just days before in Michael's office.

"We'll be nearby," Tuan said. "While we're gone, perhaps you will find this interesting to examine. What most people call a Chinese puzzle box, the kind one buys in the so-called 'Chinatowns' of various cities, is actually a Japanese configuration. Historically this has disallowed inquiry into something uniquely Chinese—a different configuration and puzzle strategy, now overwhelmed by the more common Japanese variants. This one is authentic. Its purpose is not to test skill at solving a mere puzzle . . ."

"But to test the mettle of the solver," Gabriel said, feeling a tiny surge of dread: of all the ways Tuan might have chosen to test him . . . !

Tuan and Qingzhao repaired to a curtained alcove to speak in hushed whispers while Gabriel considered the box in his hands.

He wanted to set it aside and perhaps wander near enough to the curtain to eavesdrop on the conversation, but he suspected that neither would be advisable. His host had been cordial so far—but he was clearly a dangerous man and not one to anger.

Gabriel reluctantly focused on the box in his hands. Classic puzzle boxes, he remembered, always featured sliding panels. But no part of this one appeared to slide in any direction. Thinking back to the Rubik's Cube that had so confounded him in New York, Gabriel began exerting mild stress on different parts of the box and sure enough, a triangular corner came free on a little interior hinge, now hanging out like a wing and spoiling the box's symmetry. After a one-eighty revolve, it settled back into its appointed corner upside down, completing an ideogram that had previously been bisected. He recognized the ideogram: it translated roughly into *"as above, so below."* Accordingly, Gabriel twisted free the corner that was diagonally opposite—a corner that had not budged before. It flipped out and settled back with mild pressure, and Gabriel felt something *click* definitively inside the box.

Ah. Now we're getting somewhere.

The top of the box, he found, felt loose, as if it would slide if he pressed it. He did, and realized that the entire top half of the box could be eased away from the bottom half, turned like a knob and reseated.

Each repositioning completed a Chinese character previously obscured or lost within the filigree of design.

The top half of the box displaced a quarter of its own length. Gabriel realized that if the bulky section could fold over, the box would retain its original size and shape. The engineering seemed impossible, but sure enough—*click*.

Now panels revealed themselves in the conventional manner. The wrinkle of an authentic Chinese box would be that some of the panels would be tricks, traps or dead ends. These enigmas were dependent on the user's preconceptions of how such things might or might not work.

He pressed on one panel—

"A word of advice, my dear new friend," said Tuan, returning.

Gabriel was embarrassed not to have heard his approach. He'd been more wrapped up in solving the puzzle than he'd realized. He put the box down unfinished, hearing somewhere, in the back of his head, Michael's voice chastising him. *You give up on things too easily.*

"Qi has told me of your adventures and difficulties," said Tuan. "I would say you should not expect to leave China, if that is your thought. You are on Cheung's map now. The caution you take should be threefold. Really, if it was safety you sought, you should not have even dared to come back into the city at all."

"Mind reader," said Gabriel.

They left Tuan in his den and returned, painstakingly, to where they'd first met him. The old couple was gone.

Gabriel wanted to ask Qingzhao what she'd gotten

in exchange for the priceless terra-cotta warrior this time, but he was prepared to wait to grill her—about this and her relationship with Cheung—till they were alone, far from prying ears and eyes.

Coming in and out of central Shanghai could be like stepping into a time machine. Barely outside the city limits, the terrain and people seemed to come from far in the past. Gabriel had once seen the backlots of Shanghai Film Studio, where an entire small city had been constructed for the purposes of shooting movies. During Gabriel's visit, the street had been dressed as 1933 Shanghai right down to the fake billboard for *King Kong*, in service of an epic called *Temptress Moon*; on the adjacent lot, you found yourself on the same city street, 200 years earlier. Driving through the streets of the city proper could feel a lot like that, antiquity and modernity rubbing shoulders block by crowded block.

It was easy for Gabriel to close his eyes—once again in a pedicab with Qingzhao—and imagine he was some European interloper from ages ago, racing along the cobblestones toward a meeting with Kangxi Shih-k'ai or one of his lieutenants.

The illusion was enhanced a moment later when he heard a pair of gunshots and, looking up, saw twin holes punched in the canvas flap next to his head. He had a fleeting sense of high-velocity projectiles passing inches from his face and then two more holes appeared in the flap next to Qi.

Somebody was shooting at them.

Chapter 8

Gabriel reached forward to pull the pedicab driver out of the line of fire.

The man was already dead, holed through the neck and chest.

The pedicab came to a lurching halt, pitching forward, crashing into a gent on a bicycle and sending him cartwheeling into the air.

Gabriel and Qi dived out and flattened in opposite directions, hugging cobblestones slicked with night mist.

Rolling on his back, Gabriel groped for his newly acquired Colt, still wrapped in cheesecloth and now sitting in the middle of the street as citizens, heedless to the silenced gunfire, crowded around and stumbled over him.

Then he had to claw the big .45 cartridges from his pocket. Conventional wisdom with guns like this held that one should load five shells and leave the hammer down on an empty chamber, since the gun had nothing that could remotely be interpreted as a safety. Gabriel always—*always*—loaded six.

Qi had already whipped out a sleek automatic from a spine scabbard and was seeking targets.

Several gunners in black, with hoods, materialized out of the throng to rake the pedicab with machine-gun fire. It vaporized into toothpicks and floating chaff as Gabriel rolled, sighted prone, and discharged his new gun for the first time. It kicked hard and roared like a cannon, a curling gout of fire licking from the muzzle. One of the gunners arched into the air and fell—a high center hit—knocking down several people who were stampeding at the sound and sight of gunfire.

Gabriel lifted the shattered wheel of the pedicab and with one mighty swing dislocated the jaw of a second shooter who'd run toward him. Almost instantly two more thugs focused their attention on the *guilo* and Gabriel found himself in an unwilling three-way.

He kicked out at one guy grabbing him, heard the picket crack of a blown kneecap, and swung the man into his nearest neighbor. Gabriel had dropped his gun; he retrieved it now and put a round into the chest of one attacker.

Where were the police when you wanted them? A show of force by some of China's ubiquitous uniformed keepers of order might have put an end to this melee. But the police were no more anxious to rush headlong into a situation that might get them killed than anyone else would be, a guilty reality that could cost you your existence if somebody abruptly opened fire on your pedicab.

As he took down another attacker with a slash of his gun hand across the man's face only to see two more pop up in his place, Gabriel wondered, How many shooters were he and Qi worth?

In the words of a famous bank robber: *All of them*. Gabriel rather indecorously shoved a woman laden with wicker baskets aside as he thumb-cocked the hammer of the Colt one-handed and blew a round into an assailant who surely would have shredded the woman for a chance to nail Gabriel. The big lead slug spanged off the attacker's AK-47, destroying the breech and rendering the gun useless except as a club. It also took away two of the attacker's fingers, putting him out of the fight.

Bullet Number Four reaped a lucky hit, passing through one gunner and into the guy behind him. They would probably live, too, but they dropped their weapons and fell down, and that was all that mattered to Gabriel at the moment.

Gabriel looked around furiously, finally catching sight of Qi as she discarded her now-empty weapon and took on a barreling adversary by imploding a wire birdcage over his head and then delivering an expert pointed-toe kick to a nerve bundle near the man's groin that put him down, spasming. Qi swiftly took charge of her victim's pistol.

Gabriel reversed-out to a kneeling position and fanned his last two shots, blossoming two bright glurts of blood across the chest of another black-clad man seconds away from doing the same to him.

Gabriel leaped to his feet and barreled toward Qi, taking advantage of an instant's lull. If there were a second wave coming, it was stalled long enough for Gabriel to locate Qi and turn an ambush into hot pursuit.

"Come on!" he yelled, grabbing her hand and almost spoiling her aim as she plugged a masked gunner.

"No, this way!" she yelled back. Gabriel accepted the change of direction; she'd know the streets here better than he would.

Two blocks away, Gabriel and Qi folded into the shadows of a wet bricked alleyway. "Lose your jacket," she said, quickly stripping off her top and revealing a black lace brassiere with a thick backstrap. She mussed his hair, ripped the bandage from his head. "I'm a prostitute, you're a client, we're both drunk."

With his jacket discarded on the ground, the spent Colt was conspicuous in his hand; he had no place to hide it. He reluctantly plunged it into a nearby vendor's basket at the alley's far end. As they moved out of the shadows, Gabriel could not help a mournful backward glance at his forsaken hogleg. Its weight in his hand had been comforting and familiar. But it had done its job. It had saved his life.

Threading her arm around his waist, Gabriel led Qi back out into the seething crowds on the street. She bumped one hip into him and forced him to misstep. She was like a warm, skittish animal in his grasp. She laughed and chewed on his neck. Two gunmen were walking right toward them when she grabbed a fistful of his hair and spun him into a devouring full-on kiss, working his mouth hungrily as though she really meant it.

The gunmen split and walked around them, scanning the shadows past them in a desperate attempt to spot their prey.

Gabriel half expected Qi to turn and go after the men from behind and he raised one hand to stop her, but she whispered, "No," as if reading his mind. "We must get back to the motorcycle."

Gabriel's lips were still tingling. She tasted like mangoes and rare spice. Night-blooming jasmine. "The motorcycle," he agreed.

* * *

"Don't you dare get an erection, or I'll have to shoot you."

They were immersed to the collarbones inside a large cauldron of steaming water, which they had bucketed over from a wood fire inside the second of the leaning pagoda's shrine rooms. Pressed herbs floated on the cloudy surface. Qi had insisted Gabriel join her—for purely therapeutic reasons, she explained, after she had applied antibiotic ointment to his head wound and to a new gouge, raw and red, that he'd acquired on the side of his neck.

As she'd climbed in across from him, Gabriel had noticed that Qi had a tattoo of some Chinese character on one hipbone. Oddly ridged with skin, as though to mask a wound. He did not ask about it.

She closed her eyes. After the action of the day the heat was penetrating to the bone, making them both dopey.

"You may ask me now," she said, not opening her eyes.

"I'm not an interrogator," said Gabriel, squeezing water between his palms. "But I would like to know."

"My father used to bathe me. One day, I remember, he took very special care to make me presentable."

"Special day?"

"Mmm. The day he sold me."

Gabriel's eyes narrowed. "Sold you?"

"At the Night Market. Where we just were, today. And *he* bought me."

"Cheung?"

Qi opened her eyes, gazing at him, frank, stark, unashamed. Her eyes were like black volcanic glass in the flickering light. "It fed the rest of my brothers and sisters. This is *not* America, Mr. Hunt."

Gabriel already knew that centuries of entrenched Chinese dogma and cultural preference held that female children were "undesirable." The modern one-child-per-couple mandate had only made the situation worse. In the past, female children were abandoned; today they could be aborted if an ultrasound revealed a female child in utero—a practice some called "gendercide."

It also stacked the census deck to the point where Chinese men had begun to outnumber women by a significant degree. Far from making unmarried women more desirable, women had come to be treated even *less* humanely . . . and the world's second oldest profession—bond slavery—had come into a new underworld vogue. The border between China and North Korea was commonly called a "wife market," as thousands of female Korean refugees from economic privation flooded forth to find Chinese husbands. They were destined to be sold in the bars and karaoke clubs of the Chinese mafia, if they weren't scooped up first by the predatory "women hunters" who preyed on the exploding market. Few men were willing to say they had bought a wife, but that didn't mean they weren't willing to buy one. They knew they were getting someone pliable, hardworking and submissive. And from the women's point of view, better that than starving to death in North Korea, watching your family die around you. A Korean woman cost between 240 and 1,700 Euro (about $300–$2,500 American dollars, depending on exchange rates) in a country where the per capita rural income was little more than a hundred bucks a year. Korean customs officers were routinely greased to the tune of $80 per person to cross the border. The bought women were then provided with the birth stats and name of a dead Chinese (for an additional fee), prompting an upsurge in identity traffic among China's legitimate dead.

Needless to say, beauty, age, physical condition, virginity and health were all factored into a woman's price. Qingzhao would not have been brought to market as a mere baby factory or working wife. She was young, attractive, robust and healthy, and even more importantly, *not Korean*, and so had been brokered to the extreme high-end of the human traffic sector— the highest bidders, the shielded and protected elite who gathered at only the most clandestine rendezvous.

"My tag was here." She pointed to her left earlobe. A triangle of piercings there. Gabriel had assumed it was for jewelry.

"And this." Standing, she indicated the tattoo Gabriel had glimpsed on her hip, distorted with scar tissue. "Cheung put it there. I tried to cut it off once. It didn't hurt." She poked the area. "Now it has no feeling— none at all."

She dismissed the topic with a haughty sniff and sat down again. The last thing she wanted was pity. "In time, I became Cheung's administratrix of protection. Head of security."

"You were his bodyguard? Like that guy I saw take Cheung through a plate glass window at the casino?"

"Not like him. No simple employee could ever gain *that* much of Cheung's confidence. No woman, either." She pulled her knees to her chin in an aerobic stretch.

"Who is he?"

"Longwei Sze Xie. His given name means 'dragon greatness.' He is commonly called 'Ivory.' No one knows why."

"How did you leave Cheung's . . . employ?"

"Cheung and Ivory became convinced that I would serve as an adequate sacrifice for a bad business decision."

"Michelle Quantrill was in the same kind of situation," said Gabriel. "She was falsely implicated, too. When Cheung killed her sister, he left Michelle to take the heat. I got her out of jail and told her to stay put, but she assumed her sister's identity to come here and . . ." Gabriel trailed off. "Well you know the rest. It didn't work out."

"And why did you come?"

"To talk her out of what she was trying to do."

"Why?"

"Because I knew something bad would happen to her, like what *did* happen to her. I think she knew it, too. I just don't think she cared."

"She came as a ghost, then," Qi said contemplatively. "She was already dead. I knew we were linked when I first saw her. I just *knew*."

They sat regarding each other for a silent moment. The connections between people are not reducible to hard statistics, Gabriel knew. Sometimes attraction was a thing of looks and moments, half-drawn breaths and secret approval. Intuitive, as when things denied logic yet felt correct. He resisted the urge to lean forward, to taste the spice again.

"I betrayed no one," Qi said, "regardless of what they claimed. And I survived their attempts to destroy me. Twice now I have tried to take him, and twice I have failed. Once in the Pearl Tower. Once at the Zongchang casino. I failed the second time because your friend was in my line of fire—on a similar mission, though I did not know it."

"And you think you owe yourself another stab?" Gabriel could not quite bring himself to say, *Let it go; get past it.* Qi would just ignore him if he did. "He's not just going to forget your face. He'll see you coming."

"I want nothing less," she said quietly.

"Then you'll die, same as Michelle did."

"As long as he dies first."

Gabriel had encountered fatalism before, and zealotry, and devotion to a cause; but rarely held with this combination of unquestioning conviction and yet so little emotion.

"I know when the children will next be sold at the Night Market," she said. "Cheung will be there. From high places, the rich bid on the poor. I can kill him there. But I cannot do it alone. Think on this for a night. Do not answer now. I am going to sleep."

With a complete absence of shame or self-consciousness, Qi rose from the cauldron naked, stepped over its iron side and walked away, leaving a trail of wetness on the ground. Her body was lean and hard, muscular, pantherish. Before she'd turned, Gabriel had seen there was another ungainly X of scar tissue beneath her left breast, where some other possessive malefactor had tried to brand her, or take something away from her. Gabriel watched her until she was out of sight, engulfed by the night.

After a moment sitting alone in the cooling water, Gabriel rose dripping and got his gear, because there was work to do before sunrise.

It took the better part of two hours for Gabriel to clean, hack and chip away the main debris around the base of the giant bronze statue presumed to be warlord Kangxi Shih-k'ai, in the second shrine room. He had to work by fire and lantern-light, with brushes and chisels, the way the old-school guys had before the intrusion of modern conveniences like floodlights. Had workmen built this cumbersome thing inside the shrine? Had they built it somewhere else and hauled it here, and if so . . . how? It was impossible to calculate the sheer tonnage of the idol, but it would take an earthmover to budge it.

It had to be constructed of sections, Gabriel concluded. Components. Which meant seams. He had thought of this angle of attack while puzzling over the cunningly engineered box back at Tuan's. The base of the idol was a crude rectangular metal slab, not nearly as detailed as the rest of the statue. It was aesthetically offensive. Why? Nothing about the composition of an idol like this was an accident.

Here, on one face of the pedestal, were ideograms. Spackled with the "alpha decay" common to archeological bronze, the writing was invisible until Gabriel was able to sculpt out the calcareous accretions. Perhaps here were instructions, clues, leads; unfortunately, the language variant was one Gabriel did not recognize. And on the other faces of the pedestal—nothing. No marks at all.

The dry environment of the room and mountainside had helped retard corrosion, but nothing could stop the process. Using an improvised potter's cut-off tool he fabricated from a nail and a paintbrush handle, Gabriel was able to scrape the patina of ages from a small seam about two inches down from the top of the base. Following it, he was able to describe a small, rough rectangle about a foot high. It did not appear to want to travel anywhere laterally, so Gabriel struck it with a hammer. The metal made a loud clang like a muffled bell, but Qi did not come running.

Decay and flakes of oxidized metal sifted floorward. Gabriel hit it again.

The rectangle had sunk into the pedestal about an eighth of an inch. Maybe the pedestal was hollow. Rough acoustics indicated it might be.

Bang, again. And again.

Whatever this little component did, it had not done it for nearly a century, and it resisted easy cooperation. But every time Gabriel struck it, it retreated into the base a bit farther until it was sunk nearly half a foot . . .

. . . revealing a small inset on the right-hand side, like the dado joint on a drawer. Gabriel could just curl his fingers around it. It was meant to be pulled out, like a lever.

Using all of his strength and most of his weight, Gabriel was able to budge it about half an inch. He then lost another half hour devising a rudimentary block-and-tackle system to loop around the exposed end and leverage it.

He had to have more than one warm body on this line. He took a break to wash down some caffeine pills he found in one of Qi's bags with a draught of strong (though cold) coffee, and went to seek his mysterious partner.

He found her asleep on a pallet on the third level of the pagoda, still naked though tightly bound up inside the punctured sheet of tin, which she'd wrapped around her torso and secured with wet leather thongs that constricted as they dried. It was like a penitent's scourging corset and looked intensely painful, but Qi seemed sound asleep.

Then Gabriel caught the flickering residual tang in the air and realized that among the other provisions Tuan had supplied Qi, besides food, weapons and equipment, there had been a dose of opium. The long pipe was still at her side like a snoozing demon lover.

Chapter 9

The workings of the pedestal proved more frustrating to operate than a public telephone in Beijing.

The hidden lever freed itself by degrees, measured in Gabriel's sweat. At full cock it released a panel on the far side of the iron base. The panel was heavier than the door in a Swiss bank vault and meant to be slid horizontally backward into a recess in the wall that was clotted with decades—perhaps more than a century—of mulch, roots and earth. Gabriel spent the better part of an hour scraping dirt before he realized the sheer weight of the door would prevent him from moving it; it wasn't as though it was on ball bearings or a hydraulic arm or something.

He hit upon using Qi's motorcycle as a conscripted assistant, since Qi was definitively out of the action.

The revving four-stroke engine raised a hellacious chain-saw racket and the spinning high-treads kicked back a tsunami of dust from the floor. In the lantern light it looked as though the shrine room was on fire. Russet clouds rolled and settled on everything, including Gabriel, who had begun to look a bit like a terra-cotta warrior himself.

The iron panel, nearly a foot thick, was gradually

inched backward until there was a gap into which Gabriel could shove a lantern. He saw the boundaries of a twelve-by-twelve cobwebbed room—beneath the base of the statue—and the edge of a stoneworked archway that indicated the passage went deeper.

After more revving and straining, the space became big enough for Gabriel to wriggle through. He was parched from his exertions, though he had already drunk at least two quarts of water, and his shoulders pulsated with fatigue. He grabbed some road flares from Qi's stores along with a flashlight and an extra lantern. He'd figured he'd need all the light he could get.

The interior directly beneath the statue's base, sheeted in iron, was disappointingly vacant. It bore the musty mothball smell of old, dead air.

Past the archway was another room lined with wooden shelves, many of which had dried out, become porous, and collapsed over time. Arrayed upon the shelves that remained were hundreds of miniature warriors, each about nine inches in height and made of fired porcelain. Many of them had been unceremoniously dumped by time and the crumbling shelves; they lay in shards on the floor, which also appeared to be metal, judging by how his footsteps rang against it whenever they weren't squashing something underfoot. He was within what amounted to a big iron box, Gabriel concluded, one that could only be accessed via the statue's base—metal above, below, and except for the archway he'd entered through and another on the far wall, all around, so no one could dig their way in.

Gabriel recalled Emperor Qin's city-sized necropolis, which had been constructed in relative secrecy and then hidden away underground. Logistically speaking, it would have been much more difficult for Favored Son Kangxi Shih-k'ai to pull off such a feat at the beginning of the 20th Century, when labor was more dear and secrecy harder to come by. Perhaps he had rendered his vaunting self-tribute only in miniature, except for the handful of life-size guardians Qi had found in the room outside. Enough niches spun off from this chamber to suggest there might be several thousand doll-soldiers here.

Was this Kangxi Shih-k'ai's grand joke on history?

Was *this* the great prize Cheung sought?

From what Mitch Quantrill had told Gabriel, the would-be warlord thought he was going to claim his putative ancestor's skeleton—which the great man would've been hard-pressed to have inserted into something the size of an action figure.

Gabriel popped a flare and dropped it on the floor. That was when he first saw that the metal surface he was standing on was writhing with worms and salamanders. He examined a nightcrawler under his flashlight. It looked like some sort of troglobitic millipede with a nasty oval mouth. Some were as much as a foot long.

That meant . . .

Then he noticed the heavily ammoniac, compost stench wafting toward him from the far archway. Opening the portal had caused a tiny bit of air movement, and the flow was eye-watering.

That also meant . . .

. . . that there had to be another way in.

Quickly he drew a small automatic pistol—also procured from Qi's stores—and advanced behind his upheld light toward the second archway.

Stone stairs wound down into blackness. The stench

was already a physical thing as oppressive as wrapping your head in a piece of rotting cloth.

The stairs were long disused, crumbling, slicked with a gray organic fluid that glistened with phosphorescent mold spores. It was like walking on treacherous ice, the kind that could upend you and send you sprawling.

He was traversing downward at about a thirty-degree angle. He could hear trickling water now. He had to duck; the headroom was low.

The stairs broadened into a tiny pavilion with carved rails, all of it indistinguishable beneath caked, stinking muck.

Twin terra-cotta sentries stood mute guard over the pavilion with long-corroded weapons of bronze that had rotted away to stubs and flakes. The standing soldiers appeared to have been dunked in cake batter and left to decay for a century. Their features were not apparent. They were clotted and bloblike, runny pseudo-human monstrosities, more manlike in size and general outline than in any internal detail.

The pavilion faced a grand chamber at least the size of a football field. The distant sound of a small stream or other subterranean waterway was louder here, joining with the other ambient noises and echoing slightly, indicating that this was a *very* big room.

The whole place was a hibernaculum.

The concave dome of the ceiling was wall-to-wall with thousands of nesting bats. He could identify at least three species at this distance—the horseshoe bat, the long-fingered bat and the roundleaf bat. There were also lizards and annelids and other scavenger-parasites that fed on bat guano, which would be abundant indeed here.

Gabriel stepped forward very cautiously.

To either side of the pavilion he could now make out two large, hinged wooden constructions like catapults or small cranes. A shaft held an ironbound basket the size of a bale of hay aloft over a reservoir, which Gabriel presumed had once been filled with water, long-since evaporated.

And below, massed on the floor of the huge chamber, standing in a foot-deep tar pit of urine and guano, was Kangxi Shih-k'ai's army of life-sized figures.

Then Gabriel heard Qi calling out to him from above, as loudly as she could, and thousands of bats took wing, flying straight for him.

Chapter 10

Gabriel smashed the only fuel lantern he had to make a pool of fire near the archway during his hasty retreat, but the bats' sonar had unerringly informed them of a new way out of the cave. Some of them sported a wingspan of two feet or more.

From Qi's point of view it was as though Gabriel was propelled out of the base of the idol by an unbroken thunderhead of swarming bats.

They were not vampires or the dreadnaught-sized killers of the Amazon, but this many airborne teeth and claws could make life terribly inconvenient, especially if the horde was hungry.

Gabriel struck Qi like a linebacker, sprawling them both onto the floor, shielding her face and burying his own into her shoulder in a duck-and-cover as the black beehive madness of the bats filled the shrine room. Eventually they would peter out and find their way into the night. They were just bats. But Gabriel did not know if Qi harbored any phobias or other reactive behaviors that might complicate their survival right now.

When the first wave ebbed, they worked together

to seal the sliding iron portal. With two pairs of shoulders and thighs heaving and amped up on adrenaline, they no longer required the motorcycle to move the door.

Stragglers winged wildly about the upper reaches of the room. Gabriel looked as though he had lost a paintball fight, and this time Qi's reaction could not be dammed back. She found his appearance hilarious.

"Very funny," said Gabriel.

"I suppose you'll be wanting to use the bath again?" she said.

"Briefly," he said.

"Bats are good luck all over Asia."

"But not all over my head." Gabriel made his way to the other shrine, stripping off his shirt as he went.

"My mother used to tell me," Qi said, following, "if a bat lands on your head, you should hope the cricket sees rain coming because the bat won't get off your head until it hears thunder."

He ducked his head under the now cool water, ran his fingers through his hair. He finally came up for air again.

Qi was still beset with mirth over Gabriel's condition. It buoyed him to see that Qi *could* laugh.

He described for her what he'd found in the giant chamber below the statue.

"It's almost worth telling Cheung," Qi said. "The thought of him rooting like a pig through tons and tons of dung, looking for his precious skeleton. On his knees. Slowly being driven mad by the smell."

"Except that he'd send lackeys to do the digging while he watched from a safe distance," Gabriel said.

"Yes, and then shoot them when they finished." Qi wasn't laughing anymore. "I want to see this room for myself."

"Then why'd I bother getting cleaned up?" Gabriel said. But the truth was, he wanted to see it again, too. His explorer glands were firing hotly already, reinvigorating him; he could feel the gnawing need to *find out* burning in his brain afresh. Was one of the figures Kangxi Shih-k'ai? If so, which one? You'd think a man with an ego like that would put himself at the head of his army, leading it—but in the quick glance he'd gotten, there hadn't seemed to be such a "leader" figure. And to find any one figure hidden among the lot of them, one would have to spend hours digging through calcified strata of crap.

"Let's go," he said. "Before the lucky wildlife returns."

Gabriel's second descent yielded three bits of information.

One: That the bats obviously had some other way in and out of the mountainside, some path yet undiscovered, since a good portion of them had returned by the time he and Qi went down, and more filtered in every minute. Qi and Gabriel moved slowly and quietly, to avoid triggering another mad onrush.

Two: That the catapult/crane devices were some ancient form of automated defense against intrusion into the chamber, though fortunately they had long since rotted into inutility. Peering at them more closely, Gabriel saw they were still loaded up with fist-sized iron spheres protruding with spikes on all sides. He lifted one, hefted it briefly and dropped it back into place, then wiped his hand on the seat of his pants. He wouldn't have wanted to see even one of those flying his way, never mind the hundred or so piled up here.

And three: That Kangxi Shih-k'ai's lost terra-cotta army . . . wasn't.

"These aren't statues," Gabriel whispered, after examining one from close up. "They're bodies. Skeletons now, but bodies when they were planted here." He pointed at the metal shaft sticking up from the ground and continuing into the seat of the figure's rotting armor. "He dressed them up in battle gear and rammed them upright onto spiked poles. I'm guessing they were alive at the time."

Qi's expression darkened at the revelation.

"I can't imagine even the most devoted warrior army submitting to that sort of death," Gabriel said. "He must have conscripted a special group of victims for the purpose."

"Peasants," she muttered. "Slaves."

"I thought it was just hyperbole when they called Kangxi Shih-k'ai the 'Vlad of China,'" Gabriel said. "But this . . . There must be more than a thousand people here, all murdered at his hand. And for what? To provide him with . . . human mannequins for this display?"

They made their way carefully back up to the shrine and forced the doorway shut.

"So these are not the Killers of Men we have found," said Qi. "They are not the members of his army." She took a mouthful of water from a dipper and spat it out on the ground. Gabriel understood the impulse.

"Well, there's no way to know, but I doubt it," Gabriel said. "More likely they're people his army rounded up as a sort of mass sacrifice when Kangxi Shih-k'ai died."

Qi bowed her head. She spoke quietly. "One of the reasons this area has been abandoned as far back as anyone can remember was a belief that the area was full of ghosts. People said it was haunted by spirits in pain. My mother said people were telling stories like that when she was a girl."

"That would have been, what, in the sixties? Back then there might still have been people alive who had been children when the slaughter took place. Maybe even some who'd been adults."

"Maybe even one or two who'd participated in it," said Qi darkly, "and wanted the traces never to be uncovered."

"Maybe."

"In any event," Qi said, "it's been a no-man's-land for most of the past century. No one comes here. Except ghosts like me."

Her gaze was abstracted into the small fire they'd built.

"Qi," Gabriel said. "I know your priority is Cheung—"

"My *life* is Cheung. My death, too."

"—but there's something bigger here. The world should know about this discovery."

"So let them know. When Cheung and I are dead."

"There's no reason you have to die." Gabriel tried to take her hand, but she harshly jerked it away.

"Share this discovery with me," he said. "Let me get you safely out of China. The Hunt Foundation has influence, and once we reveal this to the world . . . we can take action against Cheung in other ways. And we can keep you safe."

"Can you? Can you really? Cheung's men came all the way to New York to murder your friend's sister.

They would not hesitate to find me, track me like an animal, and kill me like less than an animal." She fixed Gabriel with a hooded gaze. "You're going to say I could change my identity perhaps. Maybe I could get surgery to alter my appearance, the way Cheung did. No. None of it will matter, in the end. You have not accepted the inevitability of this."

"I don't believe in inevitability," said Gabriel.

"It doesn't matter what you believe," Qi said, shaking her head.

Gabriel was not accustomed to feeling impotent. The Foundation, the specialists he knew, the money he could wield—none of it mattered here in a part of China where it might as well have been hundreds of years ago, where a flock of bats had the power to defeat him and a young woman could embrace a suicide mission because she saw her own death as inevitable.

"If you wish to help me," Qi said, "you can. But there is only one way. By coming with me to the Night Market."

"And doing what?"

"You can get close to Cheung. He doesn't know what you look like. I doubt his men do either—at most they have a blurry image from the cameras on the ship, probably not even that."

"You're forgetting they found us after we left the Night Market, when they ambushed us in the pedicab."

"They were following me, not you. You could have been anyone. And no one who got a good look at your face that night lived to tell."

Gabriel thought back to the brutal firefight in the street. It was true enough. "So what, exactly, do you have in mind?"

"We can both return to the Night Market, Gabriel Hunt. I as a vengeful ghost. You—you as a bidder."

"A bidder," Gabriel said.

"A wealthy foreign guest," Qi said, reaching out with one hand to stroke along his cheek, "with a taste for young Chinese flesh. Cheung will probably pour you a drink himself."

Chapter 11

Quite abruptly, Gabriel found himself back in the world. Clean clothes, wired cash, at least semi-legitimate to all outward appearance but for the recent scars on his head and neck. Michael Hunt was in the air over the Pacific Ocean, racing to pick up the lecture series where it had so unceremoniously been abandoned. Gabriel had e-mailed him a brief, discreet summary of everything that had happened, using carefully veiled language on the theory—hell, the certainty—that all outbound e-mail sent from the complimentary terminal in a five-star hotel's business center would be read by the authorities. He'd sent another even briefer message to Lucy, at the anonymous e-mail address she'd given him before getting on the plane for Arezzo: *Am still in China, L, but M is gone—I'm sorry.* Her response: *Gone missing or gone dead?* To which he replied, *Don't know which. Doesn't look good.*

She hadn't written back.

Meanwhile, Gabriel prepared for his visit to the Night Market and his meeting with a contact called Red Eagle. Earlier in the day Qi had pulled together an assortment of goods—galvanized steel pails, tensile wire, firecrackers and cherry bombs, several large jute bags of money all in coins. She did not specify their purpose. But she had pointed out several other things to Gabriel as they toured incognito, both their faces hidden behind the popular surgical-style paper masks many pedestrians wore and shaded by wide-brimmed hats.

"Nine corners," she had said, indicating the zigzag bridge to the Tea House. "Nine turns, so that evil spirits will become disoriented and cannot pursue you." Gunmen, Gabriel knew, might not be as likely as spirits to get disoriented, but the nine turns could still help break up lines of sight—and of fire.

Qi's combat access to the Night Market was via tunnels beneath the Tea House, part of the old aqueduct system, and she'd showed him the exit she would use tonight. "Tuan has all the best maps," she noted, adding that on auction nights, Cheung would have all the surface entrances and exits heavily fortified.

She had stopped next to a stand whose sign read CRISPY FRIED ANTS—MARINATED SCORPION—TURTLE SHELL GELATIN and ordered a vile-looking beverage from the vendor, a tiny man in an Edwardian suit with the obligatory status-symbol label sewn to his outer left cuff.

"God—what *is* that?" said Gabriel, his throat constricting at the sight of it. The stuff looked like deep red cough syrup with a floating skin of herbs.

"Double Penis," she replied. "Deer and bull. Good for bones, circulation, heart, memory."

"Also is excellent aphrodisiac," said the vendor with a sly wink. He pointed out the source organs, hanging from a drying rack. The deer members looked like rawhide doggie treats two feet long. The bull penis was the size of a Louisville Slugger.

"Drink," Qi said, as though sealing some covenant between them. "It's expensive."

Gabriel downed the viscid brew, keeping his eye on a Tibetan spinning a prayer wheel in the distance. He swallowed twice, then swallowed again. It seemed there was now a smoldering lump of raw lead between his lungs.

Qi had moved on to a small shrine with an urn for burning money. She lit joss sticks, bowed and offered some bills to the pot.

"Now you," she said, gesturing for Gabriel to do likewise.

"But I don't believe in—"

"You must believe in *something*," she said, eyes flashing.

That had been their afternoon. Now it was night-time.

Showtime.

The Iron Fist was exactly what its name implied: an under-the-table combat venue hiding in plain sight, where human beings tried to beat each other to death for money. Gabriel passed through several dining rooms and then a billiard hall before he found the grand stairway for which he was looking. It swept upward into a well appointed—and well guarded—amphitheater from which he could already hear the flat, meaty sounds of flesh battering flesh, lubricated by blood.

But no crowd noise. No jeers or cheers or frantic yelling.

Gabriel was admitted through a curtained foyer. The central focus of the room was the fighting pit, an oval thirty feet across at its widest point, girdled by a chain-link barrier. Two gigantic urban predators, steroidal nightmares, sought to terminate each other in the pit. They were collared together by eight feet of chain. Each wore a spidery leather mask and a studded bludgeoning glove on one fist.

The room was opaque with cigarette smoke and crowded with bettors wall-to-wall, standing room only. They stood in total silence, like the spectators at a chess match. They wagered with nods and winks and raised fingers. Their manner was of banking, not bloodsport.

One of the fighters finally fell like a chopped oak and stayed still. He was dragged out of the ring by his feet. Then the onlookers came unglued, jabbering in fifteen languages, waving money, offering critique.

Two new opponents entered the ring. It was not obvious at first due to their masks and squarish figures, but they were both women.

"New fighters are always cause for excitement," said a voice behind Gabriel. "Their odds are not known."

"Do I know you?" said Gabriel.

The newcomer was a classically handsome Chinese man who looked like an executive or playboy, clad in an expensive tailored silk suit and obviously packing at least one sidearm in a shoulder rig. There was a fine-cut tightness to the material across his back that suggested body armor. His hair and eyes were jet. He smiled at Gabriel like a matinee idol.

"I am Longwei Sze Xie. Please call me Ivory, Mr. Hunt."

This was the part where Gabriel would discover whether any of his hasty fabrications would hold an ounce of water. They shook hands in the Western fashion.

"Do I stick out that obviously?" said Gabriel.

"Forgive me," said Ivory. "Part of my training. I always index newcomers . . . is 'index' the correct word?"

"I know what you mean."

Ivory pointed to the fighter on the far side of the pit. "That is the fresh fighter. Called Jin Huáng, for our purposes."

"Chinese for 'yellow' or 'golden'?"

"Very good, Mr. Hunt. Of course there are a hundred character variants for 'yellow' in traditional Chinese. Depending on the usage, *jin huáng* could be an expression for mulled rice wine, pornography, an eel, Hell, or . . ."

"Or, if you reverse it to *huáng jin*," said Gabriel, "it refers to the Yellow Turbans peasant uprising at the end of the Later Han Dynasty." Gabriel silently thanked his brother Michael for this tidbit from his lecture notes, hoping he would not be called upon to discuss the matter in any more depth.

"Outstanding!" Ivory clapped his hands together. "Full marks. But then, of course, you are a man who knows his history."

"That's why I'd like to speak with Mr. Cheung."

"Mr. Cheung is available later this evening, and has expressed great interest in what you may be able to tell him about Kangxi Shih-k'ai. You understand his need for a considerable degree of discretion and personal security. After we complete this diversion—and please don't feel rushed in any way, if you are enjoying yourself—I should advise you in advance that I will have to search you, although I'm certain it is quite unnecessary."

Oboy, thought Gabriel, *this guy is* really good *at his job*.

Jin Huáng danced into the fight, making her opponent swing the early blows, high, wide and powerful. None connected. She was going to air her opponent out a bit before wrecking and damage. The mob fell into library silence once more.

Gabriel and Ivory were able—and obliged—to whisper. Gabriel noticed the comm button seated in Ivory's right ear.

"I hope I'm not intruding on Mr. Cheung's, ah, other interests," said Gabriel. "I mean, I understand tonight is—"

"Do not speak further of that here," said Ivory. "That is privileged information. But rest assured I understand your meaning. You are an honored visitor here, and all courtesy must be extended."

Spoken by anyone else, it might have been a veiled threat.

"Watch the combatants," said Ivory. "There is no good or evil here. No ring characters or personae. Only a victor."

"The last person standing."

"Precisely."

Jin Huáng dropped low and launched a perfect pivot kick to her attacker's throat, which slammed the other woman down, sucking dirt in hulking gasps.

"Now, take a moment to admire that," said Ivory. "A single blow decides the outcome of the entire contest. It is always one single act. An atomic explosion or the twitch of a fly's wing—it is all the same, in all warfare, in all times. It always comes down to a single act at the correct time."

"That is what makes history," said Gabriel. "It's what makes my job interesting."

"Would you mind if I asked you what happened to your head?"

The scarlet crease from the bullet wound still defaced his temple in a spot impossible to hide or entirely cover with makeup, though he'd applied some in his hotel room. Perhaps the bullet had been fired at him by this very man, Ivory, with whom he was now conversing so pleasantly. The talk was lulling, almost coaxing or coddling, the kind of innocuous byplay that of course was just another form of warfare according to Sun Tzu.

"The Hunt Foundation jet has very small doors," Gabriel said ruefully. "Hatches. No headroom. It looks worse than it is."

"And your intelligence regarding Kangxi Shih-k'ai? What makes that special? Please forgive my natural curiosity."

"I assume you mean apart from the historical record?"

"Yes. Mr. Cheung is an expert on that particular warlord." The implications were clear, including *Don't waste our time* and *If this is a bluff, we'll know.*

"My father's journals," said Gabriel, not exactly lying. "He recorded certain information. Longitudes and latitudes. Parallel evidence. I believe he was on the verge of a breakthrough at the time of his death."

"That is a pity. A great loss."

"Maybe I can salvage some little piece of that loss," said Gabriel. "Maybe help find the Favored Son's tomb at last, with Mr. Cheung's help. It could benefit us both and become a great boon. For my father, not for me."

"Ah, now *that* I understand," said Ivory. "For you, it

is personal, a matter of legacy and duty. An emotional involvement beyond statistics and records and treasure."

"Well, treasure wouldn't hurt . . ."

Ivory permitted himself a small laugh. "Exactly. Come with me. It is time for us to go present you to Red Eagle."

Red Eagle was a florid, pashalike woman who tipped the scale at about 350 pounds. Her surroundings were garishly Japanese but she spoke with an inflection favoring an affect for the American South.

Her chambers opened onto a wide balcony about five stories up inside one of the subway-crush of tall buildings that broke up this area of the Night Market into a series of large atriums. A few other bidding balconies could be seen across the vast open space above the tents and stalls of the vendors below. From such a balcony, a select section of the Night Market could be locked down with no indication whatsoever to the outside world. Below, the Beggar's Arch and other tunneled accessways into this area would soon be sealed off by Cheung's security force.

Which was why Qingzhao had chosen to come in via the sewer.

Red Eagle took a dainty hit from a hookah and offered the pipe to a Mr. Yawuro, an Armani-suited African gangster with a complement of Masai bodyguards. Red Eagle's own guards and functionaries, Gabriel noticed, all seemed to be turbaned Sikhs. Cheung's men were all clad in black-on-black. There were three other bonebreakers in Secret Service wash-and-wear accompanying a boisterous Texan (complete with Stetson) named Carrington. The real problem of any meeting was finding a place to park all the bodyguards, and make sure their pecking order was not ruffled.

"Please try the quail eggs, Mr. Yawuro," said Red Eagle. "They're very special."

Carrington made a face and scanned the room for more whiskey.

Having satisfied Ivory's pat down, Gabriel was presented.

Carrington squinted at him. "I know you," he said. "You're that explorer guy. You was at the North Pole awhile back."

"South Pole," said Gabriel, who knew Douglas Carrington III was an oil man. Inherited wealth. Global pollution. Third World usury.

"Why, hell, son—you're *famous*," the Texan said broadly, getting the notice of everyone in the room. Gabriel watched a pit-viper expression cross the man's tanned face. "And you're rich, too. But you ain't *this* rich." He spun on Red Eagle. There were questions of privacy and decorum to be dealt with here.

"I may not have as much as you," said Gabriel, "but I figured I could pick up something small." The Texan eyed him unhappily, as though detecting the undercurrent of sarcasm Gabriel was trying so hard to hide.

"He is here for *me*, Mr. Carrington," said Kuan-Ku Tak Cheung, interceding. "Be wise and do not insult my special guest, for he is a man who has at least *earned* his reputation."

Carrington actually blushed, then gruffly apologized and retreated.

Gabriel almost felt like blushing, too, when in response to Cheung's endorsement Red Eagle began fussing over him. She giggled like an adolescent and kissed his cheek, leaving a smear of crimson lipstick.

He found himself staring at her. There was, he thought, the distinct possibility that she was actually a he. Gabriel's eye sought the seams of the illusion. Anything was possible here in this polyglot microcosm.

"I am honored to make your acquaintance face-to-face," said Cheung.

Gabriel could not help wondering what that phrasing meant: Was Cheung toying with him? Had he made Gabriel from the security footage from the casino?

"I have read your book," said Cheung with an eager smile.

"Which one?" said Gabriel.

"*Hunt Up and Down in the World*," said Cheung. "Your most incisive chronicle of excavation and underground exploration. Some of it is quite exhilarating. Exciting and improbable, almost like pulp fiction. It speeds the blood."

"I actually didn't write that book," Gabriel said, "in the strictest sense. It's more of an 'as-told-to.' Dahlia Cerras did the hard part, the donkey-work. But of course her name is smaller on the title page than mine."

"And nowhere at all on the cover," Cheung said, clucking gently. "Poetic license, then?"

"I try not to embroider too much."

He thought back on the book's compendium of snake pits, booby traps, torch-bearing locals, gunfights and wild escapes. Yes, it probably would seem ridiculous . . . to anyone who had not been there.

"No literary aspirations?" said Cheung, apparently genuinely intrigued, leaving Ivory to keep an eye on the rest of the room.

"My brother Michael is more the author type," said Gabriel. "In that respect he takes after my parents. I'm afraid I'm the roustabout."

Gabriel also watched Ivory, watching Cheung. This man knew his exits, backstops, contingencies and cover plans. But there was something off about his manner. Ivory was a man of secrets, more than simple hired muscle. He seemed to command the bodyguards and thus be ranked higher. Not quite a partner of Cheung's, but not quite an employee, either.

"Our lots tonight include adult men and women," Red Eagle told her guests, clapping briskly to draw everyone's attention. "Psychics, androgynes, jesters, amputees. Ah, Ms. Carlsen."

A tall Scandanavian woman with an elaborate Maori neck tattoo had just joined them. She drew tiny bird-like sips from a cut crystal flute of champagne.

In his peripheral vision Gabriel saw Ivory running check-ins with his sentries. Very pointedly, none of the security men in the room were drinking.

There was no way, Gabriel knew, that Qi could take Cheung from ground level. She had to be lurking in one of the buildings across the way, with a good angle on the proscenium of Red Eagle's balcony.

Her chosen tool was a "slightly used" bolt-action British L115A, a sniper rifle codesigned by an Olympic gold medalist shooter and chosen by the SAS to use against the Afghans in 2001. It could destroy the engine block of a truck at 1,200 meters. Body armor did not matter to this weapon.

Gabriel wrestled with the role he was about to play. He did not doubt that Cheung was an unsavory sort—but so far all of Cheung's crimes had been hearsay, not verified. *Someone* had killed Mitch's sister and someone had ordered the attack on the pedicab, but there was no way to be certain who. Meanwhile Qi was hardly the most stable person Gabriel had ever met. Her whole touching story (complete with pathos in all the right places) might have been fabricated to recruit him.

But perhaps Qi was right, and perhaps everything she'd told him was so. At least it jibed with what he'd heard from Mitch. That had to count for something.

Though the question of Gabriel's role remained. He was supposed to steer Cheung onto the balcony and into the path of a bullet. But why? If Qi had the capacity to shoot through a bodyguard to nail her target, why was Gabriel needed? As an on-site witness to confirm the kill?

Red Eagle rang a small gong to indicate commencement. Outside, from high above them, counterweighted cages began to lower into view on chains. The sale stock hung in the air before them like Christmas ornaments. In one cage a twelve-year-old girl stood with her hands on the bars and a tri-pronged lot tag stapled to her earlobe. He could have been looking at Qingzhao, fifteen years ago. The girl's eyes were dull with tears and she stood without energy or focus, as if she did not have any real awareness of where she was or what was transpiring.

In another cage, a Caucasian woman in her early twenties, same deal.

In another, an eight-year-old boy, twirling a black sucker in his mouth.

In another, a man with both forearms missing. He was the most active of the lot, scampering from one side of the cage to the other and calling out in a language Gabriel didn't recognize. He wore a fixed, forced smile, apparently trying to court bidder favor.

Mr. Yawuro pointed at the girl and said, "Open for ten thousand."

"Pacific dollars?" Red Eagle asked. The man nodded. Cheung countered: "Eleven. In platinum."

If Qi was to be trusted, Cheung had the advantage, when bidding, of a man who knows he is giving money only back to himself. He attended these auctions to play the players.

"Mister Yawuro?" Red Eagle prompted.

"Twelve," Yawuro said.

Gabriel took a step forward and Cheung came forward with him. They had cleared the overhang and were now in plain sight. Ivory was already moving toward the balcony, to advise his master to back up.

Though it wasn't his turn to bid again, Yawuro uttered a small sound, like a chest cough. Then he was flung backward as the incoming round blew both of his lungs out through the back of his rib cage. His blood lingered on the air as fine red mist.

A second shot sizzled through the air, spanged off one of the hanging cages, missed Red Eagle's beehive hairdo by two inches and burrowed into the wall, starting a fire. A tracer bullet. *Why was Qi firing tracers?* thought Gabriel as he hit the deck. That would only happen if—

The muzzle of Ivory's big automatic was nestled beneath Gabriel's jaw, and from his prone sprawl Gabriel saw Cheung's other bodyguards all leveling firepower directly at his head.

Quite abruptly, as one of the men swung the butt of his gun at Gabriel's injured temple, Gabriel found himself out of the world again.

Chapter 12

Qingzhao could not believe she had missed the shot, and quickly chambered her tracer—her followup round, to track and correct aimed fire.

She'd had Kuan-Ku Tak Cheung dead in her sights on the balcony across from her, with only a ten-degree angle of correction for a downward shot. The picture in the crosshairs told her that Cheung was history. Her trigger pull was a steady, clean, slow squeeze.

But the man standing next to Cheung had died instead.

Which meant that the sights on this ex–Royal Marines rifle had been tampered with.

Her tracer shot strayed to bounce off one of the hanging cages and ignited the wallpaper inside Red Eagle's eyrie. Perhaps it was because Qi, too, had seen the young girl up for sale, so much like herself, once; perhaps it was because Qi had fired with tears welling in her eyes? But no—the tracer proved the weapon's sights to be decalibrated. The scope was supposed to have been zeroed. It obviously had not been. Useless.

Even more useless: The adjustment ticks on the

scope had been shaved down, preventing a fast adjustment with a coin edge or anything else.

Cheung was under cover by now. Ivory's response was frighteningly efficient.

She could have chambered the next powerful Magnum round and taken out one of the bodyguards, but there was little point.

Her window of time had spoiled faster than burning paper. Without checking the window again she fired up her preset fuses and ran from the room, abandoning the rifle and going hot on her backup pistol—a supersized Ruger revolver, so as to avoid even the faintest possibility of a jam.

Ten seconds later, cherry bombs, M-80s and firecracker strings began to detonate around the perimeter below. This would give eager bodyguards false gunfire they would waste time trying to track. The final fuse crisped the support rope for her buckets of coins, which tumbled loose and sprayed a metallic rain of money from the sky, all jingling downward to spin and roll across the cobblestones of the Night Market. Everyone below would scramble to collect the coins, which was good for Qi's escape plan. Sentries would be blocked, hazarded, mobbed and traffic-jammed as they tried to fan out from the archways.

From the doorway into the wild free-for-all of the Night Market, it was five swift steps to the bridge to the Tea House. Qi sprinted across, zigzagging. The propane tanks she had emplaced earlier were still in position. She shot each one with modified tracers like the big hazard-striped rounds she had used at Pearl Tower. Both tanks combusted and blew spectacularly, punching the air out of the space with twin fireballs and lopping off the first fifteen feet of the bridge, which noisily redistributed itself over the surface of the pond water, blackjacking a few curious fish.

Inside the Tea House was a narrow stairway leading down to a supply room with a trapdoor in the floor. The access led down into the sewer system, where Qi had a small motorboat waiting.

Gabriel was not there to meet her as planned.

She had to leave the area now. She waited a few extra beats anyway.

At the very least, she had seen Cheung crawling on his hands and knees, clothing disheveled, panic on his face.

That would have to do until next time.

At the top of the Peace Hotel, Cheung commanded an entire floor. From the elevators one walked across his Junfa Hall, a long corridor lined with statues of Chinese warlords and decorated with ostentatious Peking Opera weapons on wall displays. But for the sliding glass doors, all bulletproofed, and the sentries at each end, the hall held the stately ambience of a museum.

Ivory found Cheung in his Temple Room, a chamber enameled in shiny black and hung with silks. Catercorner to a small shrine was a custom dentist's chair on a hydraulic riser. Mugwort leaves smoldered from a salver next to a sterile work tray.

A technician in a crimson medical tunic was meticulously inserting long acupuncture needles into Cheung's face and scalp.

Cheung indicated his eyebrow. "Here. Deeper."

Dinanath waited in one corner with the behemoth Tosa dogs on stand-down. Cheung ignored them and kept his gaze on Ivory.

Lurking silently in her usual corner was Sister Menga, a white-haired, pink-skinned Taoist soothsayer with the bearing of a lifelong martial arts practitioner. She was one of Cheung's spiritual advisors and seemed to thrive on breathing fog-thick incense smoke.

"Do we know whose base area is the Night Market?" said Cheung, already knowing the answer. Ivory nodded.

Cheung handed Ivory the small carved casket he had been tooling earlier. His expression was benign, yet made hideous by all the needles sticking out of his face.

The Tosa dogs snarled, sensing the gravity of the moment.

Ivory nodded, turned and departed.

Tuan hand-fed a toucan from his table in the Pleasure Garden and meditated on the little coffin that had just been delivered to him. He treated himself to an extra goblet of absinthe and waited for Ivory to arrive.

Ivory entered the room with no fanfare.

Tuan spoke first. "Real warlords made no such foolish rules as Cheung demands."

"This was not a personal decision," said Ivory, taking the seat across from the big man.

It was all smoke in any event, Tuan knew. "Real" warlords were rapists and plunderers, thugs and mercenaries risen to glory via massacre, whose idiom was the raid, not the bargaining table. Once they got legitimized, the rigors of politics almost always unseated them.

Ivory helped himself to the glass that had been put out for him. "Tell me about the rifle," he said.

Tuan chuckled. "You already know about the rifle."

"A very efficient weapon for its intended purpose," said Ivory, who had examined the gun once it had been recovered from the Night Market. "But tampered with so as to be useless for that purpose. Why?"

"To even the odds," said Tuan. "A last-minute change of heart. A perverse notion of fairness in combat." He lifted his big hands to the air. "What does it really matter, now?"

"You supply the rifle," said Ivory. "But you make sure the sights are skewed. You are still trying to play both sides against the middle, Tuan. Unwise, given your position in this scenario. It suggests that you would prepare to align yourself with whichever side emerged victorious. It should be clear to you that Kuan-Ku Tak Cheung is destined to rule New Shanghai. It is an inevitability, not a choice."

"You sure about that?"

"As I said, it is not a choice," returned Ivory. "We cannot abide allies who are less than committed to our purpose. Collaboration with our enemies is more than interference, it is antiparticipation."

"I supplied the terra-cotta figures, as requested," said Tuan.

"Yes. Four so far. Four figures of indeterminate origin, which Cheung found to be useless. A stalling tactic."

"By which I take it to mean that Cheung destroyed them? In his search for a skeleton or a skull or a jewel or a key or *anything* that would relate them to the dynasty of the Favored Son?"

Ivory had, in fact, witnessed Cheung knock off the heads, lop off the arms, powder the fragments with the intensity of a junkie searching for a fix. He'd found nothing to assuage him. Each time his reaction had been more terrifying. Cheung needed a breakthrough to the past so badly that he was apt to start killing his own men left and right just to vent his rage.

"Cheung's quest after his heritage is no longer a concern of yours," Ivory said. "Even in that, you have failed him."

Neither Cheung nor Ivory, nor for that matter Tuan, had any idea that the figures brought to the city by Qingzhao had come from *outside* the tomb, that they had been decoys, leftovers. Vague hints as to what lurked farther onward, nothing more.

"Further," said Ivory, "you became culpable by dealing directly with the woman formerly known as Qingzhao Wai Chiu, when you know Cheung has designated her as one of the Nameless. The figures were brokered directly through your offices."

"Guilty," said Tuan. "But I did it to further my own interests, while providing a layer of insulation between the statues and Cheung himself. I may play both sides against the middle, as you say, but I never *cheat* anybody."

"You were the conduit to the Nameless One," Ivory insisted. "You should have informed us of this detail directly. Instead, you kept it shadowed. Needless to say, Cheung can no longer trust you with the lower Bund."

"Is that why I received this delightful item?" said Tuan, meaning the little carved casket. "It's quite exquisite. Is it Cheung's own handiwork?"

Ivory nodded gravely.

"Then Cheung is serious about all this," concluded Tuan sadly. "Real warlords," he said, "found no dishonor in surprise attack, or night maneuvers, or bribery, or shifting alliances—these are our tools, the basic armament of deception."

"In theory I agree with you," said Ivory. "History bears you out. But Cheung's intention is to rewrite history. That means new rules—*his* rules. There can be no gray area."

"My friend," Tuan laughed, "all of Shanghai is one gray area." He finished his drink. "I'm not surprised by Cheung's decision," he said with a massive sigh. "I am surprised by his choice. I expected some cat-eyed assassin, skulking about in the shadows. Someone all steel and no heart."

Ivory merely closed his eyes and nodded, respectfully.

"I suppose whistling up my bodyguards would be futile," said Tuan.

"They have all left already," confirmed Ivory.

Tuan spread his vast fingers across the tabletop like two opposing camps; the tents of honor versus betrayal, love versus hate, good versus evil. "Of all people," he said, eyes down, "I hoped it would never be you."

"So did I," said Ivory.

Tuan extended his hand. Ivory accepted it. They clasped firmly.

With his free hand, Ivory drew his automatic and gave Tuan two in the chest and one in the head, to ensure a quick death. He held onto Tuan's hand until the big man's heart stopped forever.

Gabriel Hunt considered the limits of his cage.

The large, low-ceilinged room was like a pet sanctuary or a bondage emporium. A warren of floor-to-ceiling bars, wire cages, food pans, filth and dicey light. On a medical tray a series of prepared hypodermic needles was lined up like little soldiers.

His companions were the grist of the slave sale, snoring in drugged sleep or sitting in the corners of their cages with eyes full of fog, blinking little, breathing shallowly, zoned out.

This is no way to treat an honored guest, Gabriel thought.

A case-hardened padlock secured his cell; sadly, Gabriel had neglected to pack his secret agent kit. In any event he had been body-searched down to seams and naked skin before being remanded to Red Eagle's custody. He presumed narcotics came next.

He wondered if Qi had gotten out.

Thinking about her, he realized this was how Qi had begun, perhaps in this very room. He might even be tenanting her old cage. This was the place that had set the path for her whole life.

One cage over, Gabriel saw the doll-eyed twelve-year-old, barely cognizant of her surroundings. She hummed softly and twirled her hair as though she had been left too long to simmer in a madhouse.

From his restricted vantage he could see another prisoner who reminded him very much of Qi—a ruined shadow version of her, same age and same general comportment. The woman was sleeping, or feigning sleep to avoid seeing where she was or attracting the attention of her captors.

It is a general rule of the flesh trade that high profit resides in the tarting up of what is, at heart, rather rude raw material. When up for bids in the open air, the girl would look heartbreaking, done up to entice you to save or pervert her. She would be a dazzling, powerful temptress. Between shows, however, they were all cast back into this dungeon to live like animals.

"Gabriel. You are . . . Gabriel," said a voice.

He looked up, expecting a jailor or tormentor.

That is the fresh fighter. Called Jin Huáng, for our purposes, Ivory had said. *Chinese for 'yellow' or 'golden.'*

"Yellow" for her hair, Gabriel realized, seeing it now for the first time. It had been shorn, military style, to within a quarter-inch of her scalp, as he could observe now that her fighting mask was off. New wounds on her face, from the pit. One eye crusted with blood from a hard hit. The green gaze of her other eye opaque with some cocktail of drugs in her system.

But it was Mitch Quantrill, live in the flesh, back from the dead, incontrovertibly standing there in front of him.

Chapter 13

Imagine you are in another country.

One where you cannot speak the indigenous languages, know no one local, are unfamiliar with the grid, and through no fault of your own, stick out like a hangnail on a sore thumb.

You obviously do not belong here.

And it is only a matter of time before some grown-up, some authority figure, strolls in and asks what the hell you think you're doing.

So—what do you do?

Further imagine that after fewer than 24 hours on this alien planet, you have met the person who objectifies your hatred . . . and failed to kill him.

That during a mad popper-party of shooting, screams and panic, you may have caught a transient glimpse of an old ally from home—a glimpse so fleeting that it might have been a hallucination of wish-fulfillment.

But you cannot pause to debate that information because you have gained a new benefactor, a sharp Asian woman who knows how to deal with gunfire.

Your brain, playing mind tricks on you, gives you another flashpop look at the man you think you know, but already your mind is confusing the new helper with the old helper, and the endorphins are flooding because you are in wild retreat and have just stopped a bullet.

Stupid, careless, getting tagged like that.

None of this matters because in one stuttered, broken-film eyeblink of time, you're facedown in a freezing, fast-flowing river with a bullet in your shoulder.

Now imagine what your last thoughts might be.

Sorry, Val. Sorry, Lucy. Sorry, everybody. I could not save anyone, or change a single bad thing. I have disappointed every person with whom I have ever come in contact.

But strong hands fish you from the black maw of the water, telling you no one should die so ignominiously just for the sake of being dead. And your dying mind agrees that this, in fact, is a reasonable point of view.

So—what do you do?

You try to answer the question your rescuer has posed to you.

Where is Qingzhao Wai Chiu?

You say: Dead, I think. I'm not certain.

The rescuer says: Are you certain of anything?

Then he says: It is true that if I had needed to kill you, you would be dead. My offer still stands. I can show you a way out. No police. No adversaries.

But first there is the tiny matter of digging his own bullet out of your shoulder.

This is accomplished in an apartment ... some-where ... an identity-less box, a clean and well-lighted place, as Hemingway might have said. A window offers a choice view of Shanghai nightlife, far below.

You find yourself naked in an old-fashioned bucket

shower, an anomaly in this modern place. You remember a water dipper. Stitches. Candlelight. A bowl of noodles. You're disconnected, but ravenous. Ninety percent of your identity seems to have astral-projected out of your body and gone somewhere else, and you have a quick thought about the pharmaceutical painkillers that are probably coursing through your system along with the soup.

Then you forget the thought.

There is a saying in China, Noodle Man tells you. "The heat of anger burns only the angry."

Great, you think. Did you read that on a fortune cookie?

The fortune cookie was invented in America, Noodle Man tells you with a total lack of irony.

Ivory, you remember. This person is called Ivory. He even introduced himself to you, back at the casino.

I need to express my sympathy, Ivory tells you. For your sister. Is it your intention to avenge her death?

Dumb question.

I did not participate, Ivory tells you. Romero, Chino, some of the others used her very badly. Cheung ordered it. I am far from innocent. It saddens me still.

Spare me, you think. This man Ivory consorts with Valerie's murderers.

Unless he is lying about his own negligence or blameworthiness.

You feel you have begun something, Ivory tells you. A process in which you are trapped, and you feel a misguided urge to see it through to some end. The end can only be catastrophic for you. Do you see that?

Your brain tries to frame a counterargument but your thoughts are leaking out, wino-bagged in a sieve. Some drug in your blood is definitely messing with you.

Would you leave China now, if you had the chance? Ivory asks you.

So—what do you do?

It becomes very important for you to say the word NO. Aloud. Repeatedly.

Shanghai can be a very dangerous place. You are not sure if Ivory says this, or if you just think it. Fifty-fifty.

The drugs keep your brain drunk but your reflexes vital and threat-responsive, you discover later. Most likely, the prescription changed.

You are given an attacker and your entire personality reverts to instinct.

You are given a mask so you may be hidden in plain sight.

You fight through a waterlogged gray curtain, as though puppeteering a bloodless simulacrum in one of the violent games children so love to entertain themselves with back home, sitting lazily in front of the television. But there is no laziness to it here, nor even very much sitting. Just violence.

And in a way you accomplish what you came halfway across the planet to do. You kill. You prevail.

That is what you do. It is who you are, now.

The food, the drugs deftly separate you from a world that had little use for you, back there in behind-time.

It is not such a bad life, fulfilling in its primal imperatives. Fight. Survive. Eat. Sleep. Fight again.

You see a man in a cage, less fortunate than you. You are in control of your little universe. The man in the cage has no control. Perhaps you will face this Other in the fighting pit.

But a minuscule ember of memory remains. You recognize this person.

His name is Gabriel. You were introduced to him once.

"Mitch!" said Gabriel, bum-rushing his own bars. "Michelle! You're alive!"

"I won," she said, as though that were an answer. She regarded him oddly. Off-center. Head cocked. Sparse recognition in her green eyes. Yet she had remembered his name.

"Who pulled you out of the river?" Of the dozen questions Gabriel could have asked, this one floated to the surface first.

"Some man," she said.

"Don't you remember? We were at the casino. You were shot. We all went into the river together."

"The dream," she said. "The dream of being someone else."

"It's not a dream—look, Mitch, they *did* something to you. Shot you up with drugs or lobotomized you or . . . I don't know."

"Mitch," she repeated.

Gabriel watched her worry the name in her head. It was a slim hope, a doomed chance for her real self to flicker alight.

"I am Jin Huáng," she said. "I have fought five. I have won five." She showed him the Iron Fist, still strapped to her hand.

"No, you're not! You're—"

"When your time comes," she added curtly, "I'll win against you."

Chapter 14

"Jin Huáng, this is your rest period," said Ivory.

Mitch hung her head and shuffled away.

"Await me," Ivory said to her back. She stopped walking. Then started up again.

"You've drugged her into some kind of . . . robot," Gabriel said from the cage.

"A preparation from Mr. Cheung's resident mystic," said Ivory. "It subverts the will."

"I'll say."

Ivory unpocketed a pack of cigarettes and offered one to Gabriel.

"No thanks," said Gabriel. "I never got to finish my drink."

"We of course had your identity the moment you entered the Zongchang casino," said Ivory matter-of-factly, not even looking at Gabriel. "I suspected some connection between you and this woman. The cameras confirmed it when you took them both into the river."

"Well, good for you," said Gabriel. "I gather this is the part where I'm just supposed to listen to your brilliant strategy and not ask you why the hell you have me locked up in a cage."

"Unfortunately for you, you have been tricked into

consort with the Nameless One," said Ivory. "Mr. Cheung is very protective of his interests, and disapproves of those who would oppose him for shallow and misguided reasons."

"You mean like because he murdered your newest fighter's sister in New York?"

"Ah. That is the link, then." Ivory rubbed his forefinger against his lips, a nervous gesture. "And you sought to redress this injustice?"

"Mitch did," Gabriel said. "All *I* wanted to do was get her out of here. That's the honest truth." He hoped he sounded sincere. "This is not our country. Your fight's not our fight."

Ivory pondered a moment, then said, "Let me tell you a story."

"I don't see how I can stop you."

"Let us say that this story is about an imaginary person named Valerie Quantrill. Who worked quite expertly in the transfer of digital data. Let us imagine that Mr. Cheung's company hired her to bring everything in the organization online for access via the latest state-of-the-art equipment. Broadband literacy is essential to a man who aspires to take an entire country to a new horizon."

"But he didn't count on his imaginary data transfer czar being broadband-literate herself," said Gabriel. "And stumbling on things he didn't want her to know."

"There was no stumbling, Mr. Hunt. It was deliberate, premeditated and malign. She hacked firewalls, she stole passwords. All deliberate. She deliberately gained access to data that was damaging to us. We foresaw blackmail, threats, sealed envelopes in secret drops. But Mr. Cheung was not enraged—he was pleased. He saw this initiative as a valuable skill. He seeks to encourage people to their best potential—that is why so many in China take him seriously."

"He's a madman who participates in slave auctions," said Gabriel.

"You persist in Western linear thinking," said Ivory. "But I believe you to be an intelligent and perceptive man. Think of the small crime with yield for the greatest good."

"Every madman in history has justified his madness that way. Look at Hitler."

"Yes, yes, Hitler." Ivory glared at him. "Are you quite through?"

"Not quite," said Gabriel. "But I'm the one in the cage. I'm through if you say I'm through."

"Let us say that instead of chastising Valerie Quantrill, Mr. Cheung offered her a new and expanded role in his grand plan—one that would potentially have made her very wealthy, and free to move about the world as she pleased. And let us say further that she came to the meeting in New York to turn him down. That would have been an entirely honorable decision, you understand—but a bad choice. Mr. Cheung would have perceived her disinclination as a threat to use what she knew."

"You mean he lost his temper and killed her. Hypothetically speaking."

Ivory pressed his lips together and looked at the floor for a moment. He released a sigh, as though venting psychic decay.

"If this happened," he said, "I assure you it was not with my approval."

"You didn't prevent it," said Gabriel.

"Perhaps a Westerner cannot understand. It is not

my place to prevent Mr. Cheung from doing what he wishes. I am bound by my fealty to him."

"Fealty?" Gabriel shot back. "Ivory, he's not even really Chinese!"

"I know. I have accepted this."

"Look—you're *better* than this guy. You saw Mitch come to kill him and you saved his life, but you saved *her* life, too. Only now you're letting your sense of obligation hamstring you."

"I saved her out of regret for her sister's fate," Ivory said. "Were I a disloyal man, I would not have informed Mr. Cheung. Instead I proposed an alternate course, and he approved."

"And if he hadn't? If he'd told you to kill her? What would you have done?"

"I would have killed her," Ivory said, but he said it quietly, in a voice of utter commitment but also some sadness.

There was a deep conflict aboil just under Ivory's bulletproof surface. Gabriel had sensed it the first time they had met.

"You're *attracted* to her," Gabriel realized. "More than that, you've got the obligation of her sister hanging around your neck. Putting her in a human cockfight may not seem merciful, but it beats killing her—at least she has the chance to defend herself. Cheung is happy. And you get to control her. You're her steward. Her trainer. Her keeper. Her man."

Ivory shook his head forcefully, but not without a little sweat on his face.

"Beats buying yourself a wife—you didn't even have to pay anything," said Gabriel, gripping the bars. "You're the guy who jams her with drugs, I'll bet, and I'll bet you do it in the most loving way. You take care of her after the fights, don't you? Backrubs and front-rubs, all that. And this'll go on until she dies, or maybe until you get tired of her, till your aching conscience quiets down. Then what? Do you throw her away, the way Cheung discarded Qi?"

Here at last was a charge Ivory could answer and he leapt at it. "The Nameless One failed Cheung. I corrected that oversight."

"You *corrected* . . . you tried to kill her!"

"I *trained* her," shot Ivory. "She was the best of our candidates! And at the critical moment, she failed. Her failure permitted Mr. Cheung to be wounded, something that is not allowable, and I—"

"You nothing," Gabriel overrode. "You turned your back and Cheung threw her to the same pack of thugs and murderers that killed Valerie, assuming he didn't participate himself. Only Qi somehow survived to come after you. Yes, you—not just Cheung, don't fool yourself, she wants you, too. She wants to kill Cheung, but *you* . . . you she wants to humiliate. And what greater dishonor than to kill Cheung right under your umbrella of protection?"

Ivory's stilted quiet was an indictment in itself. At last he said, "Her story will end very soon. Tuan betrayed her. He betrayed us, too, of course, but that is no more than one should anticipate from denizens of the Night Market."

"And what happens to Tuan?" said Gabriel.

"Tuan's story is already over."

"I see. Did you kill him yourself?"

"It was my honor, and Tuan knew that."

"Your honor," Gabriel said. "You make it sound so very noble. Never mind the dirty, grubby politics of it—the fact that it also conveniently eliminates one of the three other power-bosses on the Bund. Who's left that isn't under your control yet? Hellweg, the water-and-power guy, right? And the fellow who runs the police; I forget his name."

"Zhang," said Ivory. "You are right—to win Zhang to our cause would be to put the entire army at our disposal."

"Why not just kill him the way you killed Tuan?"

"Zhang has not betrayed Mr. Cheung. He will be offered a deal, as Mr. Hellweg will be."

Gabriel almost wished Ivory weren't being so open in discussing his plans—it surely meant he was confident Gabriel would never leave the cage alive.

"Listen, Ivory," Gabriel said, figuring he might as well confront it head-on, "you and I can work out a deal, too."

"I am sorry for your unfortunate confinement," Ivory said, "but no. If I were to let you go, I would have to answer to Mr. Cheung. As I would if I allowed Qingzhao to continue living. There are no options."

"There are always options," Gabriel said. "And if I find one before you do, you may regret not making a deal with me."

"You speak very bravely for a man in a cage, Mr. Hunt."

"I'm not being brave," said Gabriel, "just telling you the truth. I have something Mr. Cheung wants very badly. How long do you think he'll keep me in this cage?"

Gabriel caught the fleeting expression of uncertainty that ghosted across Ivory's face at this news. But he had no time to appreciate it, because while he was watching Ivory someone slipped up from behind and jammed a spike full of joy juice into Gabriel's shoulder.

Chapter 15

Mitch's defeated opponent from the Iron Fist bout that Gabriel had witnessed turned out to be a lot more important than anyone reckoned.

The woman's name was Garima Bhatia; in her native Indian dialect "Garima" meant "prowess, strength and honor." That she had been tough and competent did not matter. That she had lost money for some bettors did not matter. That she had been defeated by Mitch did not matter.

What mattered was that Garima Bhatia had died soon after the match from a brain aneurysm.

What mattered more was that Garima had been Mads Hellweg's fighter, bonded and branded.

Mads Hellweg, the underground lord of New Shanghai's water and power, had long distrusted Kuan-Ku Tak Cheung, and had significant reservations about the fixing of matches at the Iron Fist. For the purposes of inside intelligence, Hellweg had emplaced most of the Sikh guards used by Red Eagle, having obtained these men through the same channels and business interests in India he had used to procure Garima. But over the prior months the pipeline had broken down and his Sikh spies were being kept out of the information loop. Garima's defeat had come at an inopportune time, never mind her death, and Hellweg was now in dutch with the local Triad shylocks.

Normally, Hellweg would have requested that Cheung use his influence to take some of the creditor heat off. Except he knew that Cheung was brimming over with his own plans and needed to curry favor with the selfsame Tong bosses to get what he wanted. Hellweg's request was doomed to go into channels and never come out.

Plus, Cheung was visibly becoming increasingly erratic. Assassins were trying to kill him in public. He had taken to soliciting the counsel of an astrologer. And he had fallen into the habit of murdering rivals at the least disagreement or split-hair detail. Hellweg had begun to suspect his uneasy relationship with Cheung was going to blossom into a less-than-equal partnership.

Fortunately, Hellweg had other allies. Quietly marshalling their forces against the Tongs in China were the members of the Japanese *yakuza*. Though nominally subject to a cross-cultural cease-fire, they were just waiting for the right excuse to commence full-scale gang warfare in the streets of Shanghai. Hellweg had maintained a back-door deal with some of the *oyibuns* of the 30,000-strong Kobayashi Clan just in case it ever proved necessary.

And this, he thought, could be the moment. If he deactivated the Iron Fist using yakuza mercenaries, Cheung would blame the Japanese and drag the Tongs in for reprisal. Both sides would suffer glorious losses, including the Triad loansharks trying to bleed Hellweg, and Hellweg himself would skate blame-free.

Then, when the tumult died down, he could debut his own fighting pit, one strictly under his control.

Best of all, if Cheung didn't suspect his involvement, he might even come to Hellweg for support, might ask him to help architect the retaliation against this bold, slap-in-the-face attack by Japan. This moment would bond them as equals in a way nothing else had to date . . .

Hellweg made the call on his ultra-secure landline.

The warning on the sarcophagus was clear. Basically, anybody who opened the tomb was to be cursed, blah-blah, the usual rot.

Gabriel tilted back his pith helmet and mopped his head with a kerchief once white, now gone to oily yellow. Weeks of digging to find a burial chain-of-title regarding a Second Dynastic Period ruler named either Kaires or Seth-Peribsen; scholars disagreed. What Gabriel had found instead was more intriguing—an overlooked intermediate ruler, sort of a vice president, name unknown, signified only by a unique, untranslatable hieroglyph—a bit like the Artist Formerly Known as Prince, but without all the platinum albums.

According to the glyphs, Mr. Unknown's guardian was supposed to be a kind of Frankensteinian version of a mummy assembled from the parts of all his best soldiers and consigned to an eternity of guard duty in the afterlife.

The sarcophagus creaked on hidden stone hinges—
Pause.

Gabriel snorted water and surfaced, having miscalculated his depth and evacuated the mouthpiece for his air tanks. Frequently the current stirred up the basal muck of this part of the Amazonas, and until it settled it was impossible to see anything underwater. The evidence was thin at best for the missing link between human and fish, and Gabriel was about to give it up for the day when something grabbed his leg while he was treading water—

Pause.

The arctic air in the middle of the Greenland ice cap was so cold that it could shatter a plastic bag, or solidify water thrown from a cup before it hit the ground. To his left, a hundred miles of featureless ice. Ditto for all other directions, save up, where hung nothing but blistering, cloudless sky. Beneath his boots, more ice, ten thousand feet of it, straight down. He was so far inland that there were no birds, for there was nothing here for them to eat. The air would crystallize his lungs if he inhaled it quickly enough. All blinding white, like the end of everything . . . until he plummeted through a thin scab of crust masking the treacherous layer of blown snow, and crashed into a cavern network that had last been open to the sky sometime during the Industrial Revolution. Even now, glacial drift was narrowing the rift, threatening to seal him in forever—

Pause.

The man-shaped creature, evil and desert-dry, had him by the throat. Gabriel could smell the mold—

The river throwback, an obscenely large mutation of the Paleozoic coelacanth, was in the process of swallowing his leg—

He looked up and saw the sun blotted out while he froze to death in the harsh Greenland icefall—

The narrative nature of dreams denies the concept of build, or the slow accumulation of facts necessary for deductive logic or extrapolation. As soon as your mind thinks of the eventuality, you flash-forward to the heat of it without the benefit of intermediate orts and bits of drama, as in a cinematic jump cut. The velocity of the dream-narrative can relentlessly shove your mind toward wakefulness, which is why many sleepers awaken before they "die" in the dream state.

Gabriel punched and flailed, battling the homicidal monster, kicking at the killer fish, fighting the cold and grinding ice floe. He fought for his life. He fought to breathe. He fought not to die.

And the damned dream would not allow him to wake up.

Cheung was busy carving another wooden casket.

Ivory's gaze found it but didn't linger there; he searched Cheung's eyes for illumination.

Sister Menga splashed animal entrails into a bronze bowl. Without looking up she spoke in a monotone: "Victory over an enemy. The exposure of a traitor. All as prophesized."

"Tuan was premature," said Ivory respectfully.

"Nonsense," said Cheung. "I should have killed him a year ago, for the information I did not know he was concealing. Why did *you* not bring that information to me?"

"I only suspected," said Ivory. "I did not know."

"Well, then, now that you *know* that the Nameless One shot Red Eagle's salon to kindling . . . now that you *know* I was humiliated when that creature Carrington spilled his drink on me and, even worse, when Yawuro got some of his blood on my clothing . . . now that you *know* all that, Longwei Sze Xie, tell me: when are you going to emerge from whatever dream-state has clouded your reason and return to be useful to me, other than as a shield?"

"For whom is the casket?" said Ivory.

Cheung snorted. "This is for our friend and fellow Quad Leader, Mr. Hellweg."

"What has Hellweg done?"

"It's not what he's done. It's what he plans on doing. Again, Longwei Sze Xie, your intelligence is tardy. Don't make me turn my scrutiny on you."

Cheung never gave people the benefit of the doubt, and the fact that he was doing so now made Ivory feel a twinge of fear—the kind of reflex horror one feels in the presence of a rabid animal, of some threat that cannot be dealt with rationally.

"Hellweg is as Tuan was," explained Cheung cryptically.

"If you take Hellweg out, the Tong Leaders may object."

"They won't," said Cheung. "I have purchased Hellweg's debts to them and made them good. Let him make his pathetic gesture of protest. Let him discover for himself what true impotence feels like. Then we discard him."

"How?"

Cheung smiled. "I shall resolve Hellweg's difficulties at the funeral."

"Tuan's service?"

"Yes. At the same time I shall find out about General Zhang's fidelity."

Ivory refrained from asking how. Cheung would just tell him again to permit him his "mad little schemes."

"Your path is clear," he said to Ivory. "You know what you must do. I have been patient with you, but the American woman you are babysitting at the Iron Fist has clouded your judgment. It happens to all of us, and it is better that we recognize it has happened to you, and move onward, because we have larger plans. Today you will kill the American woman. Then you will use the information we gained from Tuan's interview to kill the Nameless One. And we shall become whole once more. Sister Menga has prophesied it. Do not beg my forgiveness. It is not needed."

"I will do my duty," said Ivory.

Dinanath hurried into the Temple Room, breathless, neglecting to ask pardon because what he had to say was urgent. "Sirs," he said, sweat standing out on the bald dome of his head. "There's shooting at Red Eagle's."

"Who?" snapped Cheung, his eyes coming up to full flame.

"Apparently . . . ninjas," said Dinanath.

Gabriel woke up with his own blood crusting one eyelid half-shut and blocking the hearing in his left ear. His body felt pummeled and tender, as though someone had borrowed it, had a really swell party, and then returned it without dry-cleaning it. His wrists and knees throbbed with pain. He had bruises all over—some severe, with broken skin.

He was still in his cage at the Iron Fist.

He had suffered a dream; a dream of combat against multiple enemies, each defying description. Was that what the mystery drug did to Mitch, he wondered—make her think she was battling something else entirely when she was in the fighting pit? Geared up and heroic, still soldiering for her country perhaps?

Gabriel would've loved to analyze the stuff in the syringes, almost more than he presently wanted a sauna, a first-aid kit and a good night's sleep.

He went to work cleaning off his eye, and as he did, two of Red Eagle's Sikhs swept through the cage room. Rather than doing any of the things he might have expected—feeding, watering or doping up the prisoners, for instance—they went along the line methodically releasing cage latches and unhinging padlocks. In almost no time at all, the doors had all been opened so that everyone could escape to freedom . . . if they had enough presence of mind to do so.

Gabriel considered briefly the possibility that this might be another hallucination, or some sort of trick, but he rejected it. Something was going down. The Sikhs were gone as fast as they had appeared. Gabriel could not know that they had received a five-minute heads-up from their stealth employer, Mr. Mads Hellweg.

Then came the sounds of panic, violence and gunfire. Sporadic at first. Growing nearer.

Gabriel kicked out of the cage, his muscles protesting. He grabbed two of the syringes from the tray and pocketed them. Nothing else at hand even remotely adaptable as a weapon.

Several of the captives—the lot-tagged "merchandise"—were staying put in their cages like sheep.

"Move it!" Gabriel yelled, banging on the bars and wire mesh as he faded along a corridor of cells. "Get out! Get out now!"

But they didn't, and only steps behind him, black figures entered the holding area, swathed in hoods, bearing automatic handguns with stretch magazines. He heard their racing footsteps, the ratchet of magazines being slammed home, the chatter as they hosed anything questionable with gunfire. Glancing back, Gabriel saw several prisoners—young women, kids— shredded in their cells. They didn't even cry out. He turned and kept going.

He couldn't save everybody. He knew he'd be lucky if he could save himself. His skin was on too loose and felt feverishly hot, making his reflexes and reaction time unreliable. The only other person he could think about was Mitch, and that only because of his promise to Lucy, because she was counting on him. So: Get his ass, and hers, out. Save who he could on the way. It was the best he could do.

The cage run was a narrow grid of rows and sections, floodlit from above. Gabriel stalled between two rows in a section that held mostly lot-tagged young men, their eyes drug-dusted, the aluminum bands stapled to their ears. He ducked out of sight just as one boy stumbled from his confinement in time to block a three-bullet salvo from a gunman wielding a pistol that cycled quicker than you can blink.

Gabriel held fast and watched the shadows pass on the floor. They were sweeping the room by section, like a SWAT team following a playbook.

He fished up one of the syringes from his pocket, silently counted to three, and struck, stepping out in a wide pivot, jacking his strength from the elbow and burying the needle into the neck of a slender, lizardy man in black whose face was obscured by a classic *sanjaku-tenugui* wrap. A jetstream of carotid scarlet scribbled a high arc across the air and the man gobbled, clutching, already falling. Gabriel wrested away his pistol as he dropped. It was a Beretta nine modified for auto-fire or three-shot bursts, a nasty little puff adder of a gun.

Instead of engaging, Gabriel stayed ahead of the advancing force, moving into the next of the warren of rooms.

Mitch occupied a cell about seven-by-seven, with a

futon pad and a privy hole—the block's Grade A accommodations, in other words. She was wearing a one-piece zippered fatigue jumper and laceless tennis shoes. She sat with her ankles crossed on the pad, staring dead ahead at nothing and feeling her shaved skull with one hand as though trying to identify something in the dark.

"You're not . . . him," she said when Gabriel entered.

He leapt forward and clamped his free hand over her mouth. "It's Gabriel. *Gabriel.* Remember?"

"*Gbrl*?" she mumbled against his palm.

He tried to find her eyes. They were still there where they were supposed to be but somewhere else at the same time, distant and dilated and opalescent. He risked giving her a hard crack across the face, open-handed. Her eyes swam into focus briefly and met his, then slipped away. He slapped her again. This time her eyes locked and before he could give her a third crack her hand shot up to lock onto his throat.

"That's it," he croaked, reddening.

"Gabriel?" she said. Her voice sounded confused, disoriented.

"Yep." He freed her grip before his Adam's apple imploded. "Come on, Mitch. We've got to get out of here before—"

A burst of gunfire, from not very far away.

"Who's shooting at us?" she said.

"Time for that later," Gabriel said as he levered her to her feet and thought to himself: *You optimist, you.*

Chapter 16

Ivory surveyed the damage. According to what Dinanath could glean under mild duress from one incapacitated Sikh, Hellweg had ordered all his spies to bail out just prior to the assault. The Sikhs had attempted to liberate all the auction stock and caged fighters to add to the confusion. About twenty of these latter were dead now, sprawled on the floors, shot in their cages, incidental casualties of a sweep-and-clear by the trigger-happy intruders. If it moved, they had fired at it, and sometimes if it hadn't.

Those who were not salvaged or recovered, Ivory knew, would start going into convulsions in about two days.

Dinanath put the bore of a .357 Magnum to the Sikh's head and spared the man the chagrin of having to seek new employment.

From the invading gunmen, Red Eagle had reaped a bullet in the face for her trouble. She was spread out awkwardly across a lounging chair in her salon, trailing spilled silk saturated with blood. Her wig was on the other side of the room. She did not appear happy or fulfilled in death.

The lone enemy casualty was not talking. He had

suffocated on his own blood, losing the fight to breathe with a hypodermic needle through his windpipe. Ivory found him in a vast, fresh pool of scarlet not far from the cage where Gabriel Hunt had been parked. The intruder's weapon was not to be found.

The woman had also disappeared.

Directly or indirectly, the intervention of Qingzhao Wai Chiu had closed down the Moire Club at the Pearl Tower and disrupted the Zongchang Casino. Then it had compromised the Night Market and now, shut down the Iron Fist. This situation was metasta-sizing. Cheung was right; Ivory knew what he had to do and each incident that passed without his doing it hurled his loyalty to Cheung further into the shadow of doubt.

The manifestation of Ivory's dilemma—his demon—was Qingzhao, the Nameless One.

The engine of his new uncertainty was Michelle Quantrill.

The unexpected wild card was Gabriel Hunt.

Just kill them, Ivory thought. *Kill them all and be done with it.*

Gabriel would have dearly loved to blend into the crowd, but it was hopeless and would have been even if he hadn't been dragging Mitch along with him. Gabriel was easily a head taller than any of the Chinese cruising the Bund, and Mitch's buzz-cut blonde pate and green eyes might as well have been a search-light at a gala premiere. He was carrying the stolen gun and had no good place to conceal it, having been caged in nothing but a soiled T-shirt and trousers; he tried jamming it into a pocket, but enough stuck out to make it no concealment at all. Mitch, meanwhile, was hampered by the laceless sneakers that threatened to fly off each time she increased her speed above a rapid, shuffling walk. Together they looked like a pair of alcoholics who had just spilled out of a bar fight or escaped from a detox facility.

Mitch was slowly coming back into focus. "I don't understand," she said distantly. "It was like a dream—I was back in combat training. I wasn't in a ring waiting for a bell. I was in a desert somewhere, we'd been shot down, and I was trying to keep insurgents from killing me. But it felt absolutely real—more real than the prison. The times when I could see the cell, it felt . . . it felt like *that* was the dream, because it was the only time I knew I could rest. All the rest of the time, it was combat, nonstop combat."

"I know," said Gabriel, trying to maintain a watchful eye in all directions at once and to keep them moving. "They spiked me with that junk one time and I was in three different places at once, fighting for my life. It's as though the drug uses what you know against you. It produces hallucinations, picks and chooses from your experiences and your imagination to produce a situation of maximum distress."

"I don't see why they bothered," Mitch said. "It's not like the reality of the situation wasn't distressing enough."

"Point," said Gabriel.

As they passed the front lot of a western hotel, he tried to recall whether Michael would have landed in Shanghai yet. It hardly mattered, though; there was no good way to reach out to him. Inquiring through ordinary channels—a hotel, a university, a tourist bureau—would bring the People's Police down on their heads, and the police were controlled by Cheung's partner, General Zhang, formerly of the Red Army school of compassionate understanding. Even exposing themselves on a public street long enough to puzzle out the rat's maze of the Chinese pay-phone system was a bad idea. No, for now they were on their own and would have to fend for themselves. They needed food, clothing, disguises (sunglasses, a watch cap, *something*), money, transportation, identities on paper, and a way out, a way back to a world where the most agonizing decision they faced involved browsing a selection of tempting desserts.

Gabriel steered Mitch by the elbow toward an enclosed mall area on their right.

"We're going to have to do a little shopping," he said.

Gabriel had never classed himself as a criminal. So much for that comfortable delusion. In the world of the Night Market, everybody was guilty of something.

Right now, Gabriel was guilty of shoplifting.

Of course, in the past few days he had been present at extravagant symphonies of carnage and destruction, playing his little solos where the orchestration required it. But now he had to engineer a grand opera of distraction just to pinch a sweatshirt.

It should have been a simple snatch-and-grab—but the elderly pipe-smoking gentleman who ran the clothing stall had an eye on Gabriel. He checked back repeatedly to see where Gabriel was looking, and each time Gabriel made sure he was looking somewhere else. No point confirming the man's suspicions.

Shortly, the elder got into a spirited haggle with a young American woman, a forceful blonde who fully indulged the elaborate grammar of hand-wringing, waving, coaxing, position-jockeying and street theater necessary to a really satisfying negotiation. It was a thousand bucks' worth of production value over a one-dollar item.

Gabriel ducked low, slid two hoodies from the bottom of the rearmost stack beside the counter, and quickly scooted.

His turned one of the hoodies inside-out to hide a blazing Day-Glo logo of some boy band that had been all the rage two years ago. It was an XXL, and with it dangling to his upper thighs at least the gun was covered.

He looked around for Mitch, who, having walked away from the negotiation in a decent simulation of a huff, was now loitering near the restrooms. He saw her chatting up a tall fellow in an expensive sharkskin suit, the sort you'd have to go to Hong Kong to buy. Gabriel raised her hoodie and was about to call to her when he saw her unzip her jumpsuit a few inches and guide the man's hand inside for a sample squeeze.

More crime in the making, and the poor bastard didn't realize it. He watched her lead the man off toward the toilets.

Shouldn't take long for her to roll him, he figured. Gabriel turned to scan the space, keep an eye out for trouble, and found himself face-to-face—well, face-to-chest—with a man a good ten inches taller than him. And stronger: a pair of massive, callused hands gripped Gabriel's neck and hoisted him clear off the ground.

The guy holding Gabriel looked like a renegade circus strongman, a yard wide at the shoulders, totally hairless but for a drooping Fu Manchu mustache, sumo-sized and well north of six feet tall, with skin-stretching plugs in both earlobes and a grip like a construction crane.

Where had this guy come from? Was he on Ivory's crew or . . . ?

This was not the time to ponder such questions, Gabriel realized. Gabriel's head was struggling to pop away from his body while his neck muscles tried to keep it where it was. The kicks he landed were ineffectual; he was a dangling marionette in the larger man's grasp.

Then the old man from the clothing stall appeared, smoldering pipe in one hand. He commenced hollering in Chinese, jabbing his finger repeatedly at Gabriel and yelling a word that sounded like "queasy," over and over.

As Gabriel's brain started to shut off from lack of oxygen, he realized the man was shouting *qiè zéi*—thief.

The colossus had acres of ridged scar tissue on his bald head. Gabriel could whale on that skull all day and distract him no more than a fly. A small fly. A small, crippled fly.

He reached under the sweatshirt, pulled the gun out of his pants pocket, aimed it outward and downward.

The big man shifted so that he was holding Gabriel with just one hand and swatted the gun away effortlessly with a single swipe of the other. Then he grabbed hold of the purloined sweatshirt Gabriel had on and peeled it off him like a banana skin. He let gravity take over and Gabriel piled up on the wet cobblestones, stunned and insensate, his legs feeling far away.

The man bent down and snatched up the second sweatshirt, which Gabriel had dropped when lifted off his feet. It was filthy. He shook it in Gabriel's face while the old man came near to offer a bit more shouted admonishment. Gabriel let his eyes slide shut and shortly they left, or at least stopped yelling at him. The next voice he heard was Mitch's.

"What are you doing?" she said, one hand under his arm, helping him up. "This after you told *me* not to attract attention."

"Need to work on my Artful Dodging," he muttered. Gabriel saw she'd picked up the gun. Good. At least one of them had done something right. He limped with her away from the glare of the crowd. "How'd you make out with your new boyfriend?" he asked hoarsely.

"Let's just say he didn't have quite the good time he was hoping for. When he wakes up, unties his ankles and pulls up his pants, he'll find his wallet missing." Off Gabriel's expression, she added, "He's not hurt. Just his pride, and he had too much of that to begin with. And we needed the money."

"How much did we get?"

She flashed him a palmful of currency. Not much. Enough.

"All right," said Gabriel. He steered them on. They didn't speak till he stopped short a few minutes later.

"What is it?" Mitch said.

"We're going to need better weapons."

"And . . . ?"

"And I know a place where we can get some."

He pulled her past the half-hidden wooden sign that read SU-LIN GUN MERCHANT.

* * *

You would not think so from watching the average Hong Kong action movie, but private citizens in China are expressly forbidden to own or sell firearms. The penalties range from several years' imprisonment to a death sentence. This hard line to prevent "gun violence" is maintained by the same government that executed ten thousand lawbreakers in 2008, making China number one in the wonderful world of capital punishment. Preferred method of legal execution: a hollow-point to the head. *Boom*—done, and no one says a word about irony.

"Not to put too fine a point on it," said Gabriel, "but you can also pull the death penalty here for stealing a cultural object. Or killing a panda."

"So *how* is this all legal?" Mitch said, slack-jawed at the diversity of Su-Lin's arsenal.

Gabriel gave her a dour look.

"Never mind," Mitch said.

Capital crime was little deterrent where profit was involved. The temptation here was the same as it was for dirt farmers in the U.S. to move crystal meth. Here, a person could sell a single gun and make three times his or her yearly pay.

Gabriel moved to the dual laptops as tiny Su-Lin grinned in recognition. Repeat customers were highly desirable.

Gabriel typed: YOUR PIG MOTHER EATS NIGHT SOIL.

Mitch read this over his shoulder and gave him a look of confusion crossed with bemusement—but it was cut short by what appeared to be a sudden migraine jolt that caused her to pinch the bridge of her nose and squeeze her eyes shut, wetly.

"You okay?" said Gabriel.

She waved away his concern. "Mm-hm, yeah. It's just a spike—like brain freeze from ice cream, you know?" Gabriel knew—but he didn't think ice cream had anything to do with it.

Su-Lin typed back on her keyboard: I LOVE YOU, TOO.

I NEED A WEAPON, Gabriel typed. He took the ungainly Beretta back from Mitch, passed it across the counter. I CAN TRADE THIS IN.

Su-Lin gamely dug under her counter and came up with the same modified .36 Colt revolver Gabriel had lost after his visit to Tuan with Qingzhao. It was like seeing an old friend. He wondered how many times she'd sold and resold the same guns.

IT HAS ALREADY BROUGHT GREAT PROFIT, Su-Lin typed, SO I GIVE SPECIAL PRICE TO YOU.

DONE, Gabriel typed. NOW FOR MY FRIEND?

Chapter 17

"We need to get out of the middle of this thing," said Gabriel. "Nobody is going to back down. Everybody is going to get killed."

The leaning pagoda was within view as they crested a jut of rock. Mitch was climbing right behind him, but her attention seemed to be wandering and she had gone from breathing nasally to orally—not a good sign, for someone as fit as she was.

"You're part of it now, too," she said, her breath more ragged than it should have been.

"No, I'm not, and neither are you. We get to Qi's place, I call my brother. I'm pretty sure Qi's got a secure cell phone or can bash one up. Michael calls the embassy and the Marines and we burn our tail feathers straight out of here."

"You still don't get it, do you?"

He turned and gave her a hand over the next rise. "You're going to tell me that the guy who imprisoned you, drugged you, turned you out to fight for money, the guy who imprisoned *me*, for god's sake, has some kind of hypnotic hold over you that's going to keep you trying to kill phantoms?"

"No," she said. "Stop. Please. I've got to stop." She halted, bent over, hands on her thighs.

Mitch sat down heavily on a knobby outcrop of feldspar.

"It is the drug?" said Gabriel.

"I don't know. Maybe. I can't tell if this is an after-effect, or withdrawal, or bad chemistry, or what. But it's starting to hurt so bad I can't keep my eyes open."

"You can't go to sleep," warned Gabriel. "You might not wake up."

She took a deep breath and her vision seemed to clear slightly. "He told me a story," she said. "A parable."

"Ivory?"

"Yes. He asked if I'd ever had a crisis of faith . . . god, I can't remember what he said. It seemed to make a lot of sense at the time. He was talking about himself, I'm pretty sure, and about Valerie. He said he didn't kill her. But he didn't stop it when he saw it happening."

"That was his crisis of faith," said Gabriel.

"Exactly. His duty versus his honor. Very Chinese."

"I know how this one ends," said Gabriel. "Betrayal. It's who betrays whom I'm having a hard time figuring out."

Meanwhile, Gabriel was suffering his own crisis. He still had a syringe of the Iron Fist happy-hour cock-tail in his pocket. He'd grabbed two and only used one on the gunner in the cage room. The other he'd begun thinking he could get to a lab, have them break it down, analyze it. Synthesize countermeasures.

But if what he was seeing in Mitch was the first stage of withdrawal, he was going to have to use the needle on her. Perhaps diluted. Perhaps in increments.

But even so, the sample would soon be gone—and she'd be rendered a null-sum as a team member for the duration.

Part of his mind—the impatient part, the selfish part, the part that had so often kept him alive in tight spots— was asking what, really, did he owe her? Hadn't he picked up that check? Hadn't he been picking them up for Mitch ever since he'd posted her bail back in New York? Hadn't he paid plenty in skin and blood and gunfire; in nightmares and pain?

But his sense of justice was at stake here. That was the other part of his mind, the part that kept getting him into all those tight spots in the first place. He had allowed the undertow to drag him this far because Lucy was relying on him—and because men like Cheung needed taking down. And if Mitch's tragedy was a minuscule one for planet Earth, so what? Move a single grain of sand on a beach, everything in the world is changed. How's that for Zen?

"I'm not so sure Qi won't just shoot us on sight," said Gabriel, considering their range from the pagoda. "If Tuan knew her whereabouts, then Ivory knows, which means Cheung knows. And if she's found out that Tuan's dead, that he betrayed her . . ."

". . . she may be in a mood to shoot anyone that approaches."

"Keep your eyes open," Gabriel said.

"I'll try," Mitch said.

But Qingzhao was not to be found.

They entered the pagoda without incident and searched from room to room without turning her up. Mitch doubled over with a cramp about the time they entered the third of the shrine rooms.

"God, this feels really . . . weird," said Mitch, breaking a sudden sweat. Her temperature was skyrocketing.

The puzzle-box base of the idol was securely shut. Qi's bike was gone.

But most of her hair was still here. It lay at the foot of a narrow mirror, hacked off in clumps, apparently with the combat knife lying atop one clump.

The water in the big iron cauldron was room temperature. Gabriel decided to stick Mitch inside to keep her from running too hot. She didn't resist as he undressed her. He helped her up and over the side. She settled in, laid her head back against the rim. Her head jittered against the metal, perspiration beading on her brow.

He had ten cubic centimeters of amber fluid in the needle.

Okay, give her two.

He did not want to waste time or serum on a skin pop that might not take hold, and she was compliant when he tapped up a vein in her forearm. He uncapped the syringe. It was the sort of small, disposable plastic hypodermic found at free clinics all over America. The Iron Fist had probably went through these things by the gross.

Very carefully, he allowed about a drop and a half to enter her system.

Her response was instant. The tremor in her head and neck vanished, and she seemed to nod off. Gabriel hurriedly checked her pulse (slow), respiration (shallow), pupil dilation (considerable). Her breathing was barely audible but regular. She wasn't dead.

He checked her again about every two minutes while

he fired up a few torches and managed to get some coffee going on Qi's campstove.

It was the better part of an hour before Mitch cracked her eyes open. Her pupils were huge. Her green irises had subsided to a pale shade similar to algae.

She brought up a handful of water as though it was a rare treasure, and trickled it over her face. Droplets hung from her brow, nose and chin as she watched the water return to the tub in a stream. Her expression was concentrated, one of almost religious intensity. She ignored Gabriel checking her vital signs. Watching the water was paramount right now.

"Are you back?" said Gabriel. "You okay?"

In response she grabbed his wrist, pulled him close. "Where am I? Who are you?"

"I'm Gabriel," he said.

"Who?"

"Lucy's brother." Her face relaxed at the mention of Lucy's name. Her grip did, too. He pulled his arm free. "Lucy," she whispered. "Come here, Lucy."

"Mitch," he said. "Lucy's not here."

"Sure she is," Mitch whispered, her gaze unfocused. "She's right next to you. Why don't you say something, Luce? You mad at me?"

"It's not real, Mitch—it's the crap in the needle. Mitch, are you listening to me?" She'd begun to weep, had raised one arm from the water and was reaching out toward the empty air beside him.

"I can hear your heartbeat, Luce," she murmured. "Come here, baby. Come here. That's it, get in."

"Damn it, Mitch, she's not . . ." He dropped it. There was no arguing with someone under the influence of a hallucinogen this powerful. At least she wasn't imagining herself at war again. Who knew what she was imagining, exactly, but it seemed to be giving her pleasure. The tears had stopped, and her head was tilted back against the cauldron's edge once more. Her breathing was becoming rapid. Gabriel turned away. Let her have her privacy.

Full-blown traditional Chinese funerals are notoriously ornate, complicated and lengthy affairs. Some of the more elaborate ones last two years.

In the case of the late Tuan, many of the rites were Westernized in accordance with China's lunging urge toward modernity. But his casket was the traditional three-humped rectangular box, decked head-to-toe with flowers and literally thousands of encomia calligraphed on white paper or cloth. Tuan would be well-honored on New Year's, and on Grave-Sweeping Day.

Presentation of the casket (not sealed until after the wake) was strictly according to *feng-shui*: the head of the deceased facing the inside of his place of residence, white cloth over the entrance, gong on the left side of the doorway. Along with jewelry, red appointments or clothing were forbidden, as red was a color of happiness (exceptions were made if one died eighty or older, but Tuan had been far from this milestone). Inside the casket, Tuan was swathed in finery, a yellow cloth over his face and a blue one over his body. All of his other clothing had been burned, and a pile of ashes on a rattan mat attested to this.

Tuan's send-off was in defiance of the Communist imperatives that frowned on lavish funerals. Not only were big funerals seen as superstitious and wasteful, but their sheer level of filigree was in itself an indictment, suggesting that the deceased was a criminal, since only ill-gotten gains could pay for something this fancy. Stacked against this official modern stigma was the common belief that expensive funerals guaranteed peace in the afterlife.

Tuan's would be no simple village funeral. There would come snake dancers and professional wailers, demonstrative mourners, extravagance, fireworks, fury and a party atmosphere lit by a conflagration of burned paper effigies. So what if it implied he'd been a criminal? In his case, everyone knew it was true, and this liberated the planners to spare no expense.

But for now, the private, invitation-only elite entitled to a more privileged remembrance inside the Pleasure Garden were startled by the sight of *two* caskets on the ceremonial bier.

Mads Hellweg and his entourage cast uneasy glances around the area. No sign of Cheung or his number one, Ivory. Their absence was a disappointment to Hellweg. Entrance to this sanctum sanctorum required crawling on hands and knees, kowtowing and offerings. Hellweg had a perverse desire to watch Cheung crawl for something, even if it was only to further his intrigues.

General Zhang's group was present and the stiff-spined ex-military men gave the proper bows and acknowledgement to Hellweg's group. Others present included Cheung's customary cadre of international financiers and a scatter of the best and most influential Tong leaders. All with their bodyguards, of course.

And still, no Cheung. Which suggested deceit, possibly a trap.

No, wait—here was Ivory, acting cordial, even deferential, toward the high rollers in the room.

Then the lid of the casket next to Tuan's opened entirely on its own.

* * *

Qingzhao was surprised least of all, but surprised nonetheless. She had expected and anticipated many things, but not this.

When the casket opened, she was standing near Zhang's contingent of police enforcers. She was the only woman present in this boy's club—more non-sense about females not being worthy, here—but so far no one had pegged her as such because she had taken great pains to blend.

She had cut her hair short and combed it straight back. She wore tinted glasses with stainless steel frames to abet the coarsening of her complexion, which she had achieved with makeup. Her brows were bolder, more masculine, and she had expertly stippled her cheeks and chin to provide the illusion of shaved facial hair. She had avoided using a padded suit to keep from making her head look too obviously small in contrast to her frame. The man's suit she wore was black with a black respect band on one sleeve, and plenty of room for the hammerless automatic pistol nestled against her spine.

The secret lords of the New Bund's underworld rarely congregated in one place together, making Tuan's wake and funeral a notable occasion. Most of the important men, from Tong leaders to drug royalty, had come as a measure of respect to Cheung's influence, not Tuan's stature.

And Cheung was not present.

Qi immediately theorized a mass trap; Cheung drowning all rodents at once, slicing through the Gordian knot instead of unraveling it, and clean-slating the entire playing field. It was easy to envision the Pleasure Garden sealing up and filling with lethal gas.

But no ... if trap there was to be, then Ivory wouldn't have shown either. It was highly unlikely that Cheung would sacrifice his right hand man, and here he was as a kind of Cheung manqué, pressing the flesh and making sure everyone was acknowledged, given an equal show of respect.

Unless—

Unless Ivory had finally blown it one too many times, for instance by repeatedly failing to kill Qi.

He surely could have killed her, Qi knew—more than once he'd had the opportunity. She could not chalk her continued survival up to skill on her part or the operation of chance or luck. Ivory's failure to end her life was beginning to seem more willful than inadvertent, a choice even if only an unconscious one and one wrapped up in some other struggle, purely internal, between Ivory's ambition and sense of duty to Cheung on the one hand and, on the other, his sense of honor and duty to himself. Whatever the reason, something had kept him (so far) from completing the preordained arc that ended with Qi's death. Qi was determined not to become similarly handicapped. When she had a clear shot at him, she'd take it. Because ultimately, one of them had to die.

The unexplained second casket opened, then.

Cheung was inside, and sat up. This was his entrance, intended to impress, and he was making the most of it.

The side of the second casket dropped down on hinges so Cheung could dismount the bier.

Qi should have drawn, fired and fled in that moment. She could not. Even she was momentarily transfixed.

Stunned, rather. As was everyone else in the room who beheld the spectacle of Cheung's warlord outfit.

Qingzhao stared frankly, her jaw slowly coming undone.

In cut and architecture the costume was essentially military, following the aspirations of conquerors of the early 20th Century, such as a photo Qi had once seen of Manchurian warlord Chang Tso-lin. High, stiff, embroidered collar with pins of rank, Sam Browne belt, tasseled epaulettes, cockades, pips, chevrons and medals with maniacal emphasis on the breast hash and ribbon rack. A sash. Three red stripes on the jodhpurs, also denoting high rank. Riding boots, leather puttees and golden *spurs*, for godsake. For those who care to recall history, it was comparably flamboyant to the outrageous tanker's uniform confabulated by General George S. Patton—yes, the one said to be topped by a gold football helmet. But instead of olive or khaki, Cheung's ensemble was rendered entirely in black silk brocade. The only thing missing was a flag and a plumed helmet.

"Thank you all for coming," Cheung said, straightening his seams and perching one hand on the black leather flap holster belted around his middle. "We gather today to confer honor upon our fallen comrade, Tuan, and to help him toward the afterlife with such ceremony as he merits."

He leveled his gaze at everyone in the room, including Qingzhao.

In his hands was another of the tiny carved caskets.

"And one of you will be accompanying him to the afterlife, right now."

Chapter 18

Gabriel riffled Qi's first-aid supplies for saline with the thought he might be able to play alchemist and whip up a larger batch of the mystery drug from the eight cc's he had remaining in the syringe. Mitch had lapsed into comfortable silence in the big iron tub, much akin to a heroin nod. Without a fresh application of the drug, the slamming headaches and disorientation would soon resurge, and without a medical facility at hand, Gabriel was trying his best to preload a stopgap.

All the supplies he and Qi had ferried back from her bartering excursion were still here, indicating that whatever had happened to Qi, she had not yet abandoned her stronghold. But of saline there was none. Gabriel gently set the precious syringe down under a protective protrusion of rock and turned his attention back to the big bronze statue.

He had gathered 200 feet of climbing rope in 50-foot coils, along with a basic climbing kit—a bandolier of base hooks, rock anchors, carabiners, pitons and spikes; a vertical harness, an array of belay and rappel geegaws, plus a couple of high-impact strap-lamps. Among his other tools and gear were a crate of chemicals in plastic bottles, and a few sticks of dynamite, this last courtesy of Qi's armory.

"How're you doing, Kangxi, old fella?" he said. "Still rotting away inside? Still got bats in your belfry?"

Those bats needed to tell Gabriel how they normally got out of the cave to hunt. He presumed a hole in the ceiling somewhere, fifty or sixty feet above the dung-fouled bowl of the floor.

Only once he'd found this secret could Gabriel put the Killers of Men to work on his behalf.

Kuan-Ku Tak Cheung spoke multilingually. Leftovers were handled by interpreters.

"I particularly wish to thank our brothers from Sechen Tong for attending," he said. "It is their work in chemical engineering that will permit us shortly to commence worldwide distribution of our new narcotic, which we have elected to call 'freon' for short. General Zhang's selfless work with the constabulary of the military police and affiliated forces has proven invaluable, and his men have proven to be compassionate and worthy."

Zhang, in the dress uniform of his office, bowed slightly.

"As the West becomes more socialist, so do we inevitably become less communist," continued Cheung. "It is a new century. It is the order of things." He opened his fingers into a butterfly. "Information now flies freely through the very air. This in no way should be perceived as a threat."

Mads Hellweg shuffled foot-to-foot, waiting to be congratulated for his supposedly equal role in the coming new order.

Qi's hand drifted back toward her gun. Was it Cheung's intention to bore them all with a banquet speech?

"I further wish to assure all of our most honored Tong brothers that your Japanese counterparts have been assuaged. I have taken independent action to ensure their noninvolvement. The ruffled feathers are eased."

Hellweg narrowed his gaze. *What?*

Cheung was looking directly at him. "Your plot to disrupt was obvious and doomed," he told Hellweg. Then with the air of someone bestowing a great boon, he handed the little wooden casket to Hellweg.

Ivory saw confusion mar Hellweg's gaze. The man did not understand the meaning.

It became clear as Cheung unholstered the revolver on his belt and fired point-blank, not stopping until all six heavy-powder rounds were snugged deeply into Hellweg's chest. The cacophony of report seemed to stop time itself.

Hellweg staggered backward without a word and fell with his legs in a figure-four. Gunsmoke grayed the air.

Everyone in the room was frozen in tableau, as though posing for a Renaissance painter.

Ivory's crew had all drawn down on Hellweg's bodyguards. Qi, following suit, had pulled her pistol and leveled it at the nearest subject most likely to preserve her disguise.

The uncertainty in the room was thicker than the drifting webs of gunsmoke. Half the other bodyguards had freed their weapons, but nobody dared to aim at Cheung. Ivory had a gun in each hand, pointed at two different men.

Nobody held as much import in that instant as General Zhang, whose hand had flown down to his sidearm. It hovered there, tentative as a hummingbird.

Cheung watched him. "If I have done wrong, General, then it is your duty to kill me right now."

Zhang sought out Cheung's eyes. Their communion was massive. He slowly withdrew his hand from his holster. Cheung smiled.

"You see? The General is with us."

Ivory had to admire the sheer bravery on display, no matter how foolhardy it might have been. Cheung was showing the assembly the sort of leader he was. This was a public demonstration of his capacity to rule as well as a test of his personal magnetism. If he could swing Zhang, then he could swing the Tongs, and the traditionalists, too, especially since he had just coldly blown down another invading outsider. He'd still need to verify his true Chinese identity in the bloodline of older warlords, of course; there would be no winning over the hard core without that. But today's events would go a long way toward silencing his critics.

Hellweg's bodyguards were left dangling. Most of them were not aiming at anyone. They were gawping at their dead boss, now full of holes and slowly cooling on the cobblestoned floor. To a man, they were all hired Chinese muscle.

"We welcome you," Cheung told them. "You were misguided, but now your minds have been set free. Ivory will see to your employment needs."

Hellweg's men took their cue and departed en masse with nervous shows of respect.

Call it charisma or call it power, Cheung ruled the

room. His aspirations were not delusional, thought Ivory. This man could really do it, and he had just proven it.

It was that unmitigated show of power that had caused Qi to hesitate, just at the microsecond she should have been blowing Cheung's brains all over the tapestry.

Now Ivory's grip closed on her forearm from behind. His other hand already had her gun.

"You're coming with me," he said.

As though he had known all along it was her, Cheung gave a little nod and motioned his partners back to business.

Gabriel fired a round from the Navy Colt into the blackness of the cavern, and the bats all freaked out, taking wing.

He ducked down among the dung-encrusted impalement victims, these skeletal Killers of Men, to observe. He wore a hat borrowed from Qi's stores and the rainfall of batshit, both dislodged and fresh, descending from on high spattered on its crown and brim. He tracked their nightwing pattern with a handheld million-candlepower spotlight.

There.

There, in the back curvature of the ceiling about sixty feet from the cave floor, was a geological rupture that resembled a scowling stone mouth. The bats were piling through it in a centrifugal pattern that indicated it was fairly large. Apparently it led to a switchback to the surface, presumably S-shaped, since that would account for the fact that it admitted no light to the cavern in daytime.

Gabriel roughed out the distance and calculated as best he could the location of the rift on the outside of the mountain. It would have to be on the eastern slope—the steepest and most overgrown side, from what he had seen.

The vent was funnel-shaped, with the wide end inside the cavern. He headed toward its opening, lugging his climbing gear behind him. It should be possible to arrange a mechanism that would lift him toward the opening . . .

Gabriel had no way of knowing that, as he worked out this problem in engineering, back in the city the Hellweg Tower—sometimes called the Tower of Flame—was already burning for real, a five-alarmer that froze traffic for miles and caused firefighters from four districts to be called in as reinforcements.

He knew nothing about this. He concentrated instead on the work he was doing. Even when it was done, he still had some repairs he wanted to make. So he needed to work hard and work fast and not be distracted.

So he shut out all thoughts and got to work. Only one thought made it past the barrier he'd erected, and it was a thought about Qi: Where the hell was she?

The monastery had stood since 247 A.D. on the outskirts of Shanghai with the presence of centuries crushed upon centuries, witness to the rise and fall of monarchs and tyrants. Like Longhua Temple it was configured in a time-honored seven-hall structure. Bald monks in yellow robes glided phantomlike through halls appointed with intimidating idols while huge coils of incense smoldered like mutant beehives, rendering the air particulate and opiate.

Ivory had held Qi at gunpoint for more than an hour, all the way from Tuan's funeral to this place, and she liked to think the stress fatigue of staying alert for her every twitch and gesture was beginning to tire him. They held fast in the First Hall while Ivory conferred with a man in monk's robes.

"You bought off Buddhist monks?" said Qi.

"Pan Xiao is not a monk," said Ivory.

Only then did Qi notice the baffled gun muzzle, barely visible, winking in and out of view beneath Pan Xiao's robes as he moved. Some automatic equalizer on a shoulder sling, positioned for rapid deployment.

"Please," Ivory said, indicating Qi should precede him along the corridor. He had to stay ready to shoot her at the first sign of misbehavior or trouble.

He directed her by lantern-light down narrow wooden stairs. They were about two floors beneath street level.

A warren of disused corridors led to a now-dormant fermentation room and abandoned wine cellar. After a few more twists and turns they came to what appeared to be a vault door, anomalous in its stainless-steel frame against the ancient stonework of the wall.

Qi anticipated some sort of dungeon, cell or holding area. When Ivory key-coded the door and opened it, she was frankly startled.

Ivory had brought modernity to this modest series of rooms in the form of electric lights, motion sensors, a security system and several computer monitors arranged on an old rolltop desk. Fish paddled about in a backlit 50-gallon aquarium and a small bonsai tree thrived under an expensive multiband growth light. The furnishings were all handworked wood, apparently antiques.

Sure this was some kind of trick, Qi said, "Your apartment is in the city."

"My apartment is not my home," said Ivory. "It is necessary for appearances. No one knows of this place."

"Not even Cheung?"

Ivory pursed his lips slightly. He closed the big iron door, then showed Qi he was standing down with the gun. He would not wield a weapon in here, and he was trusting her to listen to whatever he had to say. This was implicit when he stated, "I could have let Cheung have you back at the funeral."

Then, maddeningly, he began to make tea as though it was the most natural thing in the world, even turning his back on her once or twice.

"Have you ever suffered a crisis of faith?" he said.

"Not religious," Qi said, slowly taking a seat in an armless, hardback "drawer chair."

"That's exactly what Michelle Quantrill told me when I asked her the same question. You two have much in common."

"I never saw her before the Zongchang casino," said Qi.

"Nevertheless."

"Why am I here?" Qi asked. "Why didn't you do your duty and kill me when you had the chance?"

"Because I am finding out that some things transcend duty," said Ivory. "Or at least some duties transcend others." He waved this rather significant confession away. "Your holy war is to kill Cheung. Yet despite multiple opportunities, you have not. My conclusion is that you are more interested in discrediting me through attrition. To avenge your status as a Nameless One."

"Perhaps I'm just a lousy shot," she said. They both knew it was not true.

"You were dealt with unfairly. Michelle Quantrill's sister was dealt with unfairly. It is the way of things in Cheung's vision of the world. But while I might be your adversary, I am not your enemy."

"That sounds terrific," said Qi. "But what does it mean?"

"You have heard the parable of the warrior of great honor," said Ivory, serving them both tea in small hammered cups that were both exquisite and comfortably weighty. "He was obligated to a cruel and uncouth master. He discovered such honor as his can be a trap, a snare that tightens the more you struggle against it. The more he tried to serve his master honorably, the more obligated he became, and the more implicated in cruelty himself."

"You have already betrayed Cheung by sparing me. He will not forgive this."

"He might not," acknowledged Ivory. "But I need to see you and this other woman clear of Shanghai. Then my obligations will be ended, and Cheung can take such measures as he will."

"You are wrong," said Qi, "that we two are the only ones you have wronged. You have involved this man Gabriel Hunt as well. The stain of your crisis of honor is spreading like a disease."

"You are correct. If I kill you now, my obligation to Cheung is served, but I have dishonored myself. If

I do not kill you, if I let you go free, you have sworn to slaughter the man to whom I owe loyalty. There can be no honor in that. Is there any solution?"

He took a sip of tea as though it was the last one of his life, then handed Qi his pistol.

"I leave the dilemma in your hands."

Ivory resumed his seat. And waited.

Chapter 19

Michael Hunt was met at the airport by an official car that conducted him into the city, and the waiting representatives of the Shanghai Cultural Alliance. Much bowing, many cocktails, even more handshakes as a modest summit was initiated, and Michael suffered it all graciously. As Gabriel often pointed out to him, pressing the flesh took time and patience—a patience that Michael had cultivated while his brother was gallivanting around the globe.

His brother, from whom he had not had word in days. Who was presumably somewhere in greater Shanghai; who had, by all best guesses based on personal experience, gotten swept up in yet another sideroad that rendered him incommunicado. It was Gabriel's rowdy way. If anything were truly amiss, Michael would have seen a red flag, a flare, a message in a bottle, something. Meanwhile his duty was to make nice with the academics Gabriel had jilted at the start of his trip and tell them the things they wished to hear.

Michael's schedule awaited him in his suite, printed out and laid against the stacked pillows on the king-sized bed. He was staying in a hotel off the Bund that had apparently been an embassy at some past time.

Looking over the printout, Michael saw there were the usual tours of monasteries and museums, as well as a brace of receptions, the first of which was—oh, look at that—in exactly 45 minutes, at some location he could not have found with a map, a native guide and a GPS device. He was in the hands of his handlers and had no choice but to trust himself to them.

Showered, shaved, plucked, dressed and polished, he presented himself at the appointed time (thanking all the valets and doormen in Mandarin) and found himself whisked to a phantasmagoric skyscraper-top discotheque one entered by walking through the enormous resin-cast jaws of a Tyrannosaurus Rex skull.

The throb of the music was physically assaultive, the bass notes reverberating in his diaphragm. Strangers shouted greetings he could not hear, and the best response he could manage was to smile, nod and allow himself to be swept along through the strobing neon, the dry-ice fog, the mirrored surfaces that multiplied several hundred jam-packed revelers into thousands. Everyone was smoking, drinking and whipping themselves into an aerobic frenzy.

Michael winced inwardly, but on the surface showed nothing but serenity, calm, earnest goodwill. Patience.

His stewards guided Michael to one of many private VIP rooms fanning out from the central club floor. These exclusive chambers were lozenge shaped—like railroad flats—and padded with a sort of silver lamé tuck-and-roll on the walls that made them look like high-class cells in some A-list lunatic asylum. Table pods sprouted from the floor like mushrooms. And when the door thunked shut, the music vanished to a mere background thrum.

Michael snuck his cheat sheet out of his pocket, glanced at it. This event involved city fathers and local politicos who wished to have a posed snapshot with the head of the Hunt Foundation. It was the next best thing to a grant, and seen by some of them as a likely (perhaps necessary) prelude to same. As they filtered into the VIP room one by one, he shook hands and accepted proferred drinks, which he then mostly set down on the table behind him, untouched.

Eventually the line of people waiting to meet him had dwindled to just a single, singular individual, a willowy black masterpiece that exceeded six-two in heels. She took his arm like a lover and urged him out of the room. He glanced at one of the handlers who'd been steering him around all afternoon, and the man nodded. Michael allowed himself to be led by this amazon—whose name, he gathered, was Shukuma—toward a table in the back.

A burly cosmopolite rose to greet him, an unusual-looking Chinese with stark blue eyes.

"Mister Michael Hunt," Shukuma said, "may I present Mister Kuan-Ku Tak Cheung."

"This is both a great pleasure and a deep honor," said Cheung. They shook hands briskly in the Western style. "Please join us."

Every fiber of Qi's combat mind screamed *kill him now*.

Ivory sat before her with an infuriating smile of calm, awaiting a bullet to his head.

She could tell by the weight of the sleek Glock in her grasp that the gun was loaded. This was no trick. Ivory had mentally infected her with indecision. All his buttery-smooth talk of conflicted obligations. But above all, perhaps without intending to, he had reminded her that he, Ivory, was not her target. All of her life's work of despair and foxed chances now offered her an unclear choice.

"You wish for me to kill you?" she said. "Or is it that you wish for me to kill Cheung and free you from the burden of your conflicted duty?"

Ivory shrugged.

She raised the gun, then gave him the barrel in a sweeping backhand to the temple. A tiny grunt eased from him. Bright blood appeared as his eyeballs swiveled up and went opaque. He slumped from his seat, one leg hung up, his foot jutting out. It was undignified.

She took one small moment to arrange him on the floor of his sanctuary. Then she checked the Glock for loads and made for the door.

Mitch was freshly dressed and running her hands all over herself, as though someone had slid her into a new and confusingly alien body, inside-out. She seemed mildly embarrassed when Gabriel returned to the shrine room.

She peered at him, trying to suss out her recent past. "Did I . . . ?" she said. Her tone was diminished and uncharacteristically modest. "Did we . . . ?"

"No," Gabriel said.

"You undressed me."

"I had to. You were burning up. It's that stuff they stuck you with."

"But I distinctly remember . . ." Her eyes went a little glassy. ". . . at least I *think* I remember . . . being, uh, extremely turned on."

"That part is true," said Gabriel.

"But we—you and I—we didn't . . . ?"

"No."

"Good," she said. "Thank you. Not that you aren't a good-looking man—"

"Understood," Gabriel said. "I saw you and Lucy together, back home."

At the mention of her name, a buried memory seemed to surface, and with it a deep crimson blush. "Your sister is a very special person."

"No doubt," Gabriel said. "Now, if you're through needlessly feeling embarrassed, I'd like to tell you about what I—"

Gabriel stopped speaking when he realized she wasn't looking at him any longer, that she was looking past him, over his shoulder, at a figure behind his back.

Gabriel sucked in a hasty breath and turned. Qingzhao was standing at the far end of the chamber with her arms folded.

Safe. Gabriel and his two charges were armed, safe and reasonably whole.

"Let me get this straight," said Mitch. "Now you don't *want* to leave?"

"Of course I do," said Gabriel. "But not with unfinished business, and I have business with Cheung. Mitch, you were abducted, drugged, pressed into a kind of slavery, shot at. Hell, forget 'at,' you were shot. I was, too," he said, fingering the healed scar where the bullet had creased his temple. "And it'll keep happening unless Cheung is dealt with. To us, to other people, to the whole country—the man needs to be stopped."

"Very revolutionary of you," said Qi. She was

stripping and cleaning a gun. "Very inspiring. Except it is easier to say this than to do it. Believe me, I have tried and I know. You forget that we are all fugitives now, and Zhang's police force is looking for us."

"But we have the one thing Cheung wants," Gabriel said.

The women looked at each other, puzzled.

"This place," he continued. "We know the location of Kangxi Shih-k'ai's Killers of Men."

"That is true," said Qi cautiously, "but only to a point. The army we found is not of terra-cotta and there is no sign Kangxi Shih-k'ai's remains are there. Surely the warlord did not have himself impaled on a spike. So, impressive as the display may be, it is not what Cheung seeks."

"That bothered me, too," said Gabriel. "I didn't see anything in the cave that would serve Cheung's purpose. So I looked at the statue again."

He led them to the second shrine room and to the back wall where the giant statue reposed in horrible, shadowy splendor.

"Look at the eye sockets," said Gabriel. "You see how they're angled? And there's a slight rim—as though they're settings."

"Settings? For what?" Mitch said. "You mean like a jewel? It would have to be huge."

Gabriel thought back to an expedition that had taken him to the Kalahari Desert. There had been a statue there with jewels for eyes that made even this behemoth look tiny. "I've seen larger," he said.

"Something like this?" Qi said. She climbed down into one of the deep trenches in the dirt from which she'd exhumed the terra-cotta figures she'd traded to Tuan for supplies. She crouched down, vanishing from view for a moment, then emerged holding an object nestled in decades-old newspaper. "I found this on the ground by the idol when I first came here."

It was a dusty, faceted red sphere, like a cut-glass Christmas ornament.

"It fits in the socket," she said. "I tried inserting it. But nothing happens when you put it in."

"Was there another one?"

"There was, at one point," Qi said. "By the time I got here, there was only one that was whole, and pieces of another, shattered on the ground. Fragments. Would you like me to get them?"

"No, that's okay," Gabriel said, turning the faceted sphere in his hands. It was not a gem—it was glass, worth about as much as a chandelier at a discount house. But he'd been around enough giant, ancient statues over the years to know it surely had a function. "Give me a hand here, Mitch, would you?"

Gabriel handed the eye to Mitch and scaled the idol, climbing up to its shoulder. Mitch passed the sphere up to him once he had. It fit equally well into either eye socket on the giant, glowering statue.

"Give me some light," Gabriel said. She turned a flashlight on, pointed it up at him.

After brushing away the accretions of ages with his sleeve, he could see a fine, almost microscopic line of ideograms around the rim of each eye socket.

He called down a description of what he saw. "You think you could you read them?" he asked Qi. "Give us even a rough idea what it says?"

Up went Qingzhao.

"No," she said as she perched in the crook of the statue's arm. "They look like they're upside down or backward, or both—they make no sense."

"Mitch," Gabriel called, "shine that light up toward the eye. No, the big light." He was referring to the dual-xenon job he had used in the cave, the million-candlepower one.

Nothing. Part of the ceiling turned red as the light reflected, but that was about it.

"Pass it up here," Gabriel said.

Qi descended to the lap of the idol, took the heavy lamp from Mitch and passed it up.

"The glass is faceted," Gabriel said. "In fact—" he shifted the lamp into position "—it looks like it's ground to a very fine tolerance, like optical glass."

"Like a lens?" said Mitch from below.

"You got it."

He held the lamp dead-center on the crimson eye and turned it on.

The tiny glyphs sprang into hard relief in a wide arc on the opposite wall of the chamber, each about a foot high. Optical graffiti.

"They still do not make any sense," said Qi, after straining to read them.

"That's because it's only half the information," said Gabriel, dislodging the crystal and mounting it in the other socket. Sure enough—a second set of characters appeared on the far wall, like a bi-pack cipher. "If we had both eyes and lit them at the same time, the projected images would merge on the wall and you could read them."

"So what do we do?" said Mitch from below.

A low, almost subaural hum had become present in the chamber.

"We start writing down those characters," said Gabriel, "*exactly* the way they appear."

The hum became a louder sound, a kind of chuddering bass note.

"What is that?" said Qi. "Did we start up some kind of machine?"

"No," said Mitch. "It's outside, damn it."

"What is it?" said Qi.

Before Mitch could answer, the sound became loud enough for them all to recognize it.

A chopper, incoming.

Chapter 20

Outside, crouched among the rocks, Mitch spotted the helicopter through binoculars, coming in soft about a hundred yards from the pagoda, the blades on powerful Ribinsk turboshafts spinning a silver halo above the craft.

"It's a Kamov," she said. "The kind the Russians nicknamed the Orca. Jesus, there could be twenty guys in there."

Gabriel grabbed Qi's upper arm. "Could you have been tagged somehow? Followed?"

Surprise and incomprehension sparked within her dark gaze. "No, I . . ."

Then brutal logic slapped her. "The Glock," she said with disgust.

"What Glock?" said Mitch.

Qi snorted, angry at her own lack of vigilance. "Why would he have a Glock? Ivory prefers fully automatic pistols—that is why he has that Russian monstrosity. He would not have a Glock around unless it was disposable." She drove a fist into her own hand. "Damn it. He handed it to me. He knew I'd take it. *Stupid!*"

"He misdirected you," said Gabriel. "Could have happened to any of us."

"He gave me the chance to shoot him with it!"

"Well, obviously he was confident you wouldn't take him up on it." The location of the leaning pagoda had just ceased to be a bargaining chip. They had been made, blown, outfoxed.

"Load everything," said Qi. She was obviously envisioning some kind of glorious standoff that would get them all killed.

"Wait," said Gabriel. "Let's see if they're soldiers, Red Police guys or Cheung's men."

"I see the bald guy from the casino," said Mitch, still glassing the slope, where the men from the chopper were now climbing, hunched over in a protective crouch.

"That is Dinanath," said Qi. "Number Two, after Ivory." She ducked into her armory and came up with a Nightforce-sighted LMT rifle, already zeroing in.

"Wait!" said Gabriel. "No shooting! We can still—"

Qi fired without hesitation just as Gabriel shot out a hand, bumping her aim off true. The 5.56 round spanged off a tree branch, severing it two feet from Dinanath's head.

Cheung's crew answered.

The rocks all around began to flint and chip with bullet hits, half of them silenced. The other half of the shooters didn't care if they were heard, time-delay gunshots bouncing around the hillside and trapping them in a weird Doppler cone of weapons fire. Mitch, gunless, had hit the dirt, and Gabriel was trying not to get nailed by flying frags of rock.

He took the binoculars from Mitch, peered through them. At least eighteen men were coming at them up a hillside with excellent cover.

Qi could pick some of them off one by one, pacing her fire, but there were too many. She could never bag them all.

Gabriel held her in abeyance until the first salvo wrapped.

"Don't," he cautioned her. "We have something they want. We still have the upper hand. Cheung's not even with them. Let me handle them."

Disappointment flashed in Qi's eyes.

"There will be no more shooting, Mr. Hunt," came Dinanath's voice over a bullhorn. "We have your brother Michael. You will cease fire and stand down now."

"Both of you, go now," Gabriel said to Qi and Mitch.

"What are you going to do?" said Qi, still bitter at being cheated of deaths she felt were owed her.

"They want the Killers of Men, let's give 'em what they want," Gabriel said. "If they have Michael we have to dispense with all this pawn-pushing and get right to the royalty."

"Chess," Mitch said in response to Qi's blank expression.

"You have a plan?" said Qi.

"Don't worry about it," Gabriel said. "Just worry about getting away. If either of you stay, you'll just wind up in cages. At best—that's if they don't just kill you on the spot. Go. *Now.* Take the back path down the hill."

Both women were staring at him stubbornly. What the hell did he have to do, point a gun at them?

"We can set up in the shrine rooms," said Qi. "Each of us with a rifle, and kill them as they—"

Gabriel overrode her. "No. Don't you see? That won't save Michael—and it won't kill Cheung. Please: go."

Bad trouble would have them crosshaired in moments. A tidal wave of downside was coursing up the hill toward them.

"Get out of here," Gabriel said. "Seriously. Leave them to me."

"You're giving up," Mitch said vacantly. She winced at a sudden spike of pain in her forehead. The last dose of the drug he'd given her had obviously almost worn off. It was why she was as lucid as she was—but it also meant she was just minutes away from suffering serious withdrawal.

He held her face and snapped his fingers to focus her. "I'm going to surrender to them, yes—but no way am I giving up. You have to trust me. I haven't lost my mind. I do have a plan. But if you two don't get out of sight, pronto, none of it'll work—understand?"

"No," she said—but Qi took her by the arm and began pulling Mitch away.

Mitch wrested free and grabbed Gabriel's jacket, turning him around, holding his torso between her hands, staring directly into his eyes.

"You be careful, goddamn it, or I'll come back and kick your ass," she said. "Lucy'd never forgive me if I got you killed."

He nodded and she let go. Qi led her back into the pagoda, toward the rear archway.

"Dinanath!" Gabriel shouted. "Hold your fire! I'm coming down!"

Gabriel left the Colt behind one of the stone lions

as he walked into the open, hands raised, to meet his captors.

"I think you are lying," said Dinanath as he circled Gabriel . . .

. . . who was lying on the ground of the shrine room, trussed up with rope. Before they'd tied him up, Cheung's thugs had gotten in some good punches, but when Gabriel hadn't either resisted or spilled any useful information, their hearts went out of the procedure rather quickly.

Gabriel quickly used his tongue to take inventory of his teeth. One wobbler; all still present in his mouth. His right eye was threatening to swell shut and his internals felt kicked down a stairwell—but this was all (he reminded himself) a necessary part of the plan.

"Don't believe me then," Gabriel said, his voice a little slurred. "Ignore what I say. That's your privilege. But if it later turns out I was telling the truth, Cheung will have your liver and heart for breakfast."

Dinanath wished Ivory were here to offer counsel. Hell, he wished Ivory were still in Cheung's favor at all, rather than precariously teetering on the edge of a particularly fatal variety of disfavor. Perhaps victory today would enable Ivory to return from disgrace—he had, after all, provided the tin can for the dog's tail and thus allowed them to discover the location of Qingzhao's hideout. Perhaps Dinanath himself would be able to offer testimony that would restore Cheung's faith in Ivory, whom he counted as a good colleague, if not a friend.

But that would be sometime down the line, at best; in the meantime, Dinanath was on his own and had to figure out what to do about this American and his claims.

"Put it another way," said Gabriel. "All you have to do is check it out. I'll show you myself."

"A trap," said Dinanath. "You would lead us into an ambush."

"Why? So I can knock off or incapacitate a few of your men? When Cheung still has my brother? That would be crazy. I'm offering a trade because I have something Cheung wants and he has something I want."

The other men on Dinanath's squad were starting to debate among themselves. Gabriel had uttered the magic words, in English and Chinese both: *Favored Son, Kangxi Shih-k'ai, Killers of Men.* Looking from man to man around him, he knew each of them had to be weighing how he might put the knowledge Gabriel was offering to use to advance his position with Cheung—maybe even to claim the ten million dollar reward, if they could turn up the big guy's bones.

They had carried Gabriel into the room with the idol, deposited him roughly at its base. It glowered down at them (eyeless now; Gabriel had dislodged the red crystal and stowed it back in the trench before they raced out to spot the helicopter); the statue's tarnished metal surface shone dully in the firelight and the strobe-sweep of the high-powered lamps each man carried as part of a basic assault kit. They were dressed for night-fighting, black-on-black.

"If you think it's a trap," Gabriel said, "just make me walk in first. You can walk me in at gunpoint. Or I'll go in alone. Whatever you say—unless you're not the man in charge and I should speak to someone else who can actually get things done."

Anger flared in Dinanath's sculpted face, so much like the idol itself—rough-hewn, broad-planed, admitting of no subtlety. This was, Gabriel had decided, a man who would not want his authority challenged. Third in line in Cheung's pecking order, his rank made him answerable here. He had been granted this responsibility. He would want neither to lose face nor gain demotion.

Dinanath squatted beside Gabriel and cracked him in the mouth again just to reassert his superiority.

Gabriel spat a small gob of blood onto the ground. "If I'm telling the truth," he said, "you get to bring the Killers of Men back to Cheung and Cheung will be all smiles. That's what I want for my brother. If I'm lying, you can kill me then just as easily as now."

"You do not dictate terms for Kuan-Ku Tak Cheung," Dinanath said, making sure the men heard him proclaim the chain of command.

"Then let me talk to Ivory," Gabriel said.

Dinanath let a tiny snort escape him. "Longwei Sze Xie is dangerously close to becoming a Nameless One."

"Fine. Then it's up to you. Untie me now and let me open it my way—or you can figure out the secret of the idol for yourself," said Gabriel.

"*You* will tell us." Dinanath reconsidered his inflection. "You *will* tell us."

"I'll tell you nothing. You can knock me around all you want, if you try hard enough you can kill me, but believe me, you won't make me talk that way. Better men than you have tried it, and it's never worked." Gabriel prayed his sincere, self-confident tone was convincing them; he hoped like hell they wouldn't test his claim, just to see. "Meanwhile," he said, "how long do you have? Cheung's a man who wants answers *now*. He won't give you days or weeks to figure this out for yourselves. But I can show you. I'm unarmed, for god's sake. You have nearly twenty men."

"The two women," said Dinanath. "They are armed. Perhaps they are the ambush."

"The women are gone. They ran away. I don't know where they are and that's the truth. Anyway, do you really think two women can pick off twenty armed men? If they could, wouldn't we just have done that when you were coming up the hill? What you're saying makes no sense." Gabriel shook his head. "I'm offering you a good deal."

"How *American*," Dinanath sneered. "A *deal*." He pressed his gun to Gabriel's forehead. To one of his men he said, curtly, "Untie him." Gabriel felt someone go to work on the knots at his wrists. They sprang free a moment later.

"Very well," Dinanath said. "I will trust you—but only so far." He let Gabriel get up on his knees, and then unsteadily stand. "You will instruct us now as to what needs to be done."

"I'll show you. Keep all the guns on me you want."

Dinanath's cell phone trilled then, echoing in the chamber.

"That'll be Daddy," Gabriel said. "Better answer it."

"*Silence*!" Dinanath dealt another backhand to Gabriel's face.

Gabriel felt his jaw swing and heard his neck tendons pop. His dentist was going to be overjoyed if he ever got out of this alive.

Dinanath stepped away for a hushed cell phone conference out of earshot. As he spoke, Dinanath's body seemed to shrink in on itself, diminishing. Awkwardly he returned and held the cell phone to Gabriel's ear.

"Mr. Hunt?" came Cheung's voice. The man might have been excited or he might have been furious, but you couldn't tell—he sounded as calm as still water. "My man has sketched the situation for me. If you would be so kind as to lend my group the benefit of your expertise, your trained eye, I would be greatly in your debt, and I am certain your brother would find any possible discovery to be of immeasurable value both to me and to your Foundation. Find me the Killers of Men and all debts are paid in full."

"All debts?" Gabriel said, trying to match Cheung cool for cool. He had to work his mouth back into speaking form first. "How about the women?"

"You can have them if you like. I leave that to your judgment. I would only ask that they leave the country and never return. Do you agree?"

"Yes," Gabriel said. "But your man here is eager to pound the crap out of me some more, maybe shoot me, instead of getting you what you want."

"You have found the vault and know the way in," Cheung said. "If I leave it to them, they shall still be loitering around there at this time next month. Prove your worthiness, Mr. Hunt, and rest assured that if anyone harms you further, it will be his final act on earth."

It was pretty clear who Cheung was talking about.

"That sounds good," Gabriel said, "but you're not here. I don't see how you can ensure my safety from wherever you are."

"You'll have to take that risk, Mr. Hunt."

Gabriel raised his voice. "What if there's treasure in the vault—gold, precious stones, old money? Shouldn't you be here to ensure none of it goes astray?"

"Not necessary," Cheung said. "My men have discipline. Anyway, I have another pestersome matter I must deal with first."

Ivory, Gabriel figured.

"You also want to be far away in case anything goes wrong," said Gabriel.

"We understand each other, Mr. Hunt."

"All right," Gabriel said. "We'll play it your way." He heard the call terminate. It would have been good if Cheung had agreed to come immediately, but it didn't matter much that he hadn't. Cheung would not be able to stay away for long, not when it came out that Gabriel was, in fact, telling the truth. Even if the Killers of Men were not precisely what Cheung had expected—he'd want to see them for himself.

Meanwhile, Cheung's men here in the shrine room, had very clearly heard the words *gold, precious stones, old money*. Already he could see the men whispering, plotting how they might reteam to double-cross one another.

It looked hopeless. It was perfect.

"I can't see the shrine room from here," said Mitch, giving up on the binoculars. Her hands were shaking badly and her head was hurting. "We have to go back."

"No, we have to go forward," said Qi. "It is as Gabriel said—we must take the head of the serpent. That is the thing I lost sight of."

They worked their way down the rock escarpment, closer to the reassuring cover of trees and brush, in darkness, undetected.

"Cheung really wants those skeletons you found, dung and all?"

"Yes. Although how Gabriel means to use them, I have no idea."

"You don't think he's just stepping up so we can get away?" Mitch kept glancing back, second-guessing.

"No. That would be foolhardy." Qi's eyes were like flint chips in the dark.

"Maybe just self-sacrificing," said Mitch.

"Illogical," returned Qi. "That is why I believe he has another plan. He may be a reckless man, but he is not a foolish one. If it were only his life at risk, maybe—but with Cheung holding his brother, I have to conclude his choice was tactical."

"Well," Mitch conceded, "I haven't heard any shooting yet."

They could see the helicopter in the clearing below them to the west, on a flat mesa just big enough to provide a landing zone. Mitch got a better look at it through the nightscope on the rifle Qi had thrust into her hands. She tried her damndest to hold it steady as she squinted to see through it.

The Kamov was a Russian special ops aircraft about a decade old, comparable to the Bell 430 or the Sikorsky S-76, Mitch knew. The four-bladed coaxial rotor was still now. Many iterations of the Kamov were manufactured in Russia for foreign sale; knowing Cheung's present orbits, this one had probably come into his hands via India. It was painted combat green over black and—interestingly—featured no registry numbers.

The pilot still had his helmet on, and his buddy was holding at port arms an M4 with a stretch magazine. Both were smoking. The M4 was less accurate at distance fire than the M16 it largely replaced; still, you wouldn't want to be within 150 meters of a 30-round spray . . . and Mitch and Qi were already well within the bubble.

Qi tugged Mitch's sleeve. "Can you fly that thing?"

"Depends who you ask," Mitch said. "The U.S. Air Force has some doubts."

Qi's face fell.

"But they're wrong," Mitch said. She started down the final slope.

Chapter 21

Right on cue, a wayward bat flittered out of the crack on the right side of the idol once Gabriel had worked the hidden lever. Its timing could not have been better. Dinanath's men watched it wheel crazily around the upper curve of the shrine room until it found a roost.

"Hold it," said Gabriel, raising a hand. Dinanath turned to his crew and everyone froze. "See that bat? There could be more inside. We don't know how large the chamber actually is. We have to be quiet and cautious."

Fully half of Dinanath's force was conscripted to muscle the foot-thick iron panel, which yielded by degrees. Gabriel raised a hand and pointed at the small chalk mark he had made at about the midpoint of the panel's arc—when the opening was slightly wider than a man.

"Stop," he said. "We must not open this all the way."

"Countermeasures?" said Dinanath.

"Yes—remember your history. Traps in tombs. We must be silent and very careful. Do you smell that? More bats inside. The footing will be treacherous. Excess noise will disturb the bats. Have you ever done this sort of thing before?"

"No," said Dinanath, uncertain whether his rank was being usurped.

Gabriel picked up a flashlight. "Mask these like so. Focused beams, not wide light." He was halfway through the doorway when Dinanath yanked him back, bodily.

"You could have a weapon just inside the door," the big man explained calmly.

"How could I . . . ?" Gabriel raised his hands in conciliation. "Okay. You're the boss."

Dinanath directed two men to precede Gabriel. They self-consciously stayed as quiet as mute cats in a library, whispering back a description of the hundreds of miniature warrior figures they saw inside.

The information grapevined through the rest of the men and Gabriel could witness its effect. They were eager, hoping for treasure and measuring the capacity of their own pockets for same.

Dinanath posted two gunners at the base of the idol. Two more at the mouth of the shrine room. Two more on perimeter, outside. Their check-ins were leapfrogged so that the first sign of trouble would bring a radio alert to the unit on Dinanath's belt.

"Now you," said Dinanath, directing Gabriel to step through.

The men inside were already picking up the small soldiers, examining them for traces of precious metals or jewels. The men behind Gabriel were eager to start nosing around on their own. Dinanath squeezed through behind Gabriel.

"Cover pattern," he hissed to his subordinates. "Keep sight of the man in front of you!"

Men were filing in behind them, grouping, oozing the point of the expedition through the second chamber and toward the head of the stone stairway. They had begun to notice the abundance of creepy-crawly life-forms among which they were standing, and Gabriel turned back to shush them. "They're not poisonous," he whispered. "Just move through them swiftly." Several of the men nodded. The more he asserted himself as knowledgeable and a leader, the more they would look past Dinanath to him for guidance when things went wrong.

This was Gabriel's third foray into the realm of the Favored Son's Killers of Men. His first exploration had released the bats. His second had revealed to him the ways in and out of the massive vault. Before he'd left the second time, he'd also observed the mechanics of the giant, pendulum-like iron baskets bracketing the stairway that led down from the stone arch. He had set to work on them, using the tools and climbing gear he had to restore the ancient mechanisms' original function. And then he'd paced off the distance from the entryway to the spot below the funnel that wound its way to the outside. Keeping himself precisely oriented as to distance and direction, he could now move to that exact location even in the dark.

Standing at the head of the dung-befouled stairway, Gabriel reached back to tug Dinanath forward by the sleeve. "The Killers of Men," he whispered, shining his masked flashlight forward into the void.

Dinanath's mouth dropped open at the sight. His men crowded in behind him, eager to see for themselves.

Gabriel gave Dinanath a hard shove. The big man lost his balance against the thick oilslick of guano on the floor. Then Gabriel dived onto the right-hand balustrade and slid down into darkness as everybody started shooting.

Qi and Mitch heard a sound like two congested little barks. Squirrel coughs in the darkness. The helicopter pilot and his buddy dropped, tumbling lifeless out of the open cockpit doors, their cigarettes still smoldering.

"What the hell—" Mitch said.

Qi signaled her to keep quiet. Neither of them had seen even a muzzle flash.

Qi spoke with her eyes. *Don't move. Not a sound.*

Five minutes later, still frozen and silent, they still hadn't seen anything to explain what had happened. All they could see was the two dead guys by the chopper growing deader.

"Let's take the bird," Mitch whispered, impatient.

"No—too obvious. We would be exposed. We wait."

"I don't know if I can," Mitch said, feeling her condition worsening.

"You must," Qi said.

In the hunter's-hide silence that descended around them, they could finally hear the sounds of gunfire coming from deep within the mountainside.

The iron plates of the floor inside the entry rooms were pressure-sensitive, Gabriel knew. His investigation showed that the ordeal of sliding open the large iron door at the base of the idol had a secondary purpose, which was to cock the mechanism for the long-dormant catapults. The weight of a single man could not trip it, but the weight of many would cause the floor to shift exactly one quarter of an inch.

It was similar to the bed on a truck scale. And its purpose . . .

Gabriel surfed to the floor of the main chamber in a sludgy mudslide of decay, guano and worse.

Outside, the counterbalanced door slid back into position and locked, crushing one of Dinanath's men who was half-in, half-out. Six men had been posted as sentries outside the idol. That left Gabriel with twelve inside, plus Dinanath.

As everybody unslung their hardware and started shooting, the thousands of bats in the cave awakened and began flying in every direction.

Thin flashlight beams swung wildly about the room, each extending three or four feet into the darkness before petering out. Muzzle flashes lit up the darkness as well, providing confusing snapshot contrasts of shadows and light, strobing in all directions, not aiding sight but blinding everybody.

The shooting ceased in a wave as Cheung's men furiously swatted at the bats swarming over their heads. Then another wave of shooting came, mostly wild, aimed toward the ceiling.

The floor mechanism—thanks to Gabriel's repair—was now able to do its intended job. Counterbalances clicked and cogwheeled belaying gears swung the ironbound baskets, hurling their deadly projectiles in the direction of Dinanath's desperate men. Gabriel heard two dozen impacts, some of metal into walls or floor, but many into flesh.

Dinanath was still trying to find his footing, having fallen halfway down the dung-slick stairs as everybody went berserk. The pistol in his hand was lost to a quicksand of liquid waste as though it had disappeared through pie crust.

A wheeling bat smacked him in the face and knocked him down again.

Gabriel shut his eyes and sprinted. *Five running steps, left, touch helmet of skeleton with raised sword on right-hand side, turn ninety degrees and haul ass straight out for twenty steps.*

He kept his eyes shut, depending on his rehearsal in the dark to guide him according to touchpoints. Five more steps.

"Let's just get the hell out of here," Mitch whispered. "Please. I can get that helicopter in the air in minutes from a cold start. Whoever shot the pilot can't be out there any longer. Let me do it."

They could hear the thunderous sounds of gunfire below, muffled by layers of rock. "You would just leave Gabriel in there?" said Qi.

"If Gabriel's in the middle of that, he doesn't have a hope in hell. But we still do. We've got to get back to the city. Save his brother from Cheung."

"Is that how you do it?" said Qi. "Exchange one goal for another? Your sister for his brother? Me for someone else?"

"Well, what do *you* think we should do?"

Qi thought for a moment. "I have confidence in Gabriel. I believe he had a plan. But," she said, letting her eyes slide shut, "you are right. Our object must be Cheung."

With one final glance back toward the pagoda, she came out from behind the cover that had shielded them and began to run toward the chopper.

In the harsh and uneven illumination provided by a dozen flashlights, many of which had fallen and were now casting their beams crazily into the darkness, Gabriel could see a flurry of still-circling bats and the bodies of dead men both ancient and new.

Two-thirds of Dinanath's crew seemed to be down. The spiked metal siege balls had killed a few and bloodied several more—and the bats could smell the fresh blood. The rest were struggling to regain their footing and orientation, or firing madly, their bullets pinholing the muddy air. Panic shots bounced off the cavern ceiling or ricocheted off moist stone. Scabs of encrusted dung jumped away from the impaled corpses in their warrior drag. Near Gabriel, a warrior's head—a featureless blunt point beneath waxy layers of droppings—was vaporized like a kicked anthill by a stray 9mm slug.

Gabriel caught a glimpse of Dinanath. He was furiously emptying his magazine in what he must have thought was Gabriel's direction, but he might as well have been shooting blind. One of his men, trying to claw a wriggling bat off his face, hit Dinanath from behind and the big Indian went down to hands and knees.

Falling bats pelted them like black hailstones. Other bats flew directly into the walls and dropped, unconscious or dead. The rest of the flock made for the funnel vent.

Primal fears took over. Terror of the dark, which their guns could not push back. Terror of the bats, which their guns could not track. Terror of more sharp killing objects, perhaps a second salvo of ancient metal death. Claustrophobia. Group panic, as men retreated to the sliding iron doorway only to find it cinched shut on the still-spasming arm of one of their comrades.

Dinanath was ground face-first into the sucking black mire by the panicked trampling of his own men.

Gabriel threaded himself into the vertical harness he'd left waiting the last time he'd been here, anticipating the possibility of a return under less than sanguine circumstances. He grabbed a short-handled dagger out of the scabbard at the waist of the nearest impaled skeleton, used it to saw through the anchor rope, and hauled himself toward the ceiling on his three-to-one pulley setup, which towed him at about fifteen feet per second.

Careening bats swept by him as he reached the cavern ceiling and began to corkscrew his way through the funnel. His ascent was designed to leave no dangling rope behind.

Gabriel had left himself a weapon on the eastern slope the first time he'd made this ascent, one of Qi's LMT shortie rifles. He grabbed it now, before quickly scrambling down to the nearest of the shrine rooms.

But when he reached the room, there was no one to shoot. The sentries posted outside the idol were all facedown in pools of their own blood, sniped off by throat hits.

Gabriel hustled past two more deceased guards to the other shrine room, where he dived into the iron tub to wash away some of the foul, clotted wastes clinging to him.

When he rose, dripping, he saw a man walking toward him from the shrine room's entrance . . . a man with a gun in his hand, and the gun was pointed at Gabriel.

"Hello, Mr. Hunt," said Ivory.

Chapter 22

While the engines were spinning up, Mitch noticed the helicopter was not outfitted with any exterior firepower. Kamovs were workhorses adaptable to a number of applications, including air ambulance and search-and-rescue over land or water, but they were originally developed by the Russians as antitank choppers. Not this one. Fully stocked with armament, the machine could chew up and spit out a Cobra gunship, but this one was fangless, with not a gun or bomb in sight. At least its defensive features were still in place: the energy-absorbing seats, the beefed up landing struts, the nonfragmenting fuselage. The rotor blades were made of a composite material that could withstand a hit by a 23mm projectile and keep functioning.

"This thing is a taxi," Mitch said as the rotors reached takeoff speed. "Stripped down for fast insertion and extraction."

"Good," Qi said. "We should try some fast extraction now."

Running from their abandoned cover to the chopper, both Qi and Mitch had scanned the area for any sign—any glint of metal in the distance, any sound—

that might portend imminent gunfire, but they'd reached the vehicle and the two dead bodies before it without attracting anyone's attention. The two men had been neatly shot—but by whom? They'd put the question to one side much as they did the bodies themselves, then climbed up into the cockpit and began preparations to leave. As Mitch worked the controls, desperately forcing her hands to remain as steady as she could get them, Qi held their small arsenal of guns at the ready and watched for trouble.

But none had surfaced, and now, after readjusting her seat several times and getting the feel of the throttle, Mitch was able to float their craft into the night air. They hovered at about ten feet while she triple-checked her board. Then she seemed confident enough to loft them into the sky.

The helo accident for which Mitch had been cashiered out had occurred during a soft landing on an aircraft carrier, strictly a milk run. She was an Air Force loan-out for Naval pilot trainees, occupying the Number Two slot on the MH-60S Knighthawk when wind shear and a rolling carrier made tacking on the landing platform more difficult than her superior, the pilot, had been prepared for. They counter-rolled as the ship surged upward on the tide, and the rotor blades snapped off like popsicle sticks against the deck, gravely wounding two runway rats and scratching one chopper at a cost of about $28 million. No time was wasted in assigning a scapegoat, especially since it would boil down to a Navy versus Air Force beef.

But Mitch could jockey these beasts. She knew it, and the brass knew it too, even if they'd never admit it. She'd longed for a gunship and the chance to deploy its devastating firepower in combat, just once.

This might have been that chance, but Kuan-Ku Tak Cheung, wily devil that he was, had provided no bang-bang aboard this eggbeater.

They had their rifles, and the guns taken off the dead pilot and his companion. Mitch had spotted a few racked grenades. And they had the helo.

"This puts us into the center of things," said Qi.

"Meaning?" Mitch concentrated on the rudder, which was a little slushy-feeling. She wiped sweat off her forehead.

"Cheung's helipad directly accesses his headquarters. No infiltration, no disguises. No strategy. All that is left to us is the lightning raid."

"You mean barge in, guns blazing, and hope for the best?" Mitch sucked air between her teeth. "Sorry, but that sounds a lot like your other plans, based as they were on the idea of a one-way mission. I'm no kamikaze."

"We have the Killers of Men as a bargaining chip. Cheung may hate us. He may want us dead on sight. But he is not so foolish as to risk this prize."

"So we fly right in like we own the place?"

"Exactly. Without Ivory or Dinanath, Cheung's subordinates will stand down."

"You hope."

Qi almost smiled. "Always. But I also prepare for the worst." She went to work stripping and cleaning the guns.

Ivory had a layer of bandage pads taped to his forehead and his eyes seemed to glitter unnaturally in the dim light of the shrine room, candlefire making them appear too starkly white.

He sat with his lethal OTs-33 held loosely, dangling between his knees as he perched on the canvas-tarped pile of one of Qi's caches.

"You have me at a disadvantage," Gabriel said, even though it was obvious, standing as he was in an elevated metal cauldron.

Ivory said nothing.

"It appears we may have the same enemies now," Gabriel added, waving in the direction of the neighboring shrine room, where Cheung's men lay dead. He pointed at Ivory's gun. "Quite a weapon. Russian, isn't it?"

"It is adequate to my needs."

"Yeah, I heard you weren't too fond of Glocks."

One of Ivory's eyebrows arched. "That, too, served its purpose. Mr. Hunt, is it your intention to waste time with banter? I have never understood that about Americans; their reluctance to address a point directly."

"'Warfare is the tao of deceit,'" said Gabriel, quoting Sun Tzu. He thought he saw Ivory roll his eyes. No doubt sick of Westerners quoting *The Art of War*.

Gabriel considered climbing out, then thought better of it. Any abrupt movement might get him killed.

"These two women," said Ivory without prelude. "Your dedication to them is unusual. My experience of most Westerners is that they are little more than infants incapable of seeing beyond their little personal dramas, attitudes, whims or appetites. What binds you to them?"

"Nothing," said Gabriel. "I used them to help me find the Killers of Men, nothing more."

"Ah, now you are being less than honest. Believe

me, I know. I, too, have been less than forthcoming, with Cheung. My covenant was to lead him to this place. Instead I came alone, and found you. And as you have said, we seem to be on the same path, now. But I must understand how you got here."

"All right, I'll be honest," Gabriel said. "I don't want to see either Qi or Mitch hurt. That's what I'm here for. The rest is incidental. There's also my brother—I need to get him free. The quickest and surest way to accomplish these things is to eliminate your boss. I'm sorry, Ivory, but the man is a Grade-A certified lunatic, and I think you know it. If you didn't, I'd be dead already."

"I cannot—"

Gabriel overrode him. "You don't have to. The women are on their own now—they can fend for themselves. And if you return with me to the city and present me to Cheung, I can get my brother back. You were supposed to find this place for Cheung—well, you've found it. By bringing me back to Cheung you will have discharged your duty. Cheung has already offered amnesty if I can reveal the Killers of Men to him; the women go free, my brother and I return to America."

"If you believe Cheung's word."

"I don't, not for a second. But look at what he wants versus what he's got. We have leverage. Frankly, it's what happens to you I'm not so sure of."

"I have earned no mercy in this, no special consideration."

"Except from me," said Gabriel. "I'll help you—if you let me get out of this pot."

He watched this handsome, conflicted Asian work the variables out in his mind. For whatever it was worth, Ivory had still not pulled the trigger on Gabriel.

Yet.

They could see the Oriental Pearl TV Tower coming up fast on the horizon, aglitter with nightlight.

"Spot it for me," said Mitch, meaning the landing platform cantilevered onto the backside of the Peace Hotel. It would be one of the neon-lit vertebrae of the Bund. "I can bank up and over."

"There," said Qi.

The concrete platform was a typical helicopter bull's-eye, outlined by blue landing lights. Tiny now, far below them as the chopper found its mark.

"Son of a . . . *bitch*," Mitch grunted as though she'd just taken a bullet.

"What is it?" Qi shouted. In the bounce from the console telltales it was clear that Mitch was drenched in sweat. She was vising the bridge of her nose brutally and drawing air in fast, hyperventilating gasps.

"Goddamn it," she groaned. "Not now, not *now*."

The Kamov jolted drunkenly to port as Mitch tried to correct. Tears blurred her eyes to double-vision.

With a low animal noise, Mitch unwillingly let go of the stick to grab her head. The running sounds, the rotors, were jabbing into the soft tissue of her brain.

The chopper briefly lost float and gyro'ed around like a runaway carousel, slamming Qi into the port door.

Mitch grabbed Qi's hands and posted them on the stick in front of her. "Hold this steady!" she said through gritted teeth. "I can hold the pedals. We've got to try to—"

They were already dropping like a stone. Qi saw the control dials ratchet alarmingly.

They struggled and together managed to get the copter almost level when a cramp tore through Mitch. It felt as though all her internal organs were being carelessly rearranged by a meatball medic using a rusty saw.

Qi saw the Peace Hotel landing platform whisk past on her left, at a sickening angle. They missed it by fifty yards.

"Hold the stick!" Mitch screamed, her eyes clamping shut. "We're going . . . going to have to set it down in the street."

It was academic. They were heading for the street anyway, their drop rate making lift unrecoverable.

In the street were thousands of cars, pedestrians, pedicabs, bicycles—all frantically trying to clear a path for what was sure to be a fiery crash.

The Kamov's powerhouses were redlining and worse, starting to hitch and skip.

Mitch fought the craft level and for a precarious moment it seemed like a hard but manageable job of ditching. Then the landing skids rammed like javelins through the front and back windows of a just-abandoned car and tore free, putting the Kamov into a forward roll with no landing gear.

The spinning blades were now front-most, scything like a gigantic lawn mower, snapping off and flip-flopping free as they chewed into pavement, automobiles and screaming people. Cars swerved and collided in the vain hope of not smashing into the upside-down juggernaut now sliding at speed through the congested street.

Despite their harnesses, Mitch and Qi were tumbled

and battered like dice in a cage. As the cabin compressed and imploded, jagged Plexi showered in on them. The composite armor was good, but not up to the challenge of keeping cabin-forward from crumpling. Sparks rained and scratched spot-welded highlights on their retinas as their safe cocoon clenched into a trash-compacted death trap.

Then the least lucky motorist of all plowed into the chopper from behind.

Chapter 23

Shukuma strode forward with her hands clasped behind her. She was not used to addressing Cheung as his direct subordinate. That was for Ivory, or Dinanath, neither of whom was here. Romero and Chino were dead. Tuan and Mads Hellweg had been eliminated.

Cheung was in his Temple Room, carving another little casket. Sister Menga was in her incense-clouded corner between the two Tosa guard dogs, who were sleeping at her feet like puppies. Her eyes were rolled back into her head, showing only whites to the world of mortals.

"Victory over an enemy," Sister Menga mumbled. "The exposure of traitors. All as prophesized."

"You said that before," countered Cheung. She had said it in regard to Tuan. "Are you certain your bones and animal guts are not giving you recycled information?"

"More than one victory," Sister Menga intoned, her silver eyes coming down to meet Cheung's. "More than one traitor."

"And Longwei Sze Xie is lost to me?" Cheung said. "No. He would go neutral, not virulent. Besides, I would miss him."

The tall black bodyguard knew that, other than Sister Menga's, Cheung rarely accepted counsel from females—more traditional Chinese horse manure, she thought. If the boys on the team could not handle everything falling to pieces, she could prove herself here and now. The lessons of the tenure of the Nameless One were lost on her. Venerable laws, likewise—she thought herself above their teaching, and in doing so made the error that always brings disaster to the prideful.

"The helicopter has returned," she told Cheung. "It is in the middle of the street below, burning."

"Then Dinanath failed," said Cheung. "Let General Zhang handle the rabble."

Shukuma dared to add, "You seem unconcerned."

"The Killers of Men are within my grasp. The disparate threads are all finally twining together. Binding, as Sister Menga foretold, into the pattern of the future."

"And the men that went to the pagoda with Dinanath?"

"Expendable," Cheung said. "Shukuma, you are my new Immortal. You shall assume Ivory's station from this moment forward. If you see the American woman, the Nameless One, Ivory, Dinanath or anyone else other than Mr. Gabriel Hunt, you are to retire them immediately and report to me. If there is fire and chaos in the streets, one or more of them will be coming."

"What about Michael Hunt?" she said.

"Keep him under guard until my dealings with his brother are concluded. Then you may kill all of them."

"You can depend on me, sir," Shukuma said, happy with her promotion.

The paws of the sleeping Tosa dogs twitched, as though they were dreaming at the feet of Cheung's sorceress. Dreaming of prey, thought Shukuma—human or animal, it didn't matter, we all dream of our prey.

And the first place to check for her prey would be that helicopter in the street outside.

Gabriel conducted Ivory down the mountain, and Ivory chauffeured Gabriel into the city. Neither man spoke very much during the trip. Until Gabriel finally said:

"Tell me about the drug."

Ivory inhaled deeply. Gabriel thought the man was preparing to sink into one of his stony silences as though the topic at hand was moot, beneath notice, or beyond discussion. But he surprised Gabriel with his specificity.

"The drug is a hydrochloride distillate of *xipax-idine*," he said, pronouncing it knowledgeably: *zi-PAX-eh-deen*. "It is a true synthetic, refined using the Sturges Method. Do you know it?"

"You're talking about three million dollars of equipment just to start the refining process," said Gabriel.

"Yes. There are nine steps in all to the distillate."

Gabriel recalled the nine jogs in the bridge at the Tea House. "Nine turns, to confuse evil spirits?" he said. It was a recurrent feature in Chinese design.

"Nine stages to seek purity," said Ivory, knowing what Gabriel was referring to. "At each stage the substance is highly unstable, and there is an enormous wastage factor. Also a slender margin for error. Each of these stages additionally requires a great deal of time and constant monitoring."

"What does it attack?"

"The most primary programming of the brain—fight, flight or mate. In its pure form, the distillate allows for direct suggestion without hypnosis."

"And in its impure form?"

"Each castoff stage has dangers. Psychosis, memory loss, violent self-destructive hallucinations, instantaneous addiction. The only cure for a Phase IV user is death. There is no withdrawal."

"The version you gave me and Mitch?"

"You are in no danger. She had more prolonged exposure. She would require a hospital stay for detoxification—or lacking that, regular dosages indefinitely with periodic increases due to habituation. Interruption causes withdrawal-like symptoms; they are rarely fatal, but they are always severe."

"What happens to all the impure material? Wastage at that level is incredibly expensive."

"Cheung plans to offer it to the world as a new narcotic. His 'freon' is impure Stage VII. He and I have always been in disagreement on this. The pure distillate of xipaxidine has its uses. The impure forms are unspeakably dangerous."

Gabriel's hand searched his pocket for the capped syringe with the remaining eight cc's of the drug he had given to Mitch. But it was gone, probably lost in his escape from the cavern.

Gabriel said, "He plans to sell this stuff? It'll kill people."

Ivory came back at him: "Certainly. But it will also make him rich. And warlords have always disregarded

the constraints of conventional morality. General Liu
Xiang had eight concubines all trained to play tennis,
so one would be available whenever the mood struck
him."

"Cheung may enjoy seeing himself as a warlord,"
Gabriel said, "but he's really just a two-bit criminal
with delusions of grandeur."

"This is your conclusion?"

"It's the only sane conclusion."

"You are suggesting one needs to find a new enemy," said Ivory.

"I'm suggesting that you've already found one,"
said Gabriel.

Ivory fell silent, his eyes fixed forward. Gabriel
thought the man was simply retreating into stoicism
again. Then Gabriel's mouth dropped open as he saw
what Ivory was staring at: the rolling column of smoke
and flames from the crashed helicopter in the street
ahead, and the hopeless traffic jam that would keep
them from reaching it.

Adrenaline flushed through Mitch's system and cleared
her circuits long enough for her to register the proper
response to the flames melting the synthetic fibers of
her pilot harness and licking up her arm. The pain
helped focus her.

This was no dream, no drug-induced hallucination.

She and Qi were ensnared upside down in the imploded cockpit, and everything around them seemed
to have become flammable.

Past char-fouled Perspex and wide fractures in
the canopy, they could both see elements of General
Zhang's police force advancing on them, weapons up.
They were coming from all sides, snaking between

wrecked automobiles, shoving citizens out of the firing line, and maintaining a textbook group cover pattern.

Qi wrestled her harness as though it were a living thing bent on killing her. When the latches undogged, she was still trapped—one leg bent awkwardly behind a fold of steel, blood caking her dynamic new haircut.

Mitch quickly brought up the nearest available sidearm, a Beretta 9mm with a hi-cap mag, and quickly dispatched twenty shots to pin down the approaching mercenaries with some second thoughts about an easy sweep-and-clear. She chucked the empty gun and sought another.

"Take that rifle and hit the alley, over there," Qi shouted. "I need you to cover me—I've got to get unstuck."

"No. We go together."

"Don't be stupid. We go together, we both get shot. Do what I ask."

Mitch could almost see the logic of it. One blind corner. One escape route not covered by Zhang's police. If she could make it, and then cover Qi, if they could dump weapons and fade into the crowd, they might just walk.

Mitch fielded a few more shots with the LMT rifle she had recovered, although it was awkward to maneuver the weapon inside the crushed cabin. She wished she had a full-auto pistol like Ivory's. The things had originally been designed for use by tank crews who might need to wield gunpower inside a confined space. But once she was out in the open, as Qi suggested, she'd be able to make every cartridge count.

"Go for it," shouted Qi. "Go now. I am right behind you."

Mitch scuttled out. Using the smoke and confusion as cover, she was able to crabwalk to the alleyway Qi had indicated.

Qi was not right behind her. In fact, the incoming cops had gained another ten yards on the ruined chopper. They were going to take Qi, and take her hard, if she did not move her ass double-quick.

Qi's heart surged as she saw Mitch make a break for it. It was correct that Mitch should live. Just as Mitch should not have to know that Qi could feel the ruptured metal biting through her leg all the way to the bone, trapping her in the downed aircraft, making her one with its skeleton as it burned.

Zhang's men crept closer. Qi could see the bores of their weapons, all trained on her, inside.

"Hold your fire," said a voice. "It's the Nameless One."

Shukuma was not in evening wear for this little social event, and so was not packing her unobtrusive .380. She leaned closer to the cabin behind the more awe-inspiring muzzle of a no-frills military .45.

"Cheung will want her," Shukuma told the cops.

"I have a gift for Cheung," said Qi, nearly choking on her own blood. She smiled gruesomely, her teeth outlined in red.

And opened her hands to reveal two grenades, pins already pulled.

The police were already backtracking, diving for cover. Shukuma, however, could not wrest her gaze from the bulkhead tank right behind Qingzhao that was stenciled NO NAKED LIGHT.

It was the last thing she saw.

* * *

Gabriel and Ivory were out of their vehicle and running. The explosion knocked them both to the pavement.

The secondary explosion bathed Mitch's view in white fire, sprawling her backward.

Smoke rolled to make a huge fist in the night sky.

Chapter 24

Ivory pushed up, glass fragments in the palms of both hands, to come face-to-face with General Zhang.

"I have lost men," Zhang said sternly. "What is Cheung doing? Tell me or I shall have to expedite you." He had the backup to prove he was serious.

"The helicopter was stolen by assassins," said Ivory smoothly. "The plot was to kill Cheung in the Peace Hotel."

"Massacre in the streets does not reinforce his position," said Zhang. "The Tong leaders will want an explanation."

This seemed pretty slick, coming from the man who had watched Cheung blow Mads Hellweg into the afterlife right in front of the Tong bigwigs at Tuan's funeral and not said a word against it. Of course, while that had been public violence, too, it had been less public than this.

"Do what you do best, General," Ivory said with respect. "Order needs to be restored here. Cheung shall answer fully."

Gabriel swore he could see telepathy passing between the two men, and Ivory saying: *I shall fix it.*

"Very well." Zhang turned, pointed and barked

orders to his men. "You say that this assassin—the one who has been trying to kill Cheung—is now neutralized at last?"

A quick check of the steaming wreckage of the chopper, now cordoned off by men with chemical extinguishers, confirmed this. Gabriel saw Ivory's stature warp almost imperceptibly; the cool-as-ice operative's shoulders bowed slightly in sadness.

Qingzhao Wai Chiu had been incinerated. Gabriel felt the regret settle on his shoulders as well.

But there was no sign of Mitch.

"Cheung needs to be told immediately," Ivory said. "And he will not believe it unless it comes from you or me."

"I have duties here," Zhang sniffed with harried-bureaucrat superiority. "It is *your* burden."

Ivory's performance was pretty spectacular, thought Gabriel. But damn it all, the man had not *lied* to Zhang. He had merely found a way to circumvent the truth. And in the bargain, won both himself and Gabriel an armed police escort right up to the entrance of the Peace Hotel.

Mitch finally unlocked her limbs from her frozen fetal position in the alleyway when someone, a stranger, tossed a few coins at her, thinking she was a beggar.

She could not see Gabriel and Ivory palavering with General Zhang less than fifty yards away. Too much smoke, too many people, confusion squared. Her face was scuffed, scabbed and blackened. Blood on her fatigue jersey.

She snugged her fatigues and retied a wayward bootlace. She had to make it out of this alley and into the Peace Hotel—she had to. And she could, she knew she could find some way in, if only her brain would stop slamming against the walls of her skull.

She slid the syringe from her pocket. Yes, she had deceived Gabriel back at the leaning pagoda when she'd clutched onto him and implored him to watch his ass. She'd meant what she'd said—but it had not been as important as liberating the hypodermic she knew he carried, the syringe that held all the solutions to her distress. She could seek forgiveness later, if they all lived.

She stuck the spike in her arm and gave herself the full remaining eight cc's of the drug, all the while repeating her own instructions to herself. She didn't want to lose her plan to the drug, slip away into sleep or waking dreams of unrelated combat. Somehow she needed to hold onto enough mental control to steer herself even when—

The hit when the drug took effect was similar to a great orgasm, the kind you still remember years later, yet contoured with vitamins and excellent speed, like an energy drink made with plutonium.

A deep breath, and her vision seemed to clear, though it was almost too clear at the edges, realer than real. She would have to concentrate, focus.

She moved directly to a Zhang soldier on the sidewalk who was shouting directives to an apparently deaf gentleman who wanted to argue that he could not extricate his big tricycle from the grille of a wrecked car because it was augured into a phone pole. When the soldier made to strike the man with the butt of his rifle, Mitch grabbed the gun barrel and yanked the soldier off balance. As he turned, Mitch shot a fist into his exposed throat. The weapon came free in her hands as the man went down bug-eyed and crimson-faced, unable to draw air. She gave a quick thumbs-up to the citizen, who looked horrified rather than properly grateful. No matter. She appropriated the Zhang man's helmet and moved on down the street.

The gun settled comfortably into her grasp. With the helmet and weapon, she could pass for another uniformed solider, if no one looked too closely in the midst of all the commotion.

And while Gabriel and Ivory were still occupied with Qi's few remaining molecules and the contentions of General Zhang, Mitch made straight for the Peace Hotel.

"Zhang and the Tong leaders will expect treachery," murmured Sister Menga, not looking up from her steaming chalice of entrails.

"We shall be allies," said Cheung, making the knot in his necktie hard as a walnut. He was clad in his conventional businesswear, augmented by the sort of veneered body armor Ivory had favored.

"You are children in a nursery, squabbling over toys," said Sister Menga. Each of her pronunciations seemed to issue from the haze of incense smoke just before her. "You carve coffins and hope events turn in your favor. You are losing your grasp, but not the strength of your grip."

"And *you* are starting to sound like a fortune cookie," said Cheung. "Why not feel my skull and tell me the future? I might as well burn Hell Money or seek the favor of paper gods." He spun on his adviser. "Ivory is lost to me. *Guanxi* is lost. That is what it takes to achieve what I want, and I do not shrink from it."

One of the Tosa dogs rose from Sister Menga's nest

and padded out into the Junfa Hall. The other followed soon after. Since Dinanath was gone and Shukuma was occupied, stewardship of the dogs would currently be the purview of a man named Yu Peng, who had come to be in Cheung's service from the Gedar Township of the area formerly called the Tibet Autonomous Region after the devastating earthquake there in 2006. Another Ivory recruit.

Cheung wondered how many of Ivory's recruits might turn, how many remain loyal.

The dogs' barking echoed through the museum ambience of the hall. They, too, were impatient for action.

Yu Peng would calm them down.

The other man in the hall was a Brazilian, newly hired by Cheung to salvage his skills from a murder rap in Sao Paulo. His name was . . . was . . .

Cheung hated the imprecision in his own mind. Romero? Chino? No, they were dead. Ayala, that was it. Dagoberto Ayala.

The Russian soul of Anatoly Dragunov, smoldering inside the shell of the persona he presented as Kuan-Ku Tak Cheung, resented his inability to enforce brutal fixes to essential, simple problems. In Shanghai the protocols were about ritual first, then political gain. This was frustrating. He understood peace through dominance and reflected that his plays were all logical and effective. Pawn for pawn, he reigned among ruthless men. Gabriel Hunt had come to China for a reason, and that reason had nothing to do with Valerie Quantrill's unfortunate but necessary murder, or with her deranged militant sister. All these events were threads of a tapestry of challenges and rebuttals which Sister Menga had foretold in her cloaked fashion, but which Cheung had also seen in terms of his own destiny. Gabriel Hunt was here because now was the time for Cheung to discover the Killers of Men. Gabriel Hunt's brother was here because a bargaining chip was needed in reserve. If this revelation required the betrayal of Ivory—Cheung's Immortal— then so be it. He had sacrificed his Number Ones before and would probably be required to do so again. Right now, he had no one in mind to sacrifice. While he had carved another little casket, he remained uncertain to whom it should be assigned.

According to a transmission from one of Zhang's lieutenants, the wrecked helicopter in the middle of Zhongshan Road contained none of the nearly twenty men sent with Dinanath to investigate the homing beacon with which the Nameless One, Qingzhao, had been kindly belled by Ivory. This spoke as evidence in Ivory's favor. Yet Qingzhao had no pilot skills. There was a fatal gap in information and hence, treachery was afoot everywhere today.

The soldier had reported back—not Shukuma. Another failure.

Dinanath had not reported back from the leaning pagoda.

His men, his men—were they all cowards or corpses?

Cheung was going to have to demonstrate once again that his leadership was unequalled. True generals, true leaders were unafraid to walk point.

The radiant sense of confidence with which he stood and strode forth was obliterated by the abrupt sound of a single gunshot, a hollow bang largely absorbed by all the fabric hanging in Cheung's Temple Room. Cheung's flesh contracted in a full-body flinch.

Sister Menga fell face-forward into her dish of guts,

the coals from her brazier scattering to pit the fire-proof carpeting with acrid contrails of smoke. The seer had failed to foresee the bullet that would pierce her skull right where her third eye ought to have been.

Foretell the future? The future was only told when you made it yourself, thought Cheung as he turned to face Michelle Quantrill one final time.

Chapter 25

The hairy eyeball. That is what the black-suited Cheung men were giving Gabriel. They had been vaguely alerted, but few specifics had trickled down the chain of command this far, to the ground-level enforcers. They were strictly guns, muscle, hired hands.

Further, they eyeballed every Zhang soldier who saw fit to trespass upon the Peace Hotel as though personally affronted their limited authority was being usurped by the emergency brewing out in the street.

They were tetchy and trigger-happy; itching for conflict.

"You are going to have to be my prisoner," Ivory told Gabriel. He drew his trusty OTs-33, his thumb automatically switching the gun to three-shot-burst mode.

For him to grab Gabriel's arm would be too aggressive, thus alerting the sentries. For them to casually stroll in without a declared hierarchy—Cheung operative plus prisoner—would be too casual. Ivory opted for polite formality: The captive or suspect proceeds one pace ahead, to the left. Normally this was a submissive, almost servile position for the man behind, but the guards would understand that Ivory was keeping a ready weapon trained on Gabriel's kidneys. Under normal circumstances, a jacket would be draped over the weapon in deference to public view. These circumstances were not normal—weapons were abundant thanks to the panic from the chopper crash— hence Ivory's gun would be visible, reinforcing the idea of a general alert. The guards would see the gun and the prisoner and never think this was any sort of deception. This was business, expediently out in the open, and so Ivory would be taken at face value since his disfavor in Cheung's eyes was still not widely known.

The two men bracketing the brass doors to the Peace Hotel were named Bennings and Jintao. Acquisitions, Ivory knew, from a recent canvass of Cheung security candidates based on such employment advantages as blackmail leverage, capacity for violence and general criminal records.

"For Cheung," Ivory said, indicating Gabriel. "Dinanath was sent to retrieve this top-priority guest. He failed and I have assumed personal responsibility for the delivery. Check with Constantine on the fifth floor if you must, but this is most urgent."

Gabriel did his best to look captured and cowed.

Bennings, a rangy Australian, was the guy giving Gabriel the once-over, twice. "Does this have anything to do with that balls-up?" he said, pointing to the wreck of the helicopter and the attendant madness.

"With what?" Ivory said, not even looking back.

Gabriel had to admire the ice-cold resolve of this guy.

Jintao had removed his sunglasses, silently exposing his eyes to his superior, and Ivory gave the man his own stern gaze in response. Jintao averted his gaze first.

"Is there a problem?" said Ivory.

"No problem," said Bennings, waving them inside.

They crossed the lobby in silence. The Old Jazz Bar of the Peace Hotel featured a large easeled placard that boasted *Real Shanghai Style Jazz Nightly!*

"I helped Jintao's children get into their present school," said Ivory finally, when they were out of earshot. "There are many like him in Cheung's employ—decent men who do this work from fiscal necessity. It would have been a pity to kill him."

"Would you have?"

"If it had been necessary," Ivory said. "I am glad it was not."

Cheung's floor was privately keyed, but Ivory still had the magnetic card that permitted direct elevator access.

"Wouldn't Cheung have deactivated your card if he didn't trust you?" said Gabriel once they had begun their ascent.

"Cheung does not wish to admit to himself the inevitability of my betrayal," said Ivory. "I believe that he expects me to return, in fact, of my own accord."

"So he left the door open for you," Gabriel said. "He's hoping you'll come back."

"I have come back, Mr. Hunt. And I have brought him the prize he seeks."

Gabriel was contemplating Ivory's gun, which had not lowered. "Please tell me . . . that I'm not worth a trap *this* elaborate."

Ivory's eyes indicated the ceiling, and the surveillance camera there.

"You are worth every effort, Mr. Hunt," he said. "Maximum effort."

The doors parted to admit them to the Junfa Hall.

Gabriel stepped out but was halted by Ivory, who merely said, "Hold."

He pointed.

The two Tosa dogs were strewn all over the hallway in a welter of blood. Over there, between two of the warlord statues that lined the corridor, were the protruding feet of at least one deactivated sentry.

A single shot of rifle fire resounded so crisply through the hall that you could hear the ejected brass sing. Gabriel and Ivory hotfooted it to the alcove that lead to Cheung's Temple Room.

Which is where they found Sister Menga with her brains painting the wall, and an insane-looking Mitch holding down on Cheung himself at point-blank range.

Getting past the door guards had been easy. All Mitch had to do was wait for a pair of Zhang soldiers to make for the Peace Hotel doors on some mission, perhaps to set up a triage center or summon medical backup. She blended through in their wake and made sure she was not noticed once she broke away from them. The soldiers were barely aware that they had even been tailed.

The captured helmet over her shaved head covered up a multitude of giveaways.

Getting to the top of the hotel had been tougher. Scaling the exterior wall was not an option. She might fall, be spotted or get shot. While she felt the drive and had the strength, more nimbleness than she possessed would be required for her to navigate slight brick interstices and dicey, crumbling handholds all the way up. One slip, one misplaced boot-tip, and her life and mission would end in a big wet splattered puddle. Like they'd told her in jump school, *It ain't the fall that kills you, it's the sudden stop.*

Qingzhao had warned her about guards and security elevators. Mitch was going to have to concoct a plan on the fly, and not hesitate lest she betray her own unauthorized presence. She quickly found the utility stairs and took them two at a time, as though she knew where she was going.

On the fourth floor she found a lone Cheung man patrolling the hallway. She hustled toward him with the urgent affect of a messenger, snapped a sharp salute, and hit him in the forehead with the butt of her borrowed carbine. The man's eyes crossed as he fell. She stripped him of a Beretta nine and a fighting knife the length of a bayonet. In a jacket sheath she found a silencer for the handgun that was nearly a foot long. Serious business.

She jabbed the blade into the rubber seal of the nearby elevator and levered the doors about eighteen inches apart—far enough to see cables reeling past. The car squeaked to a stop at the floor below. It was near enough for her to snake into the shaft, spider downward, and put her boots on the roof as softly as a moth lighting on a lampshade.

Mitch flattened out. It would not do to get hamstrung in a big cog or fail to see the metal girder-brace at the top of the shaft if it happened to rush at her suddenly in the near-darkness here. There were no Western numerals spray-painted on the cement stanchions, only Chinese characters. But she knew where she needed to be: the top floor.

Eventually somebody would need to go all the way up.

She ejected the Beretta's clip and verified the pistol was full up, with one in the pipe. She screwed on the hefty silencer and snugged the gun into her waistline, ruefully thinking it would take a week to draw out in combat. She slid the knife into her boot.

Her heartbeat was redlining. She could hear the thumps and clunks of the building's own metabolism—it, too, had a heartbeat. A fine, clean sweat had broken all over Mitch's body. She was an invading virus.

Another elevator car husked past on her left.

Then the car she was on was climbing, climbing.

At the apex of the shaft was a short service ladder, which led to a bolted vent. Mitch used the bayonet again. The vent led to a grate, and the grate emptied her into the Junfa Hall.

The Junfa Hall was crowded, but not with the living. Warlords lined the corridor of honor, stolid in their cast metal and forged expressions. Mitch peeked around a life-sized bronze of Zhang Zongchang, also remembered as Marshal Chang Tsung-ch'ang, who died in 1928. Perhaps Cheung had named his floating casino after this man.

Two Cheung men in the corridor, pacing like expectant fathers, sticking more or less to the row of statues, one on each side, their pace so metronomic that they always crossed in the center of the room. One Chinese, one western, Latin American, perhaps. The Chinese man looked like the boss hog, so Mitch took him first, at the end of his circuit.

When he turned, she yanked him backward by the strap on his shortie M4 rifle, chopped his throat to shut him up, and buried the bayonet in his solar plexus. Thrust, twist, withdraw. He fell into her grasp behind a Wu Dynasty bronze.

"Hey, Penga," said the man from the opposite end of the corridor, realizing his partner had vanished. Yu Peng, when alive, had wrongly assumed that Dagoberto Ayala's nickname for him was a friendly diminutive—like "Bobby" for "Robert"—but in truth, it was closer to a dirty pejorative. Ayala detested anybody higher than him on the command chain.

Ayala keyed open the bulletproof glass doors. If kept open, the doors allowed the Tosa dogs to run back and forth—endlessly—between the Junfa Hall and the Temple Room, as if the retarded mutts could not decide whose butt to sniff more, Cheung's or Peng's.

"*Podido*," Ayala griped. "You go to the can, at least tell me—"

Mitch took him. Thrust, twist, withdraw.

But the Tosa dogs in the adjacent room had already whiffed Yu Peng's freshly liberated blood, and came charging in like assault tanks. Mitch heard their claws scrabbling on the slate tile of the corridor and had no idea how to close the glass doors.

She caught the first headlong animal with her forearm, feeling the crushing jaws closing to snap her bones as she buried the bayonet to the hilt in the huge beast's chest. It rolled—and her with it—but hung on. She put five shots from the silenced Beretta into the second one, which at least slowed it down, but also seemed to piss it off.

She jammed the pistol under the dog's chin and blew the crown of its head off, swearing she could feel the slug pass right by her own arm. By then the other one had a grab on her leg at the bootline. She had to fire without hitting her foot, and abruptly realized there was blood everywhere. Her own, in part, plus a generous geyser from the first dog. Its demon pal finally relaxed its chomp after Mitch emptied her mag into it. She felt the teeth slowly withdraw from her leg as the bite went slack, but that caused even more blood to course out.

The xipaxidine would roadblock the pain, though only for a time. Her leg felt malfunctional but just now she could still stand on it.

Valerie would have been horrified. Her sister had transmogrified into a butchering monster who even killed animals. Poor doggies.

Yeah, thought Mitch, *say that when you see your own limbs hanging out of their mouths, little sis.*

Her vision zoned out for an instant, then snapped back into focus. The edges glistened now, as if she were seeing through a glaze of ice crystals.

She collected her rifle and moved for the glass doors, wondering how many more mad dogs she would have to put down before she was done.

Chapter 26

Kuan-Ku Tak Cheung was laughing. He loved the theatrical. Exaggerated gestures. Glandular suspense. Cheap thrills.

He and Mitch were pointing guns at each other. Ivory was pointing a gun at the back of Mitch's head. And Gabriel Hunt was pointing a gun at Ivory.

Alliances were more fluid than they seemed.

"Laugh at me, you bastard, and I'll blow your tongue through the back of your head," said Mitch, holding steady with the Chinese carbine. She could do it, too, with this gun—maybe twice before gravity dropped the man. Upon entering the Temple Room, Mitch's first sight was Sister Menga raising a hand against her. The seer's ornate fingernails caught the light and suggested a weapon. Mitch was aboil with endorphins and the drug coursing through her, and her body reacted without the time-delay of premeditation. She had automatically put Sister Menga down because her eyes had seen a threat. Her eyes had lied. But so what?

In response to Sister Menga's moist demise, Cheung had whipped out a Czech CZ-52 pistol, two pounds of gorgeously machined steel filling his enormous hands.

Their stand-off was about five seconds old when Gabriel and Ivory brought up the rear.

Ivory put his pistol, still set on three-shot-burst, within four feet of the curve of Mitch's occipital.

Gabriel's hands familiarized themselves with Dagoberto Ayala's M4, which he'd scooped up on the run from the Junfa Hall. Cocked, locked, ready to rock. He did not think Ivory would actually shoot Mitch, but he had to draw on *somebody*, and Cheung was already staring down the bore of Mitch's rifle. Tension ran molten-hot through the room, thickening the air. Hell, sheer trigger reflex would kill them all if somebody sneezed.

That was when that son of a bitch Cheung started laughing.

"You impress me," Cheung told her. "You have accomplished the unthinkable. You got under Ivory's skin. You have truly earned my awe."

"Mitch," Gabriel said softly. "Don't take him. Not yet. He's got my brother."

"He already got my sister."

"I could use someone like you," Cheung told Mitch, "as my new head of security." His gaze indicted Ivory, but Ivory did not waver.

"Lower the weapon, Jin Huáng," Ivory said. It was not a request.

Gabriel saw Mitch *almost* comply.

"No." She refocused on Cheung. "Valerie Quantrill."

"Who?" said Cheung.

"*My sister.* You should think more about the people you murder."

"And how many have you murdered?" said Cheung, almost avuncular. "Killed in the name of your just cause? You should thank me. I determine what people like you become."

"Don't listen, Mitch," said Gabriel.

"You may avenge your sister's death," said Cheung, "but it will cost you your own life."

Cheung smiled like a cobra and lowered his own weapon.

Gabriel's hand touched Ivory's back, but he spoke to both Ivory and Mitch: "I need him alive."

Tears were rolling from Mitch's eyes but she fought to preserve her zeroed aim.

"Cheung—let them out of the building and I will take you to the Killers of Men. I alone know the burial secrets of the Favored Son. The men you sent to the site have fallen to those secrets. I will guide you and you may do with me what you will . . . but you will guarantee the release of my brother."

"That, I believe, was our agreement," said Cheung.

Ivory put a hand on Mitch's shoulder, turned her slowly. "Please," he said. His eyes were entreating. He backed her toward the glass doors, her gun gone wayward.

"I can't just leave—" she began.

"You *must*," said Ivory. "Trust me."

Gabriel let his muzzle drift in their direction. "Get her out of here or I'll shoot you both myself," he said, not taking his eyes off Cheung.

Mitch was still trying to process what had gone wrong, and the drug inside her was not helping. Soon enough the spikes, the flares, the knifing headaches would resume, and Gabriel knew that Ivory knew that, too.

"It seems that our moment is over before it has properly begun," said Cheung as he watched them exit.

"Too bad. For just a second, there . . ." He sighed. "It would have been magnificent."

"We'll never make it out of the building alive," said Ivory as they hustled past the bloody remains in the hallway.

"What?" said Mitch. "I thought Cheung—"

"Cheung has a casket already carved," Ivory said, overriding her. "I saw it in the Temple Room. It is for one of us. Or all three of us. How did you get into the building?"

Mitch recapped. While admirable, her ingress route would not serve their escape.

"I watched Cheung shoot down Mads Hellweg," said Ivory. "It was one of the most decisive, cold-blooded things I have yet seen. And Cheung did not particularly *care* about Hellweg. He will have something much worse planned for us."

"We can always hit them frontally," said Mitch, rechecking the loads in her purloined M4. "Go out the front door."

"Not and survive—there are still too many of them."

"Then let's go up. Helipad's on the roof, right?"

"Yes . . ." Ivory's eyes showed doubt.

"And the chopper is toast, so nobody will be in a big hurry to go to the helipad . . . right?"

"True."

"So let's hit it, partner. Before my damned headache comes back."

He searched her expression for signs of xipaxidine fatigue. When she finally ran out of gas, she'd drop like a clipped puppet. And with no more drug to dose her with . . .

Together they found the access stairs that led from

the Junfa Hall to the helipad. Four Cheung men were in charge of the perimeter.

"Do you know them?" Mitch said.

"I recruited two of them." Ivory peered through mesh glass to enumerate his potential allies. He indicated a willow-tall fellow in wraparound tinted glasses that seemed to be in charge of the other three patrollers. "Parkman Ng. Kam Ng's brother; took his brother's place when Kam was killed in a yakuza counterattack two years ago. Very loyal. And Kong—" he pointed to a broad-shouldered, hairless man "—he might be sympathetic, too. The other two, I just know their names. Güyük and Breedlove. Breedlove is British."

"So take the white guy and the short-round-fat guy first?" said Mitch.

Ivory stared at her, remembering that Americans were not famous for their tact. But he nodded.

They came through the push-barred door to the helipad brisk and businesslike, Ivory in the lead.

Guns came up to meet them. Mitch dropped to a solid kneeling position and did the smart thing—she patched the two men carrying rifles, which would be more accurate in a firefight. Breedlove the Brit folded and fell with multiple hits, followed by Güyük. By then, Parkman Ng had spun like a dancer and popped a wadcutter that sang past Ivory's right ear. Return fire was instinctual, and Ivory's weapon was on full-auto cycle. Red punctures jump-stitched up Parkman's long torso and he collapsed onto his face. Mitch could see the unhappiness in Ivory's eyes as his recruit fell.

Ivory raked the autofire toward the last man standing, the one he'd called Kong. But Mitch saw Ivory do an amazing thing—he pulled his weapon up out of the firing line *while* it was firing, before his finger left the trigger. The errant shots flocked away to make someone else's life miserable.

Because though Kong had reacted professionally, cross-drawing and sighting, he had jerked his own pistol up into neutral when he recognized Ivory.

"Ivory!" Kong yelled. "Parkman said Cheung's orders were to kill you. What's going on?"

Ivory kept his weapon dead-on as he approached Kong.

"I cannot believe it," Kong sputtered. "I will not believe it! Not of you. Many of us have heard the rumors, the news you were to become a Nameless One. I say that if Cheung decides you are a Nameless One, then I am a Nameless One as well." He was as frantic as anyone might be, presented with the prospect of killing a friend. "Longwei, please, tell me, what is the truth?"

Kong actually placed his weapon on the deck, stepped away from it.

"For the things you have just said," Ivory said softly, "for disloyalty to our master, the penalty is death. You understand that, Kwong Leung Kong Ngan?"

"Yes," Kong said, lowering his gaze. "The penalty is death."

"Under normal circumstances," said Ivory, drawing even closer.

Fearing the most intimate of killings, Kong kept staring at the concrete and said, "What . . . ?"

"Under Cheung's rule the penalty is death," said Ivory. "But Cheung's covenant is false. Were I to kill anyone for such a violation, I should first kill myself. You understand the gravity of what I say."

"I—I do?" stammered Kong. He regained some of his composure. "I mean, I do." Leery of the American woman with the weapon in the background, he leaned closer to Cheung, as there were some things so toxic and important that women should never hear them. "We heard Dinanath was gone. That you were turned. All our information is unreliable. Tell me, please—what is happening?"

"The foundations of Cheung's New Bund are collapsing as we speak," said Ivory.

"Can it be?" Kong said. "At long last . . ."

"My friend," said Ivory. "I need an Immortal, and you shall do quite nicely. You say there are others of like disposition."

"Yes. Jintao. Yu Peng. Hsiang Yun-Fa."

"Stop. Do not betray them until you see with your own eyes the evidence of my intent." There was no use in telling Kong that Yu Peng was already dead. "But gather them close. If I survive, they will be needed. If I do not survive, you must—you *must*—go for yourselves, is that understood?"

Kong directed them to a secure ladder that put them onto a disused fire escape, then headed in the other direction to round up his men.

"I've never seen anything like that before," said Mitch as they descended along a rear face of the building to street level.

"I have never done anything like that before," said Ivory. "But I suspected that Kong might be with me in spirit. I gambled on that."

"You should think about it, you know? Taking Cheung's place. You could undo a lot of damage."

Ivory pressed his lips together until they were white

and bloodless. One never said such bald things out loud. Putting such words into the air was unwise.

Instead he said, "Hurry. Just because we regain the streets, it is no guarantee of our safety."

"Where're we going?" said Mitch.

"I have to take you to meet a monk."

Chapter 27

Kuan-Ku Tak Cheung stared dourly at the dead man's arm sticking out of the base of the giant bronze idol in the shrine room. His expression seemed to say: *Hmm, he almost made it.*

Gabriel was the focus of two aimed guns, in the hands of the pair of Cheung men who had accompanied them in an armored limousine to the leaning pagoda. Shorthanded, Cheung had snatched them off guard duty in front of the Peace Hotel and both men, smelling imminent promotion and favor in the boss's eyes, were eager to comply.

They seemed just as eager to fill Gabriel up with bullets.

"A booby trap," said Gabriel. "As I warned you."

"It certainly seems that the obvious way in is not *the* way in," said Cheung.

"My brother. What assurance do I have you will release him?"

"You have no assurance, Mr. Hunt. Once my needs are seen to, then I shall consider the disposition of your brother."

"Then you are not a man of your word," said Gabriel.

"And you are not naïve," said Cheung. "It is your duty to acknowledge who holds the power in our brief relationship. You have cost me immeasurable time and resources. Your help inside this tomb could compensate for all that, but in the meantime you are at my command."

The two Cheung men glanced at each other.

"I was you, mate," said the taller Cheung man in an Australian accent, "I'd answer direct questions as asked, and otherwise keep my big yap shut."

"But you're not me," said Gabriel. "Too ugly and stupid, cowboy."

The guard bristled but kept his place.

"Now, Mr. Hunt," Cheung said. "As you say in New York: Time's wasting."

Under the gaze of the guards, Gabriel climbed down into the trench and brought up the big, faceted orb of crimson glass.

"There were two at some point," he told Cheung. "Now there is only this one. Watch."

As Cheung and his bodyguards looked on, Gabriel climbed the bronze idol and mounted the jewel in the socket. Under direct lamplight, they all saw the arc of backward ideograms projected on the far wall.

"Now, if we move it to the other socket . . ."

Gabriel had a good grip on the jewel and hated to let it go. The thing was at least a century old and surely unique. But survival called for sacrifice. He made a show of carelessness and let an expression of not entirely false horror emerge on his face as he allowed the orb to slip from his fingers. It shattered into a million crushed-ice fragments on the floor.

"What have you done?" demanded Cheung, growing red in the face, but when he looked up again he was staring into a pistol in Gabriel's hand. There'd been more in the trench than just the jewel.

The Australian leveled his .45 automatic at Gabriel, but Gabriel said, "Don't move or your boss gets it."

"Shoot him," said Cheung, regaining his composure. "Just not fatally. We still have need of him."

A pair of gunshots erupted—but not from the Australian's gun and not from Gabriel's. The blasts came from the other guard's M4. The Australian, Bennings, clenched tight with hits and fell down dead.

Cheung quickly raised his own pistol and blew the other man apart at the seams with three perfect shots.

"Poor Jintao," said Cheung. "I was hoping Ivory had not gotten to him." He prodded Jintao's corpse with the toe of one boot. "You see, Mr. Hunt? Betrayal at every turn." He waved his gun in Gabriel's direction. "Come down off that statue, please. And throw the gun away. You will not shoot me, not when I hold your brother's life in my hand. Let us stop wasting each other's time, shall we?"

Slowly, reluctantly, Gabriel tossed his gun and began to descend.

"Tell me how my sister died," said Mitch. She was having difficulty keeping focus. The headaches were starting to belabor her skull again.

Pan Xiao had conducted them to Ivory's safe haven deep within the monastery. From supplies he had on hand, both herbal and medical, Ivory had prepared an injection that would help Mitch cycle down from the effects of the xipaxidine.

"You will feel weak," he said. "The effect is compensatory. This is a buffer, it is not a cure. Your body will have to cure itself. But while that happens, this will at least keep you from hurting yourself or suffering too severely."

"Thank you," she said, shivering.

Ivory lowered his gaze. "Do you trust me?" he said.

She extended her arm to him to accept the waiting needle.

"Your sister Valerie was a very strong person," Ivory began as he swabbed alcohol over her skin. She felt the prick as the needle went in. "As you may have guessed, Cheung is tied into banks all over the world. Stocks, securities, laundered money, much of it from illicit business enterprises. Big money, high security. Valerie gained intimate knowledge of this information stream. But Cheung is not the only man with such connections—all men at his level of wealth and power have similar secrets, and Cheung asked your sister to tap into their information streams on his behalf. To engage in industrial espionage. He wanted details on his enemies' activities, their resources. Valerie had learned so much so quickly about him; Cheung simply tried to turn this talent to more useful ends."

"And she balked," said Mitch, beginning to drift, her eyes growing large and dark. "She found the line she would not cross."

"But here is the unusual part," said Ivory, his voice low. "Cheung wanted to convince her so badly that he flew to the United States himself. He exposed himself to capture, to great physical danger, even possible assassination, hoping that his gesture would impress your sister. Valerie showed no appreciation. It wasn't just that she said no—that he might have accepted. But she didn't respect the gesture."

It's a face thing, Valerie had told her jokingly before heading off to the late-night in-person meeting. *It's all very Chinese.*

"Cheung told Valerie he thought she was extremely talented. He wanted to leave the door open for a possible future reconciliation. Valerie said no. She would be happy to return any file Cheung requested, sign any release, pay back the salary she had received, but her decision was final."

Ivory also remembered how Cheung's gaze had gone flat, reptilian and metallic, as he merely answered Valerie by saying, "A pity."

"I asked you how she died," Mitch said again, half-asleep.

"It was . . . unpleasant."

"That's not what I asked you."

Ivory called up strength. "He struck her, one time. Not too brutally. I think she expected that to be the end of it. But then he gave her to his men, instructed them to ruin her. There were five. One to hold each arm, one for each leg, and the fifth to . . . to defile her. They switched off the fifth spot, each man took a turn. She was unconscious before long. They brought her to with water, waited till they knew she could feel it, then continued. It went on for more than an hour. And then they cut her throat."

"You stood by and watched this," Mitch mumbled. "You did nothing."

"My responsibility was Cheung's security," Ivory said in a voice redolent with shame. "I did my job. And they did theirs."

Mitch tried to lift her head but it seemed to weigh a million pounds. "And you have suffered ever since," she said softly.

"Yes," Ivory said.

"And then you saved me, when you could have let me die."

"Yes," Ivory said.

Mitch felt herself slipping out of consciousness, felt oblivion creeping up on her. "I forgive you," she murmured. "Valerie forgives you."

She was swept away, as on a gently rocking boat, to the sound of Ivory's tears.

Chapter 28

"The vent is corkscrew-shaped, with a switchback," said Gabriel when they had reached the rockfall that disguised ingress to the cavern. The climbing had been steep, and Cheung had made Gabriel go first, knowing of his physical abilities and desirous of keeping his gun.

"The Killers of Men are inside?" said Cheung.

"Just inside. I can show them to you."

"And this climbing equipment?" Cheung indicated the gear still scattered around the vent.

"Turned out to be unnecessary," said Gabriel.

"This is an interesting conundrum, Mr. Hunt. If I let you precede me, you might enact some futile ambush. If I go first, you could conceivably slam the door on me."

"Maybe you shouldn't have shot your other bodyguard," said Gabriel.

Cheung steamed briefly. "Pah! Bodyguards are no more than physical extensions of my command. Without my authority, no power exists in the first place, do you understand? Kangxi Shih-k'ai, the Favored Son, was unafraid to lead his men into battle. No warlord fears to put himself at risk above all. That is why I do not fear you."

Gabriel said nothing. He knew his brother's life was dependent on making Cheung believe that whatever happened next was Cheung's own decision.

"Snap these tight, so I can see them," said Cheung, tossing Gabriel a pair of manacles retrieved from some inner pocket of his jacket.

"The funnel is difficult to negotiate."

"You will cuff yourself and hold the lamp as we both proceed." The ever-present gun terminated further debate.

Gabriel dropped the loose climbing gear back into the pile. Why hadn't he thought to leave himself an extra gun here as well? He cinched the cuffs onto his wrists. Cheung checked them, tightened each to make sure Gabriel was secured. Then they went into the hole.

With his hands locked together by four links of tempered steel, Gabriel was reduced to the motility of a snake, his own lamp blinding him as Cheung squirmed through close behind. The rock jags made even a lucky kick impossible.

Several strands of climbing rope were threaded through the passage, like bright blood vessels.

"What are these for?" demanded Cheung.

"I was going to haul out some of the artifacts," said Gabriel. "There wasn't time."

"Yes—robbing the graves of other cultures is a pastime of yours, isn't it? And what is that *smell*?"

"There are bats in the cave."

"And my men?"

"I doubt any survived." Gabriel had to fold up, then extend himself to scoot along, clearing the way for

Cheung to follow, never forgetting the pistol pointed at him from behind. The way widened slightly as they proceeded toward the wide end of the funnel. "Kangxi Shih-k'ai rigged the entryway with a series of traps. Once the idol locked shut, there was no way in or out."

"Except this way."

"Yes—see for yourself."

Gabriel expected Cheung's lust to get the better of him as he approached his goal, and sure enough, Cheung was wriggling past him now like an eager child. But there was no room to move. No leeway for a blow or a chokehold. Gabriel felt the gun against him as Cheung passed.

Cheung swept his light across the blunt heads of the Killers of Men far below, his heart pounding, his breath short with astonishment.

"There must be . . . thousands of them," he said in awe. Then he levered his fist right into Gabriel's throat. "You didn't say anything about there being a drop! You climbed out!"

"I thought that was obvious," Gabriel said, chocking his boots against the nearest outcrop of rock.

"Damn you! It must be twenty meters to the floor!"

"I know," said Gabriel.

In another two seconds, Cheung would be angrily backtracking to get all the mountaineering gear. Which made this the time to act. Gabriel lunged to his knees, swung his chained hands over Cheung's head, pushed off like an Olympic swimmer, and launched them both into the black sky below.

Together, Cheung and Gabriel fell from the ceiling of the cavern for half a heartbeat, plunging into the void. Their lights and Cheung's gun toppled away.

Then the carabiner locked around Gabriel's belt cinched hard enough to compress several of Gabriel's internal organs into a space rather too small to hold them all.

He had clipped it on before cuffing his hands during his dalliance over the equipment. The lifeline ran anonymously among the other ropes depending down the funnel. Now it convulsed to guitar-string tightness against the anchor pitons in the rock outside, which groaned with the impact and load, but held.

Leaving Gabriel swinging in darkness, nine feet below the vent, with his arms coiled around Cheung's collar. It was the stiff, reinforced collar that saved Cheung's life, since had the chain of the manacles been around his bare throat, he'd have been hanged for sure.

They heard the lights smash against the rocks below; two, maybe three entire seconds after they had dropped.

Gabriel could hardly even see the man below him desperately trying to fight gravity. His arms reached down into an absolute absence of light.

In credit to his nerve, Cheung did not holler or panic. He did not kick his legs. He hung on with grim determination and focused hatred, trying to crawl up Gabriel's arms. Choice was out of the question. Gabriel could not drop or hold, and all Cheung could do was try to maintain his grip against the beckoning fall as they pendulumed in a slow, lazy arc in the damp darkness. Every movement weighed Cheung's collar more heavily against the cuff chain . . . which burden threatened to unsocket Gabriel's already fatigued arms.

Disturbed bats were beginning to flit around them. Daredevils, safe crackers, heart surgeons and crazy psychiatrists call it "supertime"—the moment that elongates under stress. It seemed that they dangled on the tether for an hour, when in fact it was mere seconds.

Every dram of oxygen was vital to both men; for Gabriel, head-down, to keep the blood vessels in his face from exploding, and for Cheung, lathered with terror-sweat, choking on his own knuckles while trying to hang onto the cuff chain that was cinching his hard collar into the flesh of his throat.

"Where . . ." Gabriel managed to choke out, "is . . . Michael?"

The body below him twisted in his grasp, but didn't reply.

"*Where?* I'll . . . save your . . . life if you . . . tell me."

Cheung barked out a laugh.

Then, chinning himself with an iron grip on Gabriel's forearms, Cheung lifted his throat out of the constricting embrace of the chain. "I'll order him killed," he spat in a single breath, his face inches from Gabriel's, "while you hang here for eternity." Then with a monumental effort he shifted one of his hands to grip Gabriel's belt. He began hauling himself upward along Gabriel's body with a fierce, almost incomprehensible strength.

"He's in the Peace Hotel," Cheung taunted. "Eighth floor, west side, last room. And what good does this knowledge do you Mr. Hunt? What can you do with it now?"

"This," Gabriel said, and bending one knee, kicked Cheung hard in the face.

For a moment, Gabriel continued to feel Cheung's weight pulling him down like a lead apron; then just the scrabbling of the man's fingertips against his chest;

then nothing, a burden lifted, and seconds later he heard a wet crunch followed by a long, keening wail. All was darkness—but in his mind's eye he saw Cheung far below, impaled on one of Kangxi Shih-k'ai's spikes, the previously impaled skeleton crushed to dust beneath him by the impact of his fall. Here was a Killer of Men indeed to add to the ancient warlord's collection.

Gabriel felt no satisfaction or fulfillment—merely relief that he could draw air again. His vision was spotting and his sense of direction was shot. He tried to pull himself up by the rope, but made little progress; he had no more strength in his arms.

The bats continued flitting around him; he could not have said for how long.

The next thing Gabriel knew, he was being pulled out of the hole on the line that had nearly garroted him at the waist.

Strong hands brushed debris away. Sat him down. Gave him a blessed sip of water.

"You have shown Kuan-Ku Tak Cheung the Killers of Men?" said Ivory.

"Yes," said Gabriel, finding his voice.

"Then your business here is concluded?"

"You mean, in China?"

"No. This mountaintop."

"For now," said Gabriel.

"You must permit me to give you a lift back to the city."

A moan drifted up from the funnel vent, amplified by the cave acoustics, muffled by the mountain.

"Did you hear that?" said Gabriel.

Ivory nodded. "The history of the Killers of Men is well known. This entire area is full of ghosts, and sometimes the ghosts speak to those who will listen. Come."

Gabriel and Ivory picked their way carefully down the mountain.

Behind them, the moaning from the cave became louder, more insistent, interspersed by hysterical laughter, and finally devolving into a long, drawn-out scream. But there was no one there to hear it.

Chapter 29

The jazz band at the Peace Hotel was actually quite good. All the musicians looked to be over sixty, and the saxophonist seemed to be channeling Coleman Hawkins directly when he blazed out the solo to "Body and Soul."

Gabriel caught Ivory tapping his foot more than once to the music.

"I still don't understand how I could have been duped so thoroughly," complained Michael Hunt. "It never occurred to me I was a captive. I just assumed, you know—gunfire in the street, my floor on lockdown, no cell phone service . . ."

"You blamed China," Mitch said. "I made the same mistake, I suppose. In my own way."

The barman in the lounge had talked Gabriel into sampling a drink that was essentially vodka on the rocks with most of a lemon squeezed into it. Gabriel considered the beverage moodily. It was good but somehow the celebratory atmosphere seemed askew.

"It turns out the coordinates in our parents' notes were about five miles off," said Michael. "They were amazingly close to discovering the Killers of Men."

"The official discovery now must be handled with

utmost delicacy," said Ivory. "I agree with your brother, Gabriel—he should finish the lecture series as planned and in that context he can provide a clue that our own scholars may follow to deduce the location. Let it be done that way. Credit will accrue to our cultural historians and you will not be blamed for the damage discovered at the site."

"And what of Cheung?" said Gabriel. "Or should I say Dragunov."

"That was also not his real name," said Ivory. "It is just the identity he used in the Soviet Union. I believe he was born in Ukraine, and from what few facts I learned over the years, it is entirely possible that his birth mother really was Chinese." His voice had a tinge of sadness to it. "We met in the midst of a gun battle, you know. It was a long time ago. He was a bad man even then—a drug smuggler. But not yet an insane one."

Mitch shifted uncomfortably at the mere mention of drugs. She wasn't drinking, just nursing a tall glass of seltzer. The purge program for xipaxidine worked on her by Pan Xiao, the monk-who-was-not-a-monk, had been effective but fluidly gruesome, and her insides were still fragile.

"What about the big payoff?" she said quietly. "The gold statue, or the treasure, or whatever it was that was supposed to be there?"

Gabriel and Michael looked at each other with an air of conspiracy.

"What?"

"We went back," Gabriel said, keeping his voice low. "After putting in a call to the Foundation and having a truckload of gels and gems and lenses overnighted. We tried them all in the statue's eyes, various combinations. Eventually got an arrangement that mimicked the jewels and allowed the ideograms to converge on the far wall."

"And what did they say?"

"It took a while to translate and some of it is still obscure," Michael said, "but—"

"But it boiled down to 'Dig here,'" Gabriel interrupted. "Kangxi Shih-k'ai's burial place is behind about a foot of rock directly across from the idol—the idol's looking right at him."

"The ideograms describe his tomb," Michael said. "His body was apparently installed inside a hollow jade carving of a warrior. It is described as weighing five hundred pounds."

"*Five hundred pounds of jade?*" Mitch said this a little too loudly and some heads turned their way.

Michael waited till the eavesdroppers had returned to enjoying the music. "Yes. And supposedly his body was completely outfitted in gold. Gold armor, gold clothing, gold weapons. Please don't shout."

Mitch restrained herself. "And this will all now be discovered by the Chinese government."

"It is their treasure," Michael said. "Their history."

"And what of Cheung?" Gabriel asked again.

"He perished, sadly, in his sleep," Ivory said. "It seems to have happened the night of the unfortunate helicopter crash in the street outside this hotel. It may have been a heart attack, perhaps brought on by the shock. He has already been cremated, in keeping with his instructions."

"And who's going to take his place on the Bund?" Gabriel said.

Ivory lowered his gaze in modesty. "There are

enough of us. Enough loyalists to repair the New Bund without the incursion of gangsterism."

"Will Zhang give you trouble?"

"General Zhang is content to run the People's Police," said Ivory.

"You won't have an easy time of it," said Gabriel. "Cheung left quite a mess behind him."

Ivory nodded in agreement. "Yes, but . . . I have excellent advisors."

When he said this, Mitch took Ivory's hand.

"I'm staying," she said.

Gabriel and Michael exchanged their second glance of the evening, less conspiratorial this time than incredulous.

"You're staying?" Gabriel said.

"What have I got to return to? My sister was my only family. She's dead. The Air Force doesn't want me back. I have as much to offer here as anywhere."

"What about—" He'd been about to mention Lucy's name, but realized that doing so in front of Michael would be opening a can of worms; in front of Ivory, too.

But Mitch knew what he'd held back from saying. "I'll see her again," she said. "When the time is right."

"Who?" Michael said. "That nurse from Khartoum?"

"Yes," Gabriel said. "The nurse from Khartoum."

The four of them drank their drinks, and the music played on.

"What about you, Gabriel?" Michael said finally. "Would you like to come with me on the lecture circuit or would you prefer to go home?"

Gabriel was sunk in thought. He'd spent the past

day trying to make amends and lay ghosts. He'd sought out the little old lady in charge of the Su-Lin Gun Merchant shop and crossed her palm with enough money to fund her retirement in the country and out of the firearms trade. On her little translating screen she had typed: I THANK YOU AND TUAN THANKS YOUR GRACE.

It had made him feel better, briefly.

"What about me?" Gabriel repeated. "I was thinking I might take a trip someplace quiet."

Which is how Gabriel Hunt found himself winging back to America all by his lonesome on the Hunt Foundation jet, his trusty Colt revolver never drawn nor used, his collection now enriched by the Colt .36 wheelgun from Su-Lin's. He stared out the window and composed in his head the e-mail he'd send to his sister when he landed, the one in which he'd explain to Lucy what Mitch had decided to do and why. It wouldn't make any sense to her if he started there, at the end of the story. He'd have to tell her the whole lengthy and unimaginable tall tale of what she had started.

If they'd been children still, she'd have sat at his side and soaked it in wide-eyed, believing every word. But childhood was far behind them, and now he imagined she'd parse every word cynically. Assuming the message even reached her—assuming she hadn't skipped house arrest, fled to another country and abandoned her last anonymous e-mail address for a new one he didn't know.

But he would try. She deserved to know the story.

There was just one part Gabriel would leave out; one memory that was his alone, not for sharing.

The taste of Qingzhao Wai Chiu's lips on his own, during the only time they had ever kissed, there in the life-threatening panic of the Night Market, the two of them trapped in their own transient bubble of supertime, the scant seconds that became days where they were briefly in love. The taste and smell of mangoes and rare spice, of night-blooming jasmine.

And now—a sneak preview of the next
Gabriel Hunt adventure:

HUNT THROUGH
NAPOLEON'S WEB

Gabriel Hunt's grip on his pickaxe was slipping.

He had been in worse scrapes before; it's just that he didn't particularly relish the thought of dying while caving for fun and practice. That would be an embarrassment. When it was truly his time to check out, Gabriel would much rather have his obituary say that he'd been eaten alive by an angry tiger or felled by gunshots from enemy assailants. Or old age. That wouldn't be so bad.

But to fall into a gaping pit because he had slipped on bat guano? *Preposterous!*

Gabriel called down to his friend and caving partner, "How you hanging, Manny?"

Horizontal and belly-down, Manuel Rodriguez dangled in midair on the end of the static nylon rope, fifteen feet below Gabriel's legs. His only hope for survival was Gabriel's grip on the pickaxe.

"Is that a joke, *amigo*?" Manny shouted. He was trying to keep the terror out of his voice but wasn't doing a very good job.

It had happened quite innocently. Every two or three years, Gabriel made an excursion to one of various caves around the country so that he could hone his skills. His travels sometimes required that he perform a bit of spelunking—an outdated term, but Gabriel liked the sound of the word. It had a certain romance to it.

Dangling within an inch of one's life over a dark abyss, though, didn't have any romance to it at all.

Manny lived in New Mexico near Carlsbad Caverns National Park. Besides the exceptional landmark that was open to the public to tour on a daily basis, there were several other caverns in the park that were available only to experienced cavers. All it took to access them were a small fee and a license. Gabriel had done it many times, very often with Manny, a fifty-eight-year-old former ranger at the park and an expert spelunker.

They had been in one of the more "challenging" (as Manny had described it) caves for a little more than three hours when Gabriel and Manny—secured to each other by a fifteen-foot-long buddy rope—sat down to rest on a ledge above a black pit that supposedly led to a chamber of noteworthy formations. The hole was ninety-six feet to the bottom. They had come equipped with all the right gear. They each wore the necessary helmets, grubby clothing, knee and elbow pads, sturdy boots. Both men carried plenty of light sources and extra batteries, as well as water, snacks, trash bags, empty bottles in which to urinate, and a first-aid kit. For the vertical descent, Manny had brought along an assortment of tools such as carabiners, rope, waist and chest harnesses, Petzl stops, rappel racks, handled ascenders, pitons, chocks, hammers, and a couple of pickaxes. The goal, however, was to accomplish the journey without damaging the cave at all. Hammering pitons into the rock face was to be avoided if possible. It was best to use noninvasive tools such as Spring-Loaded Camming Devices that wedged into already-existing cracks or in between stone protrusions. "Leave nothing but footprints" was the motto amongst serious cavers.

Gabriel had finished eating a power bar, coiled a long section of rope around his shoulder and back, and stood on the ledge to locate a convenient spot to install a chock or SLCD for what was called an SRT—Single Rope Technique—descent into the hole. The plan was that Manny would follow him, staying tethered to him throughout the excursion. But when Gabriel had stooped to examine a possible position, his boot slipped on something wet and slick. He slammed hard into the ledge, facedown, and continued to slide across the slimy ridge until his body was falling through space. He must have plummeted twenty feet or so before he realized that he had pulled Manny off the ledge as well. Another dozen feet shot past before Gabriel swung the pickaxe that was, miraculously, still in his right hand. He chopped the rock face in front of him as hard as he could—and broke his fall. Hanging on to the axe's handle was another thing altogether. It had a ridged rubber grip and a lip at the bottom against which the side of his right hand collided painfully—but it was enough to enable him to hold on. He gripped the axe handle as tightly as he could with both hands, but already he could feel the strain in his fingers and arms. Making matters worse, his palms were moist from the sudden shock. And when Manny reached the end of the tether with a violent jerk, Gabriel really did damn near lose his grasp.

Then Gabriel was presented with the ultimate

insult—he smelled the stuff he had slid across. It was all over the front of his pants and shirt.

Bat turd.

Gabriel winced, remembering a cave full of bats he'd found himself in half a year earlier in China. The smell was the same all over the world.

"This is the last time I go caving with you!" Manny called. His added weight dangling at the end of the line was slowly pulling Gabriel's shoulders from their sockets. "I'm a fool for letting you talk me into this again!"

Gabriel resorted to an old ploy—bravado could cover up genuine terror every time. "Come on, Manny," he yelled down, "you know you have to stay on top of the game. Sharpen your skills every now and then."

"I'm nearly sixty years old. I don't have anything left to sharpen."

Gabriel attempted to flex his arms and pull himself up, but with the extra load hanging below him it was impossible.

"What the hell do we do now?"

"Relax, Manny. I've got it under control."

In fact, Gabriel had no idea how to get out of the predicament they were in. The rock face sloped inward in front of him, so there was no foothold within reach. The more serious problem was that he had only two hands, and they were busy holding on to the pickaxe for dear life.

After a few seconds of silence, Manny asked, "Anytime you want to start letting me know how you've got it under control is okay by me."

"Your light's still working, isn't it?"

Manny had a light affixed to his helmet. As he

twisted slowly on the end of the line, the beam traced the pit's circumference.

"It's the only part of me that isn't failing," Manny answered. "My bowels are gonna be the next to go."

"Hold on, Manny. Take a look around you. Is there a ledge you'd be able to stand on if you could get to it?"

During his next 360-degree turn, Manny replied, "Yeah. Over on the other side. Behind you. But I can't reach it."

"All right. Let's see if we can get a little swing going, okay?"

"We need music for that, *amigo*."

Sweat poured off Gabriel's forehead beneath his helmet, ran over his brows and stung his eyes. Another problem on the rapidly expanding list.

"Shut up, Manny, and see if you can swing over to the ledge. Slow and easy. I'll try and get you started with my legs."

Gabriel managed to grip the taut tether with the insteps of his boots. He then strained to wiggle the rope enough to send some movement down to his partner. At the same time, Manny flapped his arms and legs as if he were trying to fly—anything to propel himself back and forth in the air.

"You look real graceful," Gabriel said through his teeth. It was becoming much more difficult to hold on.

"Not half as graceful as we're going to look when we're flat as tortillas on the bottom of the cave."

Gabriel was glad that Manny was keeping his sense of humor. A good sign. But as his friend attempted the circus feat, the pickaxe started to squeak. As if it were about to come out of the rock. Gabriel needed to lessen the weight on his body in a big way. The sooner Manny got over to the ledge, the better.

He tugged on the rope with his legs some more and felt his partner's momentum increase a little. Manny was now a human pendulum, swaying feet first toward the target ledge, back and forth at a 20-degree angle . . . which soon increased to 30 degrees . . . and finally to 35 degrees. And then Manny's boot touched the edge of the stone outcropping.

"Almost there, Gabriel!"

The pickaxe creaked again.

Manny swung back to the ledge and came close enough to push off from it with his legs. The maneuver gave him more speed and force—but it also placed much more strain on Gabriel's wrists and the pickaxe. The metal lip at the bottom of the handle was deeply embedded in the flesh of Gabriel's hands. Then the axe slipped a few millimeters with a painful wrenching sound.

"One more push and I think I can make it!" Manny announced.

Gabriel was unable to speak. He simply closed his eyes and willed his partner over to the other side of the pit.

Anytime, Manny, anytime . . .

Manny returned to the ledge and pushed off hard. He swayed so far to Gabriel's side of the hole that he was able to touch the wall there. Then, on the way back to the ledge, he hurtled himself up and over— and fell onto the ledge with a *smack*.

"I made it!" Manny rolled and came to a sitting position. He panted for a few seconds and said, "Pardon me while I say a few Hail Marys."

The subtracted weight relieved the pressure on Gabriel's arms. He was now able to concentrate on the next problem at hand—saving himself. Manny was on the opposite side of the cave from where Gabriel hung and a couple of yards lower. The two men were connected by a fifteen-foot tether. Gabriel could simply let go, fall and hope that Manny was able to pull him up to his ledge. But then they'd be stuck there. Most of the ascending equipment was back at the top, on Bat Guano Ridge.

No, wait.

He had some tools in his pack and in his trouser pockets. A few pitons. A couple of ascenders. A rappel rack.

Gabriel thought that if he could place an anchor in the rock face, he just might be able to attach his rope and a carabiner. He could then use the assembly to raise himself a few feet. Then he'd have to plant another . . . and another . . . all the way to the top. If he ran out, he could pull out one of the lower ones and re-use it. The trip would be slow going and painfully tedious . . . but it could be done.

Now if he could just grow another arm or two . . .

"So now what?" Manny called. His voice echoed in the well. "Dying from the fall would've been better than starving to death here."

"Don't be a pessimist, Manny," Gabriel growled. "I'll get us out of here. Trust me."

He took a deep breath. What he was about to do required concentration.

Gabriel squeezed the axe handle harder with his right hand . . . and let go with his left. Hanging by only one arm, he reached back with his free hand and dug into his pack. His fingers found one of the pouches—he hoped it was the correct one—and wormed them into it. He felt something cold, hard and metallic. A piton! The angle was awkward, but he managed to grasp it. The next step was to pull it out of the pouch without . . . *dropping it . . .*

The piton fell into the darkness below.

He and Manny heard the clang when it hit bottom. Gabriel rarely cursed, but he did so—loudly.

Let's try that again . . .

Still clinging to the handle with a very sore right hand, Gabriel reached back to the pack a second time. He dug into the pouch and took hold of another piton. This time he made sure he had it firmly in hand before removing it.

His right shoulder and upper arm were killing him. The strain was becoming unbearable.

To hell with not damaging the rock.

With the piton in his left hand, he eyed the rock face in front of him. A small crack ran diagonally across the limestone. Aiming as best as he could, Gabriel jabbed the piton's point into the crack. The first attempt only chipped some of the stone away. The second try created a small hole. With the third stab, the piton stuck.

Gabriel grabbed the axe handle with his left hand to relieve some of the tension on his right arm. Then, with his weakened but now free arm, he reached for the small hammer that hung on the right side of his belt. He succeeded in pulling it out of its sheath . . . but since the piton was to the left of his body, he now had to switch it to his other hand. He'd never be able to hammer it with his right hand.

Only one thing to do, and Gabriel knew he had only one shot to do it. There would be no second attempt.

Okay, the left hand is holding the axe. The right hand has the hammer. Let's do it . . . Ready? . . . One . . . two . . . THREE!

Gabriel tossed the hammer into the air and grabbed the axe handle with his right hand while simultaneously releasing the handle with his left. The hammer had reached the top of its arc while he was making the exchange and was now plunging downward. Gabriel's left hand shot out and snatched the hammer out of midair as it fell.

He had to stop and breathe for a moment after that little stunt. Compared to it, hammering the piton into the limestone was easy.

Still using one hand, he unwrapped the rope from his shoulder and stuck an end in his mouth. He gripped it with his teeth, and then dug a carabiner out of a pocket. It was yet another awkward operation to secure the end of the rope to the 'biner with a bowline knot one-handed, but he did it. He then hooked the carabiner into the eye on the exterior end of the piton. The rope was now fixed and safe to use.

Then his cell phone rang.

"What the . . . ?" He looked back at Manny. "You mean to tell me there's actually *service* down here?" Gabriel took hold of the rope with one hand and his legs, let go of the axe handle, and hung there, suspended.

The phone rang again.

"You're not gonna answer that, are you?" Manny asked.

Gabriel hated cell phones the same way he hated most modern technology—but that didn't stop him from feeling compelled to answer the thing when it rang. He fished it out of his trouser pocket and brought it to his ear.

"Hello?"

"Gabriel?"

"Michael?"

Gabriel immediately pictured his younger brother sitting at his desk back in the luxury of his clean and comfortable New York office. He'd rarely envied his brother his stay-at-home life—but at this moment he came close.

"Are you sitting down?" Michael asked.

Gabriel grimaced. "Not precisely."

"It's Lucy, Gabriel."

The urgency in Michael's voice gave him pause. Lucy—short for Lucifer—was the youngest sibling in the family. Their imaginative parents had named each child after one of the archangels in the Bible. It didn't seem to matter to them that their daughter would have to bear the ignominy of her moniker for the rest of her life. In an attempt at kindness, her brothers called her Lucy, but ever since she'd run away from home at age seventeen, she'd taken to calling herself "Cifer" instead. Pronounced like *cipher*, it made a fine name for the scofflaw computer hacker she'd turned herself into.

"What *about* Lucy?" Gabriel asked.

"Are you sitting down?"

"*No*, Michael, I'm not sitting down! Just tell me!"

"She's in terrible danger. You need to come back to New York as quickly as you can."

"How is she in danger?"

"It looks . . . it looks like she's been kidnapped."

He wasn't sure he'd heard Michael correctly. "Say that again?"

"She's been *kidnapped.*"

"Are you serious?"

"Yes. And there's a ransom demand."

"How much do they want?"

"They don't want money, Gabriel. They want *you.*"

*DON'T MISS THE NEXT EXCITING
ADVENTURE OF GABRIEL HUNT!*

INTERACT WITH DORCHESTER ONLINE!

Want to learn more about your favorite books and authors?
Want to talk with other readers that like to read the same books as you?
Want to see up-to-the-minute Dorchester news?

VISIT DORCHESTER AT:
DorchesterPub.com
Twitter.com/DorchesterPub
Facebook.com (Search Pages)

DISCUSS DORCHESTER'S NOVELS AT:
Dorchester Forums at DorchesterPub.com
GoodReads.com
LibraryThing.com
Myspace.com/books
Shelfari.com
WeRead.com

☐ **YES!**

Sign me up for the Leisure Thriller Book Club and send my FREE BOOKS! If I choose to stay in the club, I will pay only $4.25* each month, a savings of $3.74!

NAME: _____

ADDRESS: _____

TELEPHONE: _____

EMAIL: _____

☐ I want to pay by credit card.

☐   ☐ MasterCard. ☐ DISCOVER

ACCOUNT #: _____

EXPIRATION DATE: _____

SIGNATURE: _____

Mail this page along with $2.00 shipping and handling to:
Leisure Thriller Book Club
PO Box 6640
Wayne, PA 19087
Or fax (must include credit card information) to:
610-995-9274

You can also sign up online at **www.dorchesterpub.com**.
*Plus $2.00 for shipping. Offer open to residents of the U.S. and Canada only.
Canadian residents please call 1-800-481-9191 for pricing information.
If under 18, a parent or guardian must sign. Terms, prices and conditions subject to
change. Subscription subject to acceptance. Dorchester Publishing reserves the right
to reject any order or cancel any subscription.

GET FREE BOOKS!

You can have the best fiction delivered to your door for less than what you'd pay in a bookstore or online. Sign up for one of our book clubs today, and we'll send you *FREE* BOOKS* just for trying it out...**with no obligation to buy, ever!**

If you love fast-paced page turners, you won't want to miss any of the books in Leisure's thriller line. Filled with gripping tension and edge-of-your-seat excitement, these titles feature everything from psychological suspense to legal thrillers to police procedurals and more!

As a book club member you also receive the following special benefits:
- **30% off all orders!**
- **Exclusive access to special discounts!**
- **Convenient home delivery and 10 days to return any books you don't want to keep.**

Visit **www.dorchesterpub.com** or call **1-800-481-9191**

There is no minimum number of books to buy, and you may cancel membership at any time.
*Please include $2.00 for shipping and handling.